It Is Finished

God Has Been Placing Me Into Position

A Memoir

by Thierry R. Lundy

DORRANCE PUBLISHING CO
EST. 1920
PITTSBURGH, PENNSYLVANIA 15238

The contents of this work, including, but not limited to, the accuracy of events, people, and places depicted; opinions expressed; permission to use previously published materials included; and any advice given or actions advocated are solely the responsibility of the author, who assumes all liability for said work and indemnifies the publisher against any claims stemming from publication of the work.

All Rights Reserved
Copyright © 2018 by Thierry R. Lundy

No part of this book may be reproduced or transmitted, downloaded, distributed, reverse engineered, or stored in or introduced into any information storage and retrieval system, in any form or by any means, including photocopying and recording, whether electronic or mechanical, now known or hereinafter invented without permission in writing from the publisher.

Dorrance Publishing Co
585 Alpha Drive
Suite 103
Pittsburgh, PA 15238
Visit our website at www.dorrancebookstore.com

ISBN: 978-1-4809-4895-2
eISBN: 978-1-4809-4918-8

to those who are searching for the truth

Contents

Acknowledgments vii
Prologue: God, The Great Initiator ix

Section 1: My Imperfect Plan 1
Chapter 1: My First Love 3
   Origin
   A Deep Passion
Chapter 2: My Golden Opportunity 9
   Moving Out of Miami
   Basketball Tryouts
   A Road Block

Section 2: God's Perfect Plan 19
Chapter 3: Right on Time! 21
   Early Church Experiences and Growing Up in Miami
   Invitation
Chapter 4: The Calling 29
Chapter 5: Walking Away 41
   I'm Baptized
   My Mom's Influence on Me
   The Offer

Section 3: Searching 53
Chapter 6: Pharmacy 55
   An Empty Feeling
Chapter 7: Spoken-Word Poetry 59
Chapter 8: Covering More Ground 63
Chapter 9: Journalism, Activism, and Acting 71
Chapter 10: Film & Stage Plays 81
Chapter 11: My One-Man Shows 93
Chapter 12: Acting School 97
   That Empty Feeling Again

Chapter 13: Stand-Up Comedy 103

Section 4: Sinking 109
Chapter 14: Ravaged by the World 111
    Placing my Faith in Men
    Destroying the Temple
    I Want to Join the Bloods…Again!
    "All Black" Poem
Chapter 15: Struggling 121

Section 5: Found 129
Chapter 16: I Hear Him Calling 131
    Being Groomed to be a Preacher?
    "Something Is Calling Me Out There"
    "You Are a Minister!"
Chapter 17: Go Back to Church 139
Chapter 18: No Glory in the World 147
Chapter 19: "…Take a Leap of Faith." 151
Chapter 20: He Brought Me Full Circle 157
    Original Plan
    Lansdowne
    Actively Ministering to Others
    My Poetry

Section 6: God's Goodness 167
Chapter 21: "It Is finished…" 169
    The Vision and Commission
Chapter 22: God Has Been Placing Me into Position 181

Epilogue: God Is Good 241

Acknowledgments

I would first like to thank God for being good to me, despite my shortcomings. If it were not for Him, this memoir would not exist. I would also like to thank my good friend, Junior Bennett, for allowing God to use him. Last but not least, I would like to thank my mom, Prucienne Lundy, for doing such a great job in single-handedly raising me. Thank you for the sound morals that you have instilled in me, for they have functioned as road signs on this road of life. The strength and work ethic that you have displayed has not gone unnoticed. It has inspired me to remain diligent in my personal endeavors.

Prologue

God, The Great Initiator

While looking at the depressing state of this dark world and their current circumstances, many question, "Is God truly good?" They are easily deceived into believing the lie that He is not. This belief causes those who were once in the faith to stray away from it, and keeps those who were never in the faith from coming into it. I am a witness that God is not only good, but He is also the initiator of goodness towards us. He is the Great Initiator! In the gospel, God's goodness was shown on Calvary. When we didn't ask Him to, He took the initiative and reconciled a sinful people unto Himself through His son, Jesus Christ. Better yet, God himself came in the form of man to save us from our sins. He is the one who initiated this goodness towards us, not us towards Him!

In the gospels, Jesus Christ declared, "It is finished..." right before taking his final breath on the cross. With these words, he was signifying that his perfect substitutionary sacrifice had come to a completion. It is because of this work on the cross that our sins can be forgiven and we can appear blameless before a holy God. To emphasize God's goodness, this work of salvation was solely initiated by Him, and not us. God is the great initiator, not us.

Out of His goodness, God's invisible hands are still heavily involved in our lives today. In the same way He did on the cross, God is still finishing things in our lives for our good. In the year 2013, God brought a beautiful story to a completion in my life. In a sense, in completing this story, He was saying, "It is finished." With that said, I can testify of the depths of His goodness, by painting a clear picture of how good He has been to me. It is one night in September 2013, and lately God has been bringing a chapter of my life to completion. Over the past several months, several drastic events have been taking place in my life, to mark the completion of this particular work. Though these events seemed to abruptly rush into my life, they are far from random. There is a certain familiarity about them. I know that these events are God's way of trying to get my attention and to steer me into a particular direction. This direction is one that He has always wanted me to go in. Over the past several years, full of ambition and relentless drive, I sped like a freight train down another direction, a direction filled with heavy toiling, dark uncertainty, and tears of pain. It was necessary that these events were as powerful as they were, for I had grown to be very ambitious on the course that I have been on the past several years of my life. This became a determination that only a powerful force could break and as a result, stop me in my tracks. In these past several years, I have marinated in negative ways and have picked up bad habits. I have become deeply submerged in these ways, and fully committed to the course that I had been on, and these events have come to extract me from the quicksand that I have progressively placed myself in over the period of several years. They have come to remove me from this quicksand and to place me on solid ground. They have come, full of power, to steer me into a whole new direction that also meant a whole new purpose.

As a result of now being extracted from the life I had come to know very well, I now felt like a fish out of water. I have reached another pivotal moment in my life, and I could feel it in my whole being. This pivotal moment now lingers in the atmosphere around me like a dark cloud that does not want to go away. Even after having experienced a few episodes of these drastic events, as it turns out, this wave of events were far from being over. Extremely shaken up by what I had experienced thus far, I still found myself going back to the very ways that these events were aiming to take me away from. One night in Atlanta, Georgia, I found myself sitting in the living room of my friend's apartment. I was sitting on his couch (which was my bed for the night), having a phone conversation with another friend of mine when my phone conversation was suddenly interrupted! It was not interrupted by my friend (the one allowing me to crash in his apartment on this night), who had already gone to sleep. It also was not interrupted by a disturbing noise or anything like that. The conversation was interrupted by something greater. It was interrupted by God! On this momentous night, as I sat on that couch, the all-knowing Creator of the universe revealed something to me that was so unimaginable, that it made my jaw drop! What He revealed to me transcended everything I thought the past several years of my life was about. What He revealed to me was how He used an unwise decision I made years before this night to do something great! He showed me the good results of Him being the Great Initiator. For you to get a better sense of how I got to this point, it's a must that I start at the chapter in my life that will give you a better appreciation of God's goodness. Welcome to my memoir, It Is Finished.

"For he satisfies the longing soul,
And fills the hungry soul with goodness."

Psalm 107:9

SECTION 1
My Imperfect Plan

Instead, you should say, "If the Lord wants us to, we will live and carry out our plans."

James 4:15

Chapter 1
My First Love

Origin

As a child, I developed a love for the game of basketball. Growing up in North Miami Beach, my mother and I lived in a 4-story apartment building called Tiffany Squares. In our neighborhood, there were no parks where my friends and I could go and play. So Tiffany Squares became our playground. Here at Tiffany Squares, my friends and I escaped boredom by playing all types of games together. This included hide and go seek, freeze tag, football, and the fun sport of basketball. To play football, we used a long patch of grass that was located in front of Tiffany Squares. It ran the length of the building. To the naked eye, it was simply a long patch of grass, but to us it was a 100-yard football field.

When we played tag or hide and go seek, all the four floors of Tiffany Squares were fair game. The floors provided us with great escape routes, numerous staircases to run into, and an ample amount of room to run. Sometimes while running from the enemy on the second floor, as a panic move, we would jump from the second floor onto the first. Of course we thought about safety first. To cushion the drop, we would first dangle our little bodies from the second floor of the apartment building, before letting our bodies drop to the ground below. Not only were playgrounds non-existent, but there was also no basketball courts that were close enough for us to go to. So the question now was, "How were we going to play a game of basketball with no hoop?"

At any given time, riddling the parking lot of Tiffany Squares, were abandoned shopping carts. Out of place, they had the appearance of beached whales. The tenants who brought these shopping carts home to Tiffany

Squares were people who didn't have cars. So after grocery shopping, they utilized the shopping carts like some kind of U-Haul to transport their groceries back to Tiffany Squares. Little did those tenants know, but they were providing my friends and I with the basketball hoop that we desperately needed.

After my friends and I chose a shopping cart we would immediately go make good use of it. On the first floor of Tiffany Squares, there was a wall that functioned as a partition that separated the parking lot area from the swimming pool area. We placed the right or left side of the shopping cart directly up against the wall so that the shopping cart could not only be fixed in position, but also so that the wall could function as our backboard. In this imaginative way, my friends and I played countless exciting games of basketball. Often times when we shot the basketball too hard into this makeshift hoop, it would bounce back out of the shopping cart after making a loud crashing sound, but the shot still counted for 2-points. When we did not use shopping carts, my friends and I came up with another creative way to play basketball. Tiffany Squares had a total of four floors. At each of those staircases right before you entered onto each floor there was a door. A special hinge that created a basketball rim-like structure held this door, one part of the hinge connected to the door and the other part connected to the doorframe. This hinge became our makeshift basketball hoop. The only downside of this rim was that we could not play using a regulation-sized basketball. This truth did not keep us from playing the game we loved. We just simply found a kiddie basketball that was small enough to go through it. Right there in the staircase we played competitive games of basketball as if we were NBA players trying to win a championship game.

A Deep Passion

As a child living at Tiffany Squares, I attended an elementary school called Fulford. This school had a big field that was often utilized for football games and periodic field days. It also had monkey bars and outdoor basketball courts. Needless to say, I spent most of my time on those courts. Every morning before the start of class, I made it a priority to play a game of basketball with the other boys. Before we could get this game of basketball going, we had to wait on the arrival of our Physical Ed coach so that he could make some school-owned basketballs available to us. To me, our P.E coach was like a Santa Claus who came to give me the exact gift that I wanted for Christmas--a basketball.

Upon arrival to the school, he immediately went into a closet that was under a pavilion that was near the basketball courts. Once he went into what I would like to call the "treasure trove," he instantly made available to all the kids things like jump ropes, and of course the most important thing--basketballs. The coach would throw the basketballs towards us where we stood on the basketball court. Since he was a Santa Claus, when he threw out those basketballs and all the other things we used to play various types of games, it was almost like he was saying, "I come bearing gifts!"

After receiving the basketball, I along with some of the boys, played basketball until our first class began. There was no feeling like sinking a shot, and hearing the "swish" sound that the net made when I made the shot. The girls would stand on the sideline and watch us play. In our minds, we were basketball stars, and the girls were our cheerleaders. With this fantasy in our heads, we showed off frequently as the girls watched on. We played basketball almost every morning before class, so often times we walked into our first class of the day with our clothes drenched in sweat. It seemed like we just came from taking a dip in the pool with all of our clothes on.

One of my favorite games in P.E class also involved basketballs. If the P.E. teacher had it in his plans for us to play this game that day, he would already have the game set up before all of the kids arrived to class (which was held outside on one of the basketball courts). Once all of us students arrived to P.E. class, the coach would create several teams, and these teams would line up on two sides of the basketball court. In the center of the court there were circular rubber rings organized in a circle shape, and a basketball was placed on top of each ring. Every person on each team was assigned a number. When the game started, the coach sat on a chair alongside the basketball court and would yell out a random number. Everyone waited with anticipation for his or her number to be called. The person who was assigned this number would then dart up from where they crouched towards the basketballs that were positioned in the middle of the court. They would then grab a basketball and run to whichever basket they wanted to. Then they would shoot the ball until they made a shot and quickly run back to place the ball back on the ring. The person who got to their team first, would earn their team a point. Every time I arrived to P.E to see the basketballs waiting for us in their designated rubber rings, a feeling of excitement would quickly rise up within me.

When I was about 12 years old, my mother moved from our North Miami Beach apartment, Tiffany Squares, to a 2-story apartment in North Miami. I was so passionate about the game that I risked getting stranded at Fulford Elementary one afternoon after school, just for one more chance to step on those basketball courts. Getting stranded at Fulford would be a predicament, because I no longer lived as close to the school as I used to when I lived in the North Miami Beach apartment building, Tiffany Squares. My new home in North Miami was now 10-times farther from my school than it was when I lived at Tiffany Squares. Since my home was a little further from school, my mother would sometimes have a friend of hers (who lived in the same apartment building) come pick me up along with the daughter of this friend, who also attended Fulford Elementary. While this little girl and I waited in front of Fulford one afternoon for her mother to come pick us up, I could not help but hear the excitement of some boys playing the game of basketball at the back of the school. The boys sounded like they were having so much fun, and I was tempted. I could not take it anymore, and I informed this little girl that I would go play some basketball. Then I instructed her to notify me when her mother arrived, so that I would not miss my ride home. When I gave her the instruction, she didn't say a word. Regardless of the fact that she did not give me a response, I could feel the game calling me! Leaving her there standing in front of the school, I headed straight for the basketball court where all the fun was happening. I played a few games that afternoon, but the little girl never came to notify me that her mother had arrived. So I thought to myself, Maybe our ride didn't arrive yet. To my dismay, when I walked back up to the front of the school expecting to see the little girl right where I left her, I found that she had disappeared. I immediately knew that our ride did in fact come, but only picked up the girl and left me behind. I was stranded and I had no choice but to walk home that day. I don't remember how long of a walk it was, but I do remember that it was early afternoon when I started walking, and by the time I arrived home the sun had already set. I bit the bullet that day of having to walk this long distance home, just for a chance to step on the basketball court one more time.

Not long after I graduated from Fulford Elementary, I attended a school called North Miami Middle School. Right next to North Miami Middle School was a park named Cagni. This park was composed of a baseball field, outdoor skating rink, and four full basketball courts. On these basketball courts I often played basketball with my friends and other people who I didn't know that well. I would play during P.E and I would also play during my free time. I was so passionate about playing basketball that I was willing to walk from my house to Cagni Park (which was about 30 minutes away) just so I could play the game that I enjoyed. My passion for the game of basketball also drove me to find basketball courts whenever I was in a new neighborhood. For a while, I thought that Cagni Park was the only basketball court in the area, until I found another basketball court that was only about 15 minutes walking distance from my house. This basketball court was located behind an elementary school that was near our home. It had a few full basketball courts. With my basketball in hand, I would walk those 10 minutes to the school to play the game that I loved. Depending on how I felt on a certain day, I would walk 30 minutes to Cagni Park or 10 minutes to this elementary school to get my basketball fix. In the same way a smoker needs a nicotine fix, I needed a basketball fix. Over time, my mother grew more aware of my passion. One day, very excitingly, she said to me, "I had a dream that the NBA basketball legend, Michael Jordan, came knocking on our apartment door looking for you." To her, this was a revelation that I would one day make it to the NBA.

Chapter 2
My Golden Opportunity

Moving out of Miami

At the end of my freshman year at North Miami Senior High School, I was informed that I would have to attend summer school. Summer school was for students who failed a class during the year. I was one of those students. Summer school allowed students to makeup a class that they failed during the year. If you did not attend summer school, you would not be able to move on to the next grade. Having to attend summer school also meant that your summer break from school would be almost non-existent. Like many students, I looked forward to summer break. It was our opportunity to not have to do homework for three months! With the boring, fun-zapping drag of summer school looming in my near future like an oncoming terrible storm, I was not looking forward to it at all. Then something happened to make my undesirable situation do a 180-degree turn to work in my favor.

    My mom broke the news to me that we would be moving out of Miami. I was born and raised in Miami, so Miami was all I knew. When my mother broke the news to me that we would be moving to another city, it caught me off guard. I felt like a fish being pulled out of water. With my water being the city of Miami, Florida. Despite my initial reaction to this unforeseen news, I was still excited. I was excited because this meant that I would be escaping the boring drag of summer school by transferring to a high school in a different city. What a good feeling it is for a teenage boy to know that his whole summer would no longer have to be wasted sitting in a classroom. The reason why my single mother decided to move from Miami to another city was for the sake of better job opportunities. Before moving out of Miami, my mom had already been working in West Palm Beach. She would often commute from Miami to

West Palm, leaving me with a babysitter, as she applied for job opportunities. While she was working in West Palm Beach, she was in the process of finding a place for us to live in this city. Though she didn't have a place ready for us, she wanted to live in Palm Beach so that she could be closer to her job. In the summer of 2001, we moved into her cousin's townhouse in the city of Boynton Beach, which was a city not too far from West Palm Beach. Her cousin's home functioned as our transition home until we found a place of our own.

Though moving to Boynton Beach allowed me to escape the boring drag of summer school, there was still an even greater benefit. In the city of Boynton, there was a new high school that had just been built only minutes from my mom's cousin's home. This school was Boynton Beach High, the school that my mother had plans for me to attend in the fall of 2001. With this new high school just having been built, it hit me that it did not yet have a basketball team as yet. I viewed this as a great opportunity to finally be on an official basketball team. By this time, in my early teens, basketball became a passion that shaped my future goals. It was now my long-term goal to make it to the NBA. This new high school being opened up for the first time marked an opportunity for me to begin my journey towards this goal by being accepted onto an official high school basketball team.

With the upcoming basketball tryouts fresh in my mind, I used the summer to keep my basketball skills sharp. Since I was no longer in the familiar territory of my hometown of Miami, Florida, I didn't know the location of the nearest basketball court. This was not a hard problem to fix. My passion for this sport led me to uncover the nearest basketball court, no matter where I was. While living with my mother's cousin, the question I posed myself was Where was the nearest basketball court? With my basketball in hand, this is the question that I also asked some of the locals until I finally uncovered the basketball court that would provide me with the gateway to feed my passion.

The basketball court I found was located about 15 minutes walking distance from my mom's cousin's house. This one full-court was located directly behind a local elementary school that was closed for the summer. So there was never anyone there. Most days with my basketball in hand, I walked to this "sanctuary" of mine. Many times, the hot sun would still be high in the sky when I arrived to the court. With that said, many times I would be the only one on the basketball court this early in the afternoon. Other young men were scared of the scorching heat, so they would wait until the sun went down before leaving their homes to join me. But my passion for the sport did not allow me to wait for them to play the sport that I loved so much. Right there on that court, I repeatedly shot my basketball from early afternoon until the sun went down.

Basketball Tryouts

I practiced all summer until the start of my sophomore year that fall at the new Boynton Beach High. The school had a total of three teams. There was the freshman, junior varsity, and varsity team. When Boynton Beach High School opened for the first time in the fall, my first order of business was to inquire about basketball tryouts. The coach who I inquired about basketball tryouts was a tall, slim, white male. He was the varsity team coach. He told me when tryouts would begin. The great opportunity had arrived! I've never been on an official basketball team before. I've been playing street ball for as long as I could remember. From shooting basketballs into a shopping cart as a child at Tiffany Squares to playing basketball on outdoor courts. I was now finally trying out for my first official basketball team! This was no longer the non-regulation experience of street ball. I was trying out for an official team with official referees and official coaches! Most importantly, being on an official team leads to being seen by college scouts. Being on a team like this was like the first hurdle I had to jump if I wanted to make it to the NBA, which is what I wanted to do.

The first day of tryouts had finally arrived. I could remember walking into the shiny, indoor basketball court of the newly built Boynton Beach High. There were many other young men like me who showed up for tryouts. As I watched these talented young men run up and down the shiny, new, indoor basketball court, I found myself starting to question my own skills. I was a little uneasy at the sight of these boys because it was obvious that many of these young men were very skilled players, maybe way more talented than me.

Nervous as I was, by the time I got on the basketball court, my nervousness faded away. I did what I knew best, and that was play basketball. When on the court, I was like a fish in water. With that said, the junior varsity coach quickly took notice of me. During tryouts, the coach would have the boys run five on five on the indoor court. I could remember one time, one of my teammates had possession of the ball, and he passed it to me as I ran to the other end to lay the ball into the hoop. While I was about to lay the ball into the basket, I looked off to the baseline (where the JV coach was sitting) to make sure that he saw what I just did. He was smiling as I laid the ball into the basket. To me, this smile of his spoke volumes. It said to me, "You are doing a great job Lundy!" To me, this smile of his told me that I was in good standing to make this year's junior varsity team. The thought of having a good chance of making the team gave me a great confidence boost.

Basketball tryouts were not always as fun as playing a five on five full-court game. The coaches were also concerned about getting our bodies into great shape for the upcoming season. Most of the time we had to do a lot of other things that were a part of the process of conditioning. One of them was called "suicides" and the other involved running around the track field. None of the young men who were trying out were exempt from the grueling activity called suicides. This tedious exercise did not only make you realize how out of shape you were, but also as the name suggests, by the time you were done with this rigorous exercise, you were so exhausted that it felt like your lungs were about to explode and that you were having a near-death experience. When we did suicides, all the young men who were trying out for the team would all line up on the baseline of the basketball court. Then as soon as the coach signaled us, we would run from the baseline, then we would run to touch with our hands the free throw line that was on that side of the court. Then we would run back to touch the baseline where we started. Then we ran from the baseline, past the free throw line to touch with our hands the 3-point line. Then we ran back to the baseline. We would continue this back and forth rhythm until we touched the half court line, the three-point, free throw, and base line that was on the other side of the court. We would then complete the suicides by running as fast as we could from this baseline all the way back to the baseline on the other side of the court where we started. When we completed the suicides, everyone felt like they were about to pass out. My legs felt like they were about to give out. This exercise made me realize how out of shape I was. Since I was accustomed to playing street ball, suicides were new to me. I didn't have an ounce of experience with playing with a real team. I quickly learned that I was in a different realm. I was no longer playing street ball where things were often unorganized, and just thrown together. I was now trying out for an official basketball team. Despite how hard conditioning was at times, I still had a relentless drive to make the team.

Another conditioning exercise that us boys had to do was to run one mile around the track field. Once again, the JV coach would do things that made me think that I had a good chance of making the team. To time us, the coach carried a stopwatch to clock us once we completed that mile. At one point while I was running that mile, I fell way behind the other boys who were also trying out for the JV basketball team. Noticing this poor performance of mine, the coach became angry and yelled out to me, "You are the point guard, you are supposed to be ahead of them." When the coach told me that I was the point guard, it gave me an alleviated feeling that--in his mind--he had already chosen me as his point guard for the JV team this basketball season. Once again, this boosted my confidence even further. So much that I felt like I was in good standing. As soon as he told me to speed up on that track field, I mustered up the little strength that I had left, and quickly sped up to the front of the pack. I ran to the front of the pack and successfully completed that mile. When I reached the end, I asked the coach, "How did I do?" and with that same familiar smile on his face, he answered, "Good." With this response, he once again made me feel like I had already made the basketball team. Like the deal was already in the bag. Now, all I had to do was just stick it out until the end of tryouts, and I would undoubtedly be on Boynton Beach High's 2001-2002 JV basketball team.

A Road Block

In the last few days of tryouts, all the young men trying out for the JV team had to learn something called "options." Options were the plays that the team would execute on the basketball court, during the season. So it was very important that we knew them like the back of our hands.

During tryouts, the JV coach hinted that I was the point guard. That day that I was trailing behind all the boys on the track field, he yelled to me, "You are the point guard. You are supposed to be ahead of them!" In the eyes of our coach, I was the point guard, the position that was responsible for calling out the options on the basketball court to the rest of my teammates in the midst of a game. In a sense, I would be the commander and the young men who occupied the other positions would be my troops. As this point guard, there was no way around having to learn the options.

Like I mentioned earlier, I never played regulation basketball a day in my life, so having to learn options was a new experience for me. A new experience that would breed difficulty. One day, on the outdoor basketball court located behind Boynton Beach High School, the coach started to do option drills. To me, this experience was like a baby trying to learn to walk, and continuing to fall to the ground in the process. When we would run the plays, I would pass the ball to the wrong player. When it was my cue to run to a certain spot on the court, I would run to the wrong spot. Nothing about the options sunk in! It was almost as if my ability to remember things was hindered by something, preventing me from remembering these important plays. Growing impatient due to these mistakes that I was making, the coach often took me out of the option drill, and replaced me with another young man also trying out for the point guard position. He did this in hopes that the point guard that took my place could do a better job in retaining the options, and he would. The coach gave me more opportunities to learn these options, but I just could not get them to sink in. And over and over again, he would pull me out and substitute me with another point guard that did a way better job in executing the plays. The confidence that I had of making the team quickly faded.

Determined to make the team, every day I would set my mind to learn those options. Once again like that baby learning how to walk, I would always fall on my behind. Tryouts were coming to an end, and I never learned how to walk. I never learned how to stand on my two feet. I was never able to remember those options. Then, just like that in the blink of an eye, that momentous day had arrived. The time had come for all the young men to find out if they had made the basketball team or not.

At the completion of tryouts, all the boys lined up outside of one of the high school classrooms. In this classroom, the varsity and junior varsity basketball coaches sat behind a desk ready to reveal the fate of each and every young man who tried out for the team. One by one, every young man was called into the classroom. When it was my turn, I walked in and I could feel the bad news in the air. It was thick like a dense fog. I felt like I was walking to the electric chair. Walking into the classroom, I was still being haunted by the fact that I failed to remember the options (one of the most important things a person occupying the point guard position had to know). Walking into that classroom that day, I just knew that this would cost me big time.

Nonetheless, I still had a sense of hope. I hoped that the smirk that my JV coach wore often was the prelude to good news, but it was not. I walked before them and sat on one of the student desks in the classroom. After the JV coach confirmed to me that I was a good basketball player, he told me that he would not be able to work with me if I could not remember the options. I was cut from the team. As I sat there on the desk before these coaches, I could feel my dreams of making it to the NBA go down the drain. It felt as if a dark cloud was hovering directly over my head, a dark cloud that would continue to follow me throughout the rest of the evening.

The chief reason why I did not make the cut on the Boynton Beach High School basketball was because I had a great difficulty remembering the options. No matter how hard I strained my brain to commit those options to memory, they did not stick. I was trying out for a position as a point guard, which is the person who lets all the other members on the team know the plays that they will be running during the game. These were plays that played a key role in putting points on the board during a game. So me not being able to remember any of the plays posed a major problem. This would mean that I would be ineffective if I were a point guard on the team.

Me not being able to remember those plays was an anomaly. I've always proven to be good at memorizing and retaining information. My mother was always aware of this ability of mine. When I was young, when she wanted to remember something, she would entrust it to me so that I could regurgitate the information to her later on. And with impressive accuracy, I would remind her of the thing that she told me to remember. But now, even with great effort, I was having extreme difficulty with remembering a simple basketball play. No matter how hard I tried to learn those options, they did not sink in. Something was wrong with this picture. Why couldn't I remember something so simple? I never had a problem remembering things before!

Me not making the high school basketball team did not only hit me hard, but it also surprised many people. Some of the people who were in shock were some young men who my cousin Wallace and I played basketball with in his neighborhood. I've played basketball with these young men on several occasions, so they knew my capacity to play basketball. When I played basketball with them, it was evident to them that I was very talented. The day that they found out that I did not make the team, they were shocked. I could sense their confusion. It was almost like they were thinking to themselves, How can someone so talented not make the team? or If he didn't make the team, then I definitely would not be able to make the team, because he can play way better than I can.

I had always placed my eggs into one basket. A basket labeled "Basketball." When I found out that I did not make the basketball team, it felt like this basket fell out the window of a three-story building, resulting in the loss of all my eggs. I felt very broken and defeated. I felt as though the ground had been ripped right from beneath me, and my whole world had come to an end. I wondered to myself, What's next?

My cousin Wallace was not nearly as good as I was, and he managed to make the freshman basketball team. I felt extremely embarrassed that he made a team and I didn't. This gave me a feeling of bewilderment and jealousy that he made a team and I didn't. When my cousin Wallace walked into his house (which is where I resided until my mother came to pick me up that night) that night, his excitement showed that he had just made the cut on the freshman basketball team. His excitement submerged me deeper into my gloom. It was by far one of the darkest days that I ever experienced.

The night that I did not make the basketball team I sat in one of the rooms of my cousin's house. When my cousin got home, he asked me, "You made the team?" Very calmly and nonchalant I responded, "No." Though it seemed like it did not bother me on the outside, deep inside I was in a deep state of confusion. Though I managed to force a smile onto my face, like nothing was bothering me, I wondered, What am I going to do with my life now?

By this time, my mother and I had already moved into a townhouse in West Palm Beach, Florida. She didn't transfer me right away because she knew how much making the basketball team meant to me. She wanted me to have the opportunity to make the team. That night when she came to pick me up, I would have to break the bad news to her. That night I got in the car with my basketball cuffed tightly under my arm. My mother was aware that this was the day that I would find out if I made the team or not. As soon as I got into the car with her she asked, "Did you make the team?" I could sense the excitement and anticipation in her voice, almost as if she knew for sure that I had made the basketball team. And now I was about to break the news to her that I didn't succeed in doing so. Her excitement heightened my disappointment. With a deep sadness I mumbled, "No." She said, "What?" I replied again, "No." With my basketball clutched tightly underneath my arms, the water that had swelled up in my eyes started to roll down my face as I stared out the passenger side window into the night. As my mother, she tried her best to comfort me by telling me that the coach who cut me was the one who was missing out on me. But she was not successful in her attempt to console me.

SECTION 2
God's Perfect Plan

"For I know the plans I have for you," declares the Lord, "plans to give you hope and a future…"

Jeremiah 29:11

Chapter 3
Right on Time!

Early Church Experiences and Growing up in Miami

Reader, in Section 1, you've gotten a sense of my plan for my life, and how it failed. Thank God he has the perfect plan for our lives! As a child growing up in North Miami Beach, Florida, I could remember my mother vividly describing the scene of the second coming of Christ to me. She would say on that magnificent day, trumpets would sound to usher in the second coming of Christ to earth. I would be in awe as she described this day to me. Holding on to this hope, I could remember standing on the outdoor basketball courts before the start of school at Fulford Elementary gazing into the sky, and trying my best to imagine this breath-taking scene that would one day take place. Putting my imagination to use, I would replay this future event over and over again in my mind. My mother's description of the second coming of Christ was a part of the limited knowledge I had of my savior.

For as long as I could remember, my mother has been a professed Catholic. She was raised Catholic in her place of birth of Haiti. So the ways of this religion were deeply ingrained in her. As her child, the ways of Catholics were introduced to me very early on. On Saturdays, she would take me to a Catholic church in Miami called Cathedral of St. Mary to prepare for my first communion. I could vividly remember on Saturday mornings sitting in classes at this Catholic Church as the teachers there prepared me for my first communion. One of the first things these teachers taught me was how to cross myself. I could remember practicing crossing myself in my home at Tiffany Squares Apartments. As I pointed to my forehead, chest, right shoulder, and left shoulder respectively I would say to myself, "Father, Son, Holy Spirit,

Amen." From the outside looking in, it seemed as though I was successfully being conditioned to become a part of the millions of members of the "Great" Catholic Church, for I was quickly learning their ways. This learning would soon come to an abrupt end.

My mother got a new job opportunity that was on Saturdays; therefore she was no longer able to take me to those communion classes. Though my Catholic mother made a strong effort to get me in touch with Catholicism very early on in life, religion is something that just quickly faded away from my life. Though my mother did not force Catholicism on me, she herself fervently kept her faith. After I stopped attending communion school, she still did things to convey that she was still a Catholic at heart.

Like all Catholics did, she still prayed with her rosary. A rosary was in essence a bead necklace that had a charm of a Jesus nailed to a cross. There are other particular memories I have of my mother that spoke volumes and said that she was in the Catholic faith. These memories took place while we were living in North Miami, Florida. I would be in the car with her while she was running errands. Every time she noticed a Catholic church on the side of the road she would immediately mumble a prayer while she crossed herself. This was her way of acknowledging the church showing her loyalty as a Catholic.

Taking me along with her, some weekends, she would take a trip to downtown Miami to run some errands. When we got downtown, there was a catholic church there. When we walked into the church, we would be the only ones there. We would walk in, get on our knees behind one of the pews, and she would pray. Her custom was not deeper than that. My mother was not one to attend church every Sunday. On the contrary, it seemed like only when she was downtown or just so happened to drive by a church she would make sure that she crossed herself and prayed. Nonetheless, my mother did not force her faith down my throat. As a result, I quickly became what I would like to call a free agent. In the sports world, players are called free agents if they do not belong to a particular team, making them available to sign with any team. In my case, I was not under a particular religion and I was not involved in any particular church. My loyalty didn't lie anywhere. What I didn't know was that though I was not a member of any church, I was still a part of the well thought out creation made in the image of the all-knowing God of this universe.

Having not grown up in the church, I more rapidly became familiar with the streets of Miami than I did with God and religion. I could remember as a teenager growing up in Miami, I got into all types of trouble with my friends in the neighborhood. It seemed like stealing and fighting was all that we were about as skinny little teenage boys growing up in Miami. We would steal bikes from people's yards, then we would take them back home, spray paint them, and switch the wheels out for different ones. We did this to change the identity of the bikes so that the owner who we stole the bike from would not recognize his or her bike. We did it to avoid confrontation. One particular night, a group of my friends and me decided to burglarize our middle school, North Miami Middle. We climbed into one of the back windows of the school, which led us into the home ec room. Here we found patties, heated them up in the microwave, afterwards we continued to have a good time as we proceeded to walk throughout the school. At the same school, a group of us also decided to break into one of the school's portable classrooms. We got in, stole a whole slew of candy, and as we walked back home we met two older gangsters in the neighborhood. In the darkness, they both were standing underneath a tree having a conversation with each other. And here we walked up to these two older gangsters bragging about the crime that we had just committed. My friends and I were like little gangsters trying to earn our stripes. But the older gangsters didn't seem to be too impressed with us. One of them simply searched one of the boxes that we were carrying, grabbed one piece of candy, and then commanded my friends and I to scram.

When it came to fighting, my friends and I fought more amongst each other than against any outsiders. I could remember playing football one day. One of my friends named John did something to make me angry with him. I could remember heading straight for John like a bull that has just seen the color red. I walked up to his face and slapped him. John was so shocked (I believe because he could not believe I had the guts to slap him) that he just froze for a split second. Before he could retaliate, the other boys separated us.

One night I fought a kid who lived right around the corner from us. My friends and I didn't like this kid. Unlike us, we viewed him as being very privileged. This kid was aware of how much we didn't like him, but for some reason (a reason that I still haven't figured out) he would always come around to hang with us. One day the dislike that I felt for this young man would cause me to pick a fight with him in the midst of a basketball game. During the game, he kept fouling me. I felt as though he was doing this on purpose and I picked a fight with him. This basketball game was on a basketball court behind a local elementary school, and it was nighttime in almost pitch-blackness that we fought. This was probably not the best time to pick a fight with a kid who was almost as dark as the night that we were fighting in. The only fighting move that I knew was to rush someone, pick them up by their legs, and to slam them to the ground. This maneuver did not work too well for me. This kid straightened his legs so that I could not lift him up. After being tied up for a moment, my friends separated us so that we could reset. Then the kid threw a punch that I did not see coming. It was not a surprise that I did not see the punch coming; after all, he was as dark as the night. He hit me above my right eye, splitting my eyebrow open, blood started to gush out of my eyebrow onto my face, and I fell to the ground. Needless to say, I had to go to the doctor that night to get some stitches.

Another particular time where I resorted to fighting was when I was about 15 years old, and my mother worked a job where she, in essence, baby-sat the foster children of a lady cop. These kids were far from angels. There was one kid in particular who was worse than all the others. His name was Joey. He was a short, curly haired kid who thought he was the baddest thing walking. I eventually came to show him otherwise. One day my mother took me along to her job. While in the living room of the house one day, Joey disrespected my mother by calling her a bitch. This ticked me off! I quickly went from calm to angry. I dared him to call her that one more time, and he did. Before I knew it I was on top of Joey pummeling away at his face. Luckily my mother did not get fired from her job as a result. Sometime after this event, my mother had some of her friends over, and I could remember eaves dropping as she shared the incident with them. She spoke proudly about the damage that I did to Joey. This gave me a proud feeling on the inside. It made me feel so tough. My cousin Garincha, who was also told about the event, said that he had a new-found respect for me for having defended my mother's honor. Once again, I was more familiar with the things I learned on the streets of Miami than I was with God and the church. I was a little rough around the edges--edges that needed a little smoothing. Even with this tough exterior, a seed had been planted in me with a small knowledge about God. This seed would be watered further when I moved to the city of West Palm Beach.

Invitation

In the fall of 2001, while I was still attending Boynton Beach High School, my mother and I moved to the city of West Palm Beach. We both moved into a townhouse complex named Breckenridge Place. The best way that I could describe this complex is rows and rows of townhouses. Though my mother and I both moved to West Palm Beach, she didn't immediately transfer me from Boynton High to a school that was closer to home. Once again, my mom was totally aware of how passionate I was about the game of basketball. So she didn't want to transfer me from Boynton Beach High until I had completed basketball tryouts. She did not want her son to miss out on the meaningful opportunity of making the basketball team. While I was attending Boynton Beach High, I would stay at my cousin Wallace's house (which was a matter of minutes from Boynton High) until my mother came to pick me up that night. She was more than willing to pick me up from there every evening and to drive back to West Palm Beach where we lived. Of course, she only continued to do this until she found out the sad news that I was cut from the team. After that, she felt no need for me to continue to attend a school that was so far from our new place in West Palm Beach. With that said, she had me transferred to a high school in West Palm Beach called Palm Beach Lakes High.

As a result of not making the Boynton High basketball team, I no longer had the hunger to try out for another basketball team or make it to the NBA for that matter. Nonetheless, I was still passionate about the game of basketball and played street ball often. There was a black man who also lived at Breckenridge Place. He owned a portable basketball hoop that he placed in the parking lot that was in front of his townhouse where he and his family lived, way in the back area of Breckenridge. Here on this basketball hoop, I played basketball often. Sometimes while shooting around on this basketball hoop, he would come and give me some tips on how to be a better player. This man looked to be about 30 years old, and he played for his high school basketball team in the past. One day he suggested that I try out for the Palm Beach Lakes High School basketball team. Still traumatized from being cut from the Boynton Beach High basketball team, I was initially closed-minded to this suggestion of his. But after much deliberation, I finally decided to tryout for the Palm Beach Lakes basketball team. When I showed up to tryouts, I was so intimidated by the incredible skills of the other players that I decided not to follow through with the tryouts. This in itself shows that I no longer had a hunger to make it to the NBA. No longer having a desire to make it to the NBA, I now had no sense of what I wanted to do with my future. I never had a Plan B. Once again, I had always placed all my eggs into a basket labeled "Basketball." When I dropped this basket and broke all of my eggs, I became a tumbleweed that was at the mercy of the winds of life. I had no sense of my future goals. There was a grey area in my life that needed to be colored in with the beautiful colors of purpose and direction. It is during this time that a person entered my life who would be used as a tool to change this status of aimlessness of mine. The name of this person was Junior.

Junior was a short and stalky, light-skinned Jamaican kid who was about a year younger than me, and he lived with his family at Breckenridge Place. The townhouse he lived in was a little further into the complex than the one I lived in. Where I lived was a little closer to the entrance of Breckenridge Place. Not only did we live in the same housing complex, but we also attended Palm Beach Lakes High School together. In the mornings, we both would wait, along with a group of other students, for the school bus that took us to school. This bus stop was a place where him and I had many laughs that strengthened our relationship. Junior and I did not only live close to each other, but we had many common interests. One of these interests was playing video games. We constantly visited each other's homes to play video games. When I would visit his home, it was an opportunity to also get acquainted with his family. This immediate family of his was composed of his father, mother, and his two younger brothers. Before long, the friendship of me and this video game and professional wrestling loving young man quickly flourished. Us living in the same complex, attending the same school, and sharing the same interests made it almost impossible for us not to become best of friends. Our sense of humor also greatly helped in building our friendship. I have always had a funny bone and I would often do things to make Junior laugh. One day after school we both boarded the school bus. We were both sitting on the bus when a heavyset black girl who we both knew boarded the bus. Seeing her, I quickly prepared myself to do an improvisational comedic routine with her unknowingly being the catalyst for my routine. When she walked past my seat, I immediately threw my slim body violently towards the window side of the bus. What I was saying with this comedic routine of mine is that the girl was so fat that by walking by me she caused my body to be thrown forcefully against the side of the bus. Junior watched my whole comedic routine from beginning to end, and was immediately overcome by laughter.

In meeting Junior, I was not meeting just an ordinary kid. On the contrary, there was something peculiar about him and his family. And that thing is that they were all Christians. To be more specific, they were Seventh-day Adventist Christians. What is a Seventh-day Adventist Christian? In a nutshell, this meant that according to God's fourth commandment, their faith consisted of believing that Saturday is the seventh day of the week, or the Sabbath Day (as opposed to the popular belief that Sunday is the Lord's Sabbath). The book of Exodus 20:8-11 reads:

> *"Remember the sabbath day, to keep it holy. Six days shalt thou labour, and do all thy work: But the seventh day is the sabbath of the Lord thy God: in it thou shalt not do any work, thou, nor thy son, nor thy daughter, thy manservant, nor thy maidservant, nor thy cattle, nor thy stranger that is within thy gates: For in six days the Lord made heaven and earth, the sea, and all that in them is, and rested the seventh day: wherefore the Lord blessed the sabbath day, and hallowed it."*

Also, as their name "Seventh-day ADVENT-ists" suggests, Junior and his family also believed in the literal second coming of Jesus Christ. The Second Coming of Christ is also referred to as the second "ADVENT." This is why these followers of Christ call themselves "ADVENT"-ists. With that said, in becoming friends with Junior, I was unknowingly becoming friends with a Seventh-day Adventist Christian who was active in the church. One day Junior invited me to his church. Once again, I did not grow up in the church, so I was not accustomed to attending church. I was the total opposite of those kids who've been in the church all their lives. I had more knowledge of basketball and the streets than of God. So, I was not quick to accept Junior's invitation into the house of God. Nonetheless, my Christian friend was not deterred by my rejections. He continued to invite me to his church every opportunity he got, until one day I finally gave in to his relentless petitions. I agreed to attend Junior's church at a time where I was vulnerable as a result of not having any sense of the direction my life was going. Junior entered my life at the right time.

Chapter 4
The Calling

One early Saturday morning (or Sabbath morning) Junior's dad drove up to where I lived in Breckenridge Place to pick me up for church. I got in the car where my friend Junior was waiting with his brothers, and we were on our way. It only took about 15 minutes for us to arrive to the church, which was located on Summit Road. The actual name of the church was First Seventh-day Adventist Church of West Palm Beach, Florida, but since it was located on Summit Road, the members dubbed it "Summit Church," or just simply "Summit," for short.

Summit was not a mega church that had the capacity to hold thousands of people. It also was not one of those small, intimate churches that only had room for only 100 people. It was somewhere between the two. I would say that it was mid-sized. This church had two main entrances. When you first turn off Summit Rd. onto the driveway of the church, the first entrance you would see was the one leading into the main sanctuary. Once you walked into the sanctuary, there were two glass double doors that led into a lobby area on the outside of the sanctuary. Past the lobby, you could choose to go through one glass door into the left side of the sanctuary, or through another door into the right side. Straight ahead, in front of all the rows of pews was a stage. Dead center down stage was a podium, and upstage was the baptismal pool.

The second entrance that I would like to describe to you was located on the opposite side of the building and away from the sanctuary. It was in this separate part of the building that I had my most memorable experiences at Summit Church. This was another set of glass double doors that led you into a short hallway. This hallway made a quick right turn, revealing two restrooms. One for males and the other for females, both separated by a water fountain.

Straight ahead past those rest rooms was a door that led into a classroom. Then the hallway made a left turn down another hallway that showed several classrooms aligned on the left side of the hallway. You are probably wondering, "Why all the classrooms?" The answer is that Summit Church also functioned as a day school. There is one part of this particular building that defined my first experiences at Summit Church. Let us backtrack. When you first walked into the first double doors, before making a right towards the bathrooms and classrooms, there was another set of double doors directly in front of you. Once you walked into these doors, you would find a big space that was used for anything. Youth church was often held in this part of the building. But early Saturday mornings, this space was used for a youth discussion called "Cornerstone." It is this weekly biblical discussion that shaped my first experiences at Summit Church.

Cornerstone was designed for the teenagers of Summit. In Cornerstone, the adult facilitating the discussion expected each young adult to read the spiritual lessons in a small paperback book called "The Quarterly." It was called the quarterly because a new one was issued to us every three months, or quarter. When we got through one book, a new one would be issued to each young person. There were various lessons inside these quarterlies. There was a lesson for each day of the week other than the Sabbath. So there would be a lesson from Sunday through Friday. Each young adult in the youth Sabbath School was expected, during the six days before Sabbath Day, to have reflected on each lesson, and to have answered the questions asked in each of those spiritual lessons. Once the Sabbath Day had arrived, each young person was expected to be prepared to discuss the Biblical topic they studied in Sabbath School. It was the adult facilitators job to ask the young adults questions and to keep them on track with the lesson. Every Sabbath Day there would be a different adult facilitating Sabbath School.

When I walked into Summit for the first time, I walked in with certain values. I was standoffish and had a wall up. I also let off an air that I was some kind of tough guy or gangster. To give you a better idea of my condition upon first walking into Summit, let me share with you a brief testimony from one of the elders of the church. Years later, out of curiosity, I asked him, "What was your first impression of me when I walked into the church?" And he responded, "Oh no, here is another one!" What he was saying with this statement was, "Oh, no! Here is another lost kid fresh off the streets!" I have no doubt that this was something that I picked up from growing up on the streets of Miami, Florida. Upon first entering Summit Church, I also challenged many of the members' beliefs in the Cornerstone discussions. This was because I was not accustomed to attending church, so I did not know much about God and His word. Consequently, I could not understand how a person could have faith in something that they could not see. One day in Cornerstone, I boldly asked the group, "How do you know that God exists?" In retrospect, I can see a young man (me) who didn't truly want to know the answer to the question, but to see if he could successfully ruffle the feathers of the elders who had been studying the word of God for many years. What I was trying to find out was if the elders believed something because someone told them to believe it, or whether they could actually support what they claimed to believe. They always did a great job in supporting why they believed that there was a God who created the universe and us.

It did not take long before Summit elders manifested a particular interest in me. In the Cornerstone discussions, the elder facilitating the discussion would be much more interested in my opinion than those of my peers. An elder who did this often was also one of the first people to show a particular interest in me. A Jamaican by birth, he was Alfred Sharpe, but we called him Brother Sharpe. It seemed like from the time I first walked into Summit, Alfred was trying to break down the wall that I had put up around myself, but he had great difficulty in doing so. He tried to do this by attempting to give me a hug one day in church. At the time, it was my fervent belief that a man was not supposed to hug another man. So when Alfred attempted to hug me, I rejected him! Nevertheless, Brother Sharpe was one of the first elders who noticed strong characteristics in me that I did not see in myself. One day while my friend DeJean and I were sitting at the kitchen table in Alfred's house, Alfred (who was getting dinner ready) suddenly directed his attention towards me. He turned around and talked directly to my friend DeJean, but referred to me, saying, "He has much more wisdom than his peers at the church." After Brother Sharpe said this to DeJean, DeJean immediately agreed with him. DeJean's quick response to Brother Sharpe's remark showed me that he totally agreed with Brother Sharpe. Their dialogue convinced me of a truth about myself, but I felt slightly uncomfortable. Brother Sharpe is also the one who said to me one day, "You have what it takes to be a great minister." When he said this to me, I looked at him as if he were crazy.

There was another time in particular where I felt God sharing with me His will for my life. One day while I was sitting in on a Bible study facilitated by a teenager about my age named Pierre, Pierre and his family were also members of Summit. Pierre had the evident calling on his life to be a pastor. He actively walked by faith in the calling that God had placed on his life. Pierre would facilitate Bible studies within the church, faithfully teaching others the word of God. One night, Pierre was holding one of these sessions in a classroom at Summit. I sat in this Bible study in a way that said, "I don't really feel like being here." At one point, as I sat there listening to Pierre teach the word of God, I felt a strong conviction come over me. I could feel the Lord telling me that He wanted me to do exactly what Pierre was doing in that Bible study, and that is to teach others the word of God. But once again, I brushed off this "crazy" notion.

Brother Mike was another member of Summit Church who was yielding to God's calling on his life. He was a slim, light skinned Jamaican who was about 6 feet tall. You could almost see his zeal for advancing the Kingdom of God dripping off of him. Every time I looked at Brother Mike, he had an air about him that said, "I'm a God-fearing man, and I will not compromise my beliefs for anyone." He was a fine example of what a Christian should look like, both on the outside and on the inside. Every Sabbath he dressed in a nice modest suit, and every time he spoke, he spoke in a gentle tone. Brother Mike had a very interesting testimony. He ran from the calling on his life, suffered in the world, and eventually surrendered to the Holy Spirit and started to walk in the high calling on his life to be a minister. By the time I met him, he had already become a strong fixture within Summit church. I remember very vividly a time when Brother Mike organized a series on health from the Bible's perspective for a local neighborhood. This neighborhood was about 10 or 15 minutes from our church. Before he started the series, I, along with some members, went into the community and evangelized the local residents. Mike created a beautiful PowerPoint presentation and presented it at the neighborhood's elementary school. When he spoke he did not only speak passionately about the subject of health, but about God. It did not take a genius to see that Brother Mike had done extensive research on his subject before he brought it to waiting ears. Brother Mike's apparent goal to advance the Kingdom of God also included guiding the youth into a closer relationship with Jesus. One day he invited a group of young men from the church, including myself, to dinner at an Olive Garden restaurant. Brother Mike used this as a tool to get close to us and to guide us closer to Jesus.

The elders of Summit have always seen something in me. So one day they asked me to preach a sermon for youth church. Having never written a sermon in my life, I didn't know the first thing about writing one. Naturally, I needed assistance! Having made himself available to work with the youth, Brother Michael was the one who helped me write the sermon. During this sermon writing process, Mike would take time out of this day to come over to my house and give me some pointers on how to properly structure a sermon. Full of wisdom, he gave me useful pointers on how to construct a working sermon. I really appreciated him for that. I did not know it then, but Brother Mike was ministering to me. Like Pierre, he had a calling on his life to be a pastor, and was fully yielding to the calling on his life. I could not say the same.

One day the youth were scheduled for a trip to a camp. The purpose of this camp was not only to have fun, but also to be fed spiritually. Also in attendance at this camp were youth and adults from other Seventh-day Adventist Churches. I came with some of my close friends from Summit. Before we arrived to the camp, we already had our minds made up that we were going to cause some kind of trouble while we were at the camp. Although I knew the bad intentions of my friends, I did not try to go against them. Instead of standing out like the leader the elders of the church earnestly tried to make me see that I was, I chose to support my friends.

While we were at the camp, my friends and I followed through with our scheme and misrepresented our church by doing something we were not supposed to do. Not too long after we followed through with our actions, Brother Sharpe, who was one of the chaperones of the trip, found out about it. He was also the father of my friend Mark, who was also involved in our mischief. Somehow Brother Sharpe found out that his son was involved in this mischief and was prepared to punish him. Mark was terrified. Instead of being true and saying that Mark was in the wrong, I thought that it was more honorable if I protected Mark. To comfort Mark, I told him that I would step in and defend him. I knew that Alfred Sharpe along with many of the other elders in the church had much respect for me, so I decided that would work on my behalf. I had a sit down with Brother Sharpe at the camp, and I told him something that makes me cringe with embarrassment every time I think about how foolish it was on my part. With a straight face, I said to him, "Brother Sharpe, you knew that we were going to cause trouble once we got here to this camp." In an attempt to defend my friend Mark, the message that I was sending to Brother Sharpe with my statement was: Don't get mad at Mark for what you knew he was going to do.

Brother Sharpe was a person who respected me because he saw me to be wiser than all of my peers. Because he respected me so much, he listened very intently to what I had to say. As I delivered those words, I stuck out my chest and spoke with bravado. I felt so intelligent as I defended my peers, but in actuality I looked like an idiot. Here I was called to be a minister! Here I was a man who was constantly being encouraged by the adults to set a better example for the youth that followed me. Instead of setting a good example for my peers, I got involved in the same mischief that they got involved in. Not only this, but I went to the man who always saw something better in me, and I defended the mischief that his son was deeply involved in. I thought I looked cool, but in all actuality I made a fool of myself.

Tugging away from the calling on my life, I even considered joining a street gang. At 15 years old, Mark was Brother Sharpe's oldest son, and he had been in the church ever since he was a child. Thus, he had been in the church for most of, if not all, of his life. Mark was very intelligent, but he seemed always to be attracted to the dark side of things. I don't recall how long it occurred after I'd known Mark, but eventually Mark decided to join a street gang called the Bloods. When he chose this dangerous lifestyle, I didn't exactly disapprove of it. On the contrary, I was attracted to it. Mark was not the only one at Summit who became a member of the Blood gang. Two other friends, Kareem and Osani, also became a part of this lifestyle. Like these friends of mine, I too adopted the hatred that they had for members of their rival gang, the Crips. I was not a part of the gang, but because my friends were in the gang, I felt the need to be against anyone that was against them. The hatred that I had for people that were members of the rival gang was in direct opposition to what the Bible teaches us about loving our neighbors.

"And the second is like, namely this, Thou shalt love thy neighbour as thyself. There is none other commandment greater than these." –Mark 12:31, KJV

One night, while playing basketball at church, I started acting hostile towards another young gentleman who was playing basketball with us. I acted this way because this young man was allegedly a Crip gang member, a rival of the Blood gang that my friends were a part of. When I was told that this young man was a part of this gang, I quickly directed aggression towards him. While playing basketball with him, I played with more aggression than I usually did. I unnecessarily pushed and shoved him just so that I could score. I also did a lot of trash talking towards him. I did all of these non-Christ-like acts only because I heard that he was Crip member. I was not even a part of the Blood gang! Not only was I running from my calling, but I was also sharing the hatred that one gang had for another.

Not after long after being in the gang himself, Mark invited me into the gang. The action of getting initiated into the Blood Gang was called "Coming home." One day while I was home, I received a text message from Mark. Very concisely, he asked me, "When are you coming home?" He asked me this a few times, and in a joking manner I turned down the invite. Though I turned down the invite, I often flipped around the idea of joining a gang in my head. To me, there was always something attractive about being a gang member. Blood gang members often wore the color red to distinguish themselves from other gangs. Being associated with Mark, I eventually started to wear a lot of red. One night some of my Summit friends, which included Mark, decided to go to the movies at City Place in West Palm Beach, Florida. Before we went, I put on a white tank top, a pair of red pants, and a red pair of Chuck Taylor Converse sneakers. On this night, I intentionally dressed up like a Blood gang member. When we arrived at the movie's parking lot I started to act up. I acted like I did not have any home training. I did not act like a Christian that night. That night I tried my best to convince everyone that saw me that I was the gang member that I was not. City Place was composed of restaurants, stores, a comedy club, and a movie theater. Before going into these places to enjoy themselves, people parked their cars within a parking garage, the primary parking for the visitors of City Place. So you can imagine this parking garage was busy on a Saturday night. There were long lines of cars entering and exiting the garage. On this particular night, upon arrival to the parking garage I held up the cars that were behind me. I jumped out of my car and started to scream at my friend Silo who was following me in his own car. In recollection, I did not have to get out of the car; I was simply looking for any excuse to get out of the car so that the people in the line of cars behind us could see my red clothes and associate me with the Blood gang. This action of mind conveyed several things. It showed that I had pride in the gang, that I thought it was cool, and shows that I did not totally reject this dangerous lifestyle. Another reason I put on a show for those people was because I wanted to look tough in front of them. That night it was as if the Blood gang attire that I was cloaked in instantly changed me into a very reckless person. After watching the movie, I continued to act wild, as if my mother had not raised me any better. Despite the fact of my proudly taking on the characteristics of the gang, I was not officially in the gang. But Mark--who was a real Blood gang member--would still continue to invite me into the gang. His persistence was impressive, and one day I finally gave into his relentless petitions.

Feeling depressed and empty on the inside one day, I felt as though joining the gang would grant me the fulfillment and joy that I was seeking. So on this day with my heart beating fast with nervousness, I sent a text message to Mark informing him of my decision to finally accept his invitation to join the gang. He then asked me "Are you serious", and I said "yes." After confirming, he said that he would talk to me further that upcoming Sabbath at church. Mark was going to guide me through the process of joining the gang. I was, to say the least, extremely nervous. I was not quite sure if I truly wanted to be part of a dead end lifestyle of a gang member. I didn't feel fully committed to the idea at all. After church that upcoming Saturday, I walked out of the church to find Mark standing next to my car. Right there as he stood next to my car he had a totally different demeanor that I was not use to, and it spoke volumes. He stood there rubbing both his hands together as if he were anticipating something. I could sense that he was prepared to take whatever action it took for him to get me into the gang. The more I stared at Mark with this prepared air about him, the more fearful I became. I don't know what happened, but I never joined the gang. Mark didn't even bother to invite me into the gang anymore. I believe that it was God that kept Mark and me from going through with the whole thing.

Another person who saw the leader in me was a woman in the church we called Sister Audrey. She was a tall, light-skinned, heavyset woman who often worked with the early teen group of Summit church. Teaching a Sabbath school for young teenagers every Sabbath, Sister Audrey was passionate about working with the young people of Summit church. On one particular Sabbath day after the church service, the elders invited all of the youth to lunch. This lunch took place at the house of one of the church elders. What we, as the young people, did not know was that there was a particular agenda behind this lunch. The elders of the church organized this lunch to address a specific problem that involved Summit's youth. Many times, during church service on Sabbath mornings, many of my peers would hang out outside of the church. The problem that the adults noticed was that many of the youth were not attending church service!

The place we had lunch on this Saturday afternoon after church was a house that had a patio in the back of it. On this patio, chairs and tables were set up for this lunch with a secret agenda. Later as my peers and I were finishing up our meal, Sister Audrey stood up. While standing there in the midst of us, she started to point to individual young people, commanding them to stand up. Each young person without hesitation, would obey her and stand up just as she commanded them to do. Once that person stood up, she told that person how they could use their character, gifts, and influence to be a guiding light to their peers. In other words she told each young person how he or she could make a positive contribution in leading the young adults in a positive direction, a direction--that of course--involved the young people attending worship service on Saturdays and not hanging around outside the church.

I was one of the last people that Sister Audrey asked to stand up. How epic! I was nervous at the thought of what she was about to say to me, and I had a good reason to be. By this time, many of the elders of the church already showed me that they not only wanted better for me, but they expected more from me. I was nervous about what Sister Audrey was going to say to me, because I was highly aware that she also viewed me as a leader amongst my peers. She--like the other elders in the church--noticed how much my peers followed everything that I did. The elders that facilitated Cornerstone always wanted to know what I had to say because they viewed me as a leader. The problem was that I was also conscious that "leader" is a title that I was not quick to claim. This was a title that I was not trying to live out at all. I was afraid of the idea of my being a leader, but I could feel this very thing running through my veins. Even though it was in me, I tried to run from it by blending in with my friends and rejecting the words of the adults when they told me how I could better myself. Instead, I allowed my peers to do whatever they wanted to do, even though I knew that some of the things that they were doing were wrong. In other words, I was conscious of the fact that I was not trying my best to set the best example for them.

After Sister Audrey verbally put all the other young people in their place, it was now my turn. I felt like a hardened criminal standing before a judge that was about to give me a jail sentence. I immediately knew that I was about to be scolded in some way for not doing what I was always encouraged to do. And what I was always encouraged to do--leading my peers in a positive direction. Then Sister Audrey directed her attention towards me. In a very authoritative voice she said, "Thierry, stand up!" I immediately obeyed and elevated my body from where I sat, but a feeling of nervousness and vulnerability came over me. I felt naked as the rest of my peers looked at me. In this position, it was not possible to hide amongst my peers. For now I was the only young person standing up. I was standing on my own like a lone soldier ready to take whatever fiery verbal assaults Sister Audrey was preparing to throw at me.

Sister Audrey told me exactly what I feared. She told me that I had a strong influence on my peers. Continuing to speak, she said everywhere I went, my peers followed. Then she said, "Set a better example for them." So her suggestion was for me to set a better example so that the youth would be bettering themselves when they followed me. Her suggestion was a fine example of simple mathematics. One plus one equals two. While she said these words to me, I could feel something inside me saying, "You know she is right! You are a leader, and you need to set a better example for your peers!"

Even though I felt the strong conviction that I was in fact a leader, I fought against it. Instead of yielding to what God was calling me to do, I wanted to keep my peers from seeing me as a goodie two shoes. With that said, instead of admitting that my peers were in the wrong--which they were--I chose to defend them. At the time, I did not know that in defending my peers for their wrongdoing, I was also simultaneously running from the calling on my life. I was ignoring the voice of God and running into the opposite direction.

I spoke out boldly. To all the adults who were in attendance at that lunch I said, "The youth do not stand outside the whole time that church service is going on. It only seems like that because before the adults walk into church service the youth is outside, and when they walk out of service, they are right where the adults saw them last." My argument was that, "This does not necessarily mean that my peers were outside the whole time." What I suggested to them at that lunch was, "The youth go into the service after the adults do and leave the service before the adults leave the service." As soon as this argument left my mouth, it felt absurd. As a matter of fact, I wish I could go back in time and slap myself for suggesting something so foolish. Right there on that patio I defended my peers, and in doing so I felt that I had also disappointed the adults in attendance who were just trying to lift me up to a better standard. With my response I was saying to them, "I would much rather blend in with my friends than to stand out as the leader that you see in me."

Chapter 5
Walking Away

I'm Baptized

Though I had a hard time yielding to the calling on my life, at Summit Church I developed a strong relationship with my Savior, Jesus Christ. The transformation power of God was evident in the way I started to live. I prayed and studied the word of God often. Many nights in the privacy of my bedroom, I diligently searched the Holy Spirit inspired scriptures in a big red Bible that Brother Sharpe gave me. I also had a stronger prayer life and dependency on God.

There reached a time where I started to receive severe anxiety attacks, and I don't know where they came from. For some reason I would have frequent worrisome thoughts. This was unheard of because I've never been the one to be afraid of much. The anxiety attacks would be triggered by these fearful thoughts. Worried, I would ask myself questions like, What if this happened? or What if that happened? The anxiety attacks would make it very difficult for me to breath. I've had bad fevers in my time and even rough colds, but nothing was worse than these attacks. I would try various techniques that I found in brochures to make these attacks go away. I would hold my breath for a few seconds before exhaling. This was only a temporary fix, the anxiety attacks would come back stronger than ever with the mission to make my life miserable. After trying all of these techniques in an attempt to make this physical nightmare disappear, I finally decided to take this ailment of mine to God. One night before bed, having grown sick and tired of this physical nightmare, I kneeled down next to my bed and prayed earnestly. With tears rolling down my face, I shared with my Father in heaven what I was going through and asked that he would deliver me. I had prayed many times before, but this prayer was way more fervent than all of my previous prayers. I guess this was because I had a deep desire for these painful anxiety attacks to go away. When I was done praying, I climbed into bed with the faith that God would deliver me. Before my prayer, for me to go a few minutes without having these anxiety attacks was unheard of. But on this morning, something had changed. I woke up expecting for this anxiety attack to constrict my lungs, making it difficult to breathe, but nothing happened. The anxiety attacks didn't creep up to cause me to have difficulty breathing. From that day on, I never had another anxiety attack. I depended on God to take away this pain from me, and with His divine power He cured me. I had faith that he would cure me and He rewarded my faith by simply lifting this physical nightmare off of me as if it were just a piece of lint on my shoulder.

Another tell tale sign of my conversion was experiencing a peace that surpasses all understanding. It was an inner peace that prevailed despite any storms that was happening around me. One day while riding through West Palm Beach on the public bus, I felt as though I was covered with this impenetrable cloak of joy. As the bus rode along I looked out the window at the beautiful scene outside of the bus. The leaves of the palm trees rustled in the breeze on this bright and sunny day. This scene, to say the least, was breathtaking. As I sat there on the bus, I thought to myself, It is my God who made this day and created these beautiful trees. I was at total peace. A peace that only a relationship with Jesus could offer.

Growing in righteousness, I finally decided to take that leap of faith that Christians take when they have decided to make the declaration that they have accepted Jesus Christ as their Lord and Savior. On May 21, 2005, at the age of 19, I got baptized into Summit Seventh-day Adventist Church. On this day, as I stood in the baptismal pool with the Pastor of Summit, Pastor Moseley, he asked for all those who supported my baptism to stand up. When he made this appeal, I watched as many people in the congregation stood at attention. My heart melted as my eyes took in this grand scene of support for my baptism into the Seventh-day Adventist Church.

These supporters of mine were not people that I have known for many years. I met them not too long after I moved to West Palm Beach, Florida. So I've only known them for only a few years before my baptism. Yet, by standing they were showing their unwavering support of me finally giving my life to the Lord. These supporters of mine watched my quick spiritual growth from the time I walked into Summit until now where I was now making the decision to give my life to the Lord. As I stood in that baptismal pool, they all looked on at the scene with reverence, as I was about to get submerged into the watery grave. It was almost like they were saying, "Thierry, we are not only your supporters, we are your family!" I suspect that this respect was not simply for me, but for the Almighty Creator who had dramatically transformed a lost kid to a follower of Christ. As the people remained standing I was submerged into the baptismal water and then lifted up again into a new life. The word of God says:

> *"Therefore we are buried with him by baptism into death: that like as Christ was raised up from the dead by the glory of the Father, even so we also should walk in newness of life."*
>
> -Romans 6:4

Alfred Sharpe is one of the elders in the church who had always seen something special in me. He was there when I first walked into Summit Seventh-day Adventist Church, and he was there to witness my baptism. He was one of the church members who tried to make me see that I had much more in me than I thought. Days before my baptism, he approached me and requested that I recite a poem entitled "I Am a Soldier in the Army of God" immediately after my baptism. The words of this poem conveyed the strong relationship that I had quickly built with my Lord and Savior, while attending Summit Church. Only because of God's grace, I made massive strides from questioning the very existence of God to now boldly declaring that I was now a willing soldier in His army. What a drastic change! This was a change that could only have been accomplished through the transformation power of the blood of Christ.

After I was baptized, I removed my wet robe and got dressed in some clothes that I bought specifically for this special day. After removing my wet robe, I put on a nice pair of black-tip, light brown dress shoes, a light brown shirt, black slacks, red suspenders, and a red bow tie. With this new attire, I stood boldly as a new man in Christ before the couple hundred Christians who were in attendance that day, and I recited the poem "I Am a Soldier in the Army of God."

I am a soldier in the army of my God.
The Lord Jesus Christ is my Commanding Officer.
The Holy Scripture is my code of conduct.
Faith, prayer, and the Word are my weapons of warfare.

I have been taught by the Holy Spirit, trained by experience, tried by adversity, and tested by fires.

I am a volunteer in this army, and I am enlisted for eternity.
I will not get out, sell out, be talked out, or pushed out.
I am faithful, reliable, capable, and dependable.
If my God needs me, I am there.

I am a soldier.

I am not a baby.
I do not need to be pampered, petted,
primed up, pumped up, picked up, or pepped up.

I am a soldier.

No one has to call me, remind me, write me, visit me, entice me, or lure me.

I am a soldier.

I am not a wimp.
I am in place, saluting my King,
obeying His orders, praising His name,
and building His kingdom!

No one has to send me flowers, gifts, food, cards, or candy, or give me handouts.
I do not need to be cuddled, cradled, cared for, or catered to.
I am committed.

I cannot have my feelings hurt bad enough to turn me around.
I cannot be discouraged enough to turn me aside.
I cannot lose enough to cause me to quit.

When Jesus called me into this army, I had nothing.
If I end up with nothing, I will still come out ahead.
I will win.

My God has and will continue to supply all of my needs.
I am more than a conqueror.
I will always triumph.
I can do all things through Christ.

The devil cannot defeat me.
People cannot disillusion me.
Weather cannot weary me.
Sickness cannot stop me.
Battles cannot beat me.
Money cannot buy me.
Governments cannot silence me, and hell cannot handle me.

I am a soldier.
Even death cannot destroy me.

For when my Commander calls me from His battlefield,
He will promote me to captain and then allow me to rule with Him.
I am a soldier in the army, and I'm marching claiming victory.
I will not give up. I will not turn around.

I am a soldier, marching heaven-bound.
Here I stand! Will you stand with me?

Unknown author

To my surprise, a powerful force came over me as I started to recite this poem. It was a surreal sensation that I never felt before. This thing took over my body and my mouth, and gave me an extra boost of power that I never felt before. After becoming more familiar with God's word through fervent research, I now know that this thing was not a thing at all, but the Holy Spirit of God that was in me. The Spirit helped me to deliver this poem in a way that I could not have done alone. It helped me to touch those in attendance in a place that I could not have done under my own power. Using the last few words of the poem "Here I stand! Will you stand with me?" I asked everyone in the congregation to stand with me. The couple hundred people who were in attendance that day immediately obeyed and stood at attention. As I looked out at them, they all looked like a sea of soldiers. After that momentous day, I was told that there were people in the congregation who cried when I recited this poem. I suspect that their tears were mostly prompted by the rapid spiritual growth that they have witnessed in me, to now having finally and consciously accepted Jesus Christ as my Lord and Savior.

I was making a strong declaration with the poem "I Am a Soldier in the Army of God." Very boldly, I was declaring to all the Christians on the day of my baptism that I would never turn my back on God or my church family. In the beginning of this poem I say:

> "I am a volunteer in this army, and I am enlisted for eternity.
> I will not get out, sell out, be talked out or pushed out."

My Mom's Influence on Me

Several strong opposing influences in my life have always kept me from God's plan for my life. One of these influences is my mother. The strong bond that I had with my mother is the reason why she had a powerful influence on me. This strong bond resulted from the fact that it has always been my mother and me. Yes, I had many stepfathers who came in and out of our lives, but none of them stuck around long enough for me to build a relationship as strong as the one that I had with my mother.

In my early childhood, I attended an elementary school called Gratigny. One afternoon after school, I missed my bus home. With no way to get home, I became very worried. Not knowing what else to do, I pitifully sat on the floor against the front of the school building. I sat there as if I were waiting on some kind of resolution. I don't remember exactly how long I sat there for, but after sometime I looked up to see my mom coming to my rescue. She came around the corner of the school building like my superwoman. Excited to see me, she had the biggest smile on her face, and both her arms were opened in a welcoming gesture. To say the least, I too was very relieved and joyous that she had come to my rescue. Every time this memory comes to mind, it warms my heart.

Another memory that I have of my mother's loving character was when I got older. I was attending a middle school in North Miami Beach, Florida, named John F. Kennedy. At the time we lived a little ways from my school, so I had to catch public transportation early in the morning to be able to get to school. Walking, the bus stop was about 20 to 30 minutes from my home. In the mornings, she would wake up early along with me just to walk me to this bus stop. Her making sure that I arrived to the bus stop safely stemmed from the love that she had for me. These are just a couple examples out of many, of why I loved my mother so much.

As a result of the love I had for my mother, she had a big influence on many decisions I made. In this way, many times I have allowed my mother to lead my life. This proved to be a major obstacle when the Lord was trying to lead my life upon entering Summit Church. Placing my mother (or anyone for that matter) above God is against His will. The Word of God says, "If any man come to me, and hate not his father, and mother, and wife, and children, and brethren, and sisters, and yea, and his own life also, he cannot be my disciple." Luke 14:26.

My family is full of what the world would call "successful people." This means that they occupied respectable positions and made a lot of money. When I think about the people who meet this criteria, the first person that comes to mind is my cousin Lenz. After a humble beginning of growing up in the small country of Haiti, he then traveled oversees to Argentina, to study to be a surgeon for an impressively long 12 years. Before I graduated high school, through my mother, I would always hear stories about his success. It always seemed like she was in some kind of competition with her older sister (which is my aunt and Lenz's mother). It appeared that both sisters had placed their kids on a figurative racetrack, and as their children, we were a part of some kind of competition. I would get a sense of this competition when I would eavesdrop on my mother's phone conversations with my aunt. My aunt would give my mother constant updates on what her kids were doing with their lives, and my mother would update her on what I was doing with my life. In this way, I could sense how proud my mother was of her nieces and nephews accomplishments. She spoke about them with a certain pride in her voice. Often times, when she became angry with me, she would say things like, "Why couldn't my kids be more like my sister's kids?" When she would say these things, it hurt me in a deep place. Nonetheless, these words drove me to impress my mother even more, leading me to fight to equal or top the accomplishments of my cousins.

I graduated from Palm Beach Lakes High School in May 2004. Before I graduated, God continued to use the elders at Summit Church to set me on the path to become a pastor. Way before I graduated, I clearly heard God telling me the direction that He wanted me to go in, but I continued to tug in the opposite direction. For as long as I could remember, I had always dreamed of making it to the NBA, so I used to always envision myself getting a scholarship to play basketball in the NBA. But now, basketball was no longer in the picture. My hoop dreams went downhill when I did not make the Boynton Beach High School basketball team a few years back. So on the cusp of graduating high school, I found myself in the position where I had to figure out what I wanted to do after I earned my diploma. I decided to attend college.

My decision to enroll in college was half the battle. Now with my own finite mind I tried to figure out what it is exactly that I wanted to study. Initially, I made the decision to study nursing. I did my research on this career and what I found out about it was very enticing. It only took four years to earn a degree in this field. Not only this but after this short time of studying, I learned that I would be making more than enough money to support myself. After making the decision to study nursing, I told my mother. But no matter how enticing nursing was to me, I didn't stick to this major. Altogether, I rejected the idea of studying nursing in hopes that I could figure out another major that I was more comfortable with. When I told my mother that I no longer wanted to study nursing, she was infuriated! She said, "You don't know what it is that you want to do with your life!" When she said this, I was to say the least, very shaken up.

Racking my brain, I continued my quest to find the right major for me. I thought about the things that I was good at and then I racked my brain to try to figure out a major that matched my talents and interests. With that said, I researched a career as a computer technician. I've always been good with computers, so I figured that I would probably enjoy a career as a computer technician. One evening my mother and I set aside some time to visit a school named ITT Tech. This was a place where future computer technicians came to learn. When we got there, one of the faculty members gave us a tour of the campus. I guess the tour was not to my liking because I never went back or even applied to the school. I continued my search.

After much deliberation, I finally decided to study pharmacy. Before settling on this career, I did thorough research on it. My thought process was the same as when I decided to study nursing. I looked at the amount of time that it would take to get a degree in pharmacy coupled with the amount of money that I could make after graduating from school. Just like when I decided to study nursing, I was highly attracted to what I found out. It only took six to seven years to attain a degree in this respectable field! This to me was highly attractive. Not only this, but I was also enticed by the idea that upon graduation, I would be making close to six figures a year. The money that I would make once I graduated from school was a big plus. This career would also be impressive in the eyes of my family members (who I was interested in looking good in front of). As a result of allowing the world and my family to dictate what I needed to do with my life, I began my quest towards a pharmacy degree at Palm Beach Community College in January of 2005. As the school's name suggests, it was located in the same county I attended high school (Palm Beach) in a city called Lake Worth.

The Offer

I always focused more on pleasing my mother instead of pleasing God. So when I initially made my decision to study nursing, I quickly notified my mother of my decision. She was so excited and started to share this information with her big sister (my aunt) like she always did. She didn't waste anytime in telling her sister about my decision. Her actions showed me that what I decided to do with my life was very important to her. Or she was, like I always suspected, living through me. I suspected that she was trying to show her sister that her child could also be successful. When I broke the news to my mother that I was no longer pursuing a degree in nursing and decided to pursue pharmacy, she was so angry that it shook me to the core. She said, "You can't make up your mind on what you want to do with your life!" I was hurt by this comment of hers, but she was right! Deep inside I could feel that I did not truly know what I wanted to do with my life. I was all over the place. What my mother thought of me mattered to me. The problem here is that the only thing that should have mattered more was what my Father in heaven thought about my decision. Once again, the influence that my mother had on me would get in the way of what God wanted me to do.

About a year after I was baptized into the church, on March 18, 2006, the members of Summit ordained me into the office and work of a Deacon within the church. Not too long after this ordination, the elders made me yet another offer that would continue to move me down this path that God wanted me on. It was an offer that conveyed the minister that the elders of Summit have always seen in me. And this offer required for me to take a tremendous leap of faith into God's perfect plan for my life.

One Sabbath morning, while I was standing outside of Summit, I was approached by one of the elders of the church. He started off by saying that he and some of the other elders of the church had a meeting, and I was one of the topics of the meeting. He then said that the elders of Summit have agreed to help me pay half of my tuition if I agreed to attend Oakwood University. Oakwood is a school that was founded by Seventh-day Adventists. To Adventists, it is "the" school for Adventist youth to attend, especially those who were pursuing a career in the ministry. That Sabbath morning the elders made me a strong offer to cover half of my tuition! But I could only get this scholarship under one condition. I had to make the decision to abandon pharmacy for a study in theology.

As this elder stood in front of me on this Sabbath morning, waiting on my decision, I could hear a voice deep inside me encouraging me to accept the offer. This voice said, "Accepting the offer is the right decision." There was also another voice that was present and going against this voice. It was a part of me that did not want to accept this great offer. As I stood in front of that elder that morning, a war was raging inside of me. The scholarship was enticing, but the other part of me was having tremendous difficulty in giving into it.

As I stood in front of that elder, I could not help but feel my fear of how my mother would react if I were to make the decision to now study theology. Once again, I allowed my mother to dictate my decision. As I stood there in front of that elder with this war raging inside of me, I thought about how my mother reacted when I told her that I switched my major from nursing to pharmacy. I thought about how frustrated and angry she was that day and how hurt this reaction of hers made me, and I didn't want to relive this reaction of hers. I thought to myself, If I change my major from pharmacy, so that I could go down the path to becoming a pastor, then my mother would really think that I am crazy. As I stood in front of that elder, I was placing my will and my mother's will before God's will. I successfully tugged into the opposite direction of the voice inside of me that was telling me that in accepting the offer I would be making the right decision. Right there as that elder stood in front of me waiting patiently on my decision, I gave him my final answer. A very unsure "No" crept out of my mouth.

Me denying the offer was not anything new. When I felt the calling on my life before, I was always afraid to fully submit myself to the calling on my life. The only thing that made this occasion different from all the others is that I was now verbally expressing my denial of what has always been happening within me. Being concerned with doing my will and my mother's will caused me to deny a very important offer that came from my church elders. Now I was placed in a position where that church elder was asking me to change my major from pharmacy to theology. I avoided this by denying the offer. In denying this offer, I was saying to him that I was sticking to pharmacy.

A second factor that kept me from accepting the scholarship was simply the fear of the high calling of being a pastor. I was scared of the whole idea of me leading in the church in this capacity.

I did not simply deny the scholarship. Along with denying that offer, I denied the leader that the elders of Summit always saw in me. Therefore, after I denied the scholarship, the atmosphere of Summit church changed. The elders of the church noticeably distanced themselves from me. They started acting differently towards me. Instead of showering me with the praise that I was used to, they now gave me a cold shoulder. As a result of this change in some of the members' attitude towards me, the atmosphere of Summit Church felt claustrophobic, almost like the walls were closing in on me. I now felt unwanted, unimportant, and shut out. I could not take this painful feeling of being closed out for long. So my solution to relieve this pain that I felt was to leave the church altogether.

For the longest time, I thought I walked out of Summit Church because of how the elders of the church acted towards me. But now as I look back in retrospect, the way that they acted towards me was a small influence. Overall, what caused me to leave the church was the strong guilt I felt of having denied the minister that the elders of the church have always seen in me. Summit was by far the longest that I have ever been at one particular church. With that said, the strangers I met years ago quickly became my family. They played a major role in my spiritual growth. Now after years of having grown close and fond of this family of mine, I decided now to leave them behind and go my separate way. These wonderful people never did me any harm. They showed me time and time again that the best was all that they've ever wanted for me. Now, without thinking twice I made the decision to leave my Seventh-day Adventist family behind as if they were merely strangers.

Section 3
Searching

"Now the word of the LORD came unto Jonah the son of Amittai, saying, Arise, go to Nineveh, that great city, and cry against it; for their wickedness is come up before me. But Jonah rose up to flee unto Tarshish from the presence of the LORD, and went down to Joppa; and he found a ship going to Tarshish: so he paid the fare thereof, and went down into it, to go with them unto Tarshish from the presence of the LORD."

Jonah 1:1-3

Chapter 6
Pharmacy

I started attending college towards a pharmacy degree in January of 2005, before I walked out of Summit Church. After I walked out of Summit, I continued my matriculation through school. Superficial is the best way to describe the factors that drove me to study pharmacy in the first place. I was attracted to the large amount of money that pharmacists made. On an entry level in the pharmacy career, you could make close to six figures! I also chose to study pharmacy because I viewed it as a career that would be respectable in the eyes of my family members. These shallow motivations propelled me to work extremely hard upon first entering college.

During class lectures I made sure I took careful notes. I also made sure that I stayed on top of homework and other assignments. To help me with my organization, I used a planner that was issued by the school. In it, I carefully jotted down all of my class assignments directly underneath the date that each assignment was due. I did this to ensure that I turned them in on time. I had a strict daily study routine. After completing my classes for the day, on the way home from PBCC, I would catch the public bus to a bus stop that was about 15minutes walking distance from my home. I would then unchain my bicycle from a post (that I chained it to earlier that day when I was on the way to school) and ride home. When I arrived home, I would grab something to eat and watch television until I fell asleep. After this brief nap (which was about an hour long) I would put on my backpack, and ride my bike 10 minutes to the library. I read somewhere that in order to be successful in school, it was recommended that students study three hours for each hour that they spent in class. Very carefully, I calculated the amount of hours I was in class for each subject, which was about an hour. As the recommendation told me, I then studied that subject for three hours of each hour I was in class for it. After locating an available study room in the library, I followed this recommendation to a tee.

Before long, I earned great accolades at PBCC. I was inducted into a National Honor Society called Phi Theta Kappa, and I also made the Dean's List. Students who earned a spot on the Dean's List were not lazy, passive students. They were the total opposite. These students achieved high grades due to their relentless work ethic. These students were active, hardworking students who took their studies very seriously. I was, hands down, one of these students. While in school, my mom did not make it a secret that she wanted me to succeed in school. I could clearly remember the night I found out that I had made the Dean's List. While deeply submerged in my studies one night at the local library, I received a call on my cell phone. It was my mother. She told me that she found a letter in the mail informing me that I had made the Dean's List. I could tell by the tone of her voice that she was proud of me. She was so happy that you would have thought that she was the one that made the Dean's List! This shows how interested my mother was in my success. So I continued to excel in school so that I could please her.

An Empty Feeling
When I began my matriculation at PBCC, I was impressively driven and highly optimistic. I moved around the campus with passion, and I consistently made good grades. All these emotions and my success in school were all driven by the idea that I would one day become a high-paid pharmacist making between five and six figures. It was also driven by the idea that a respectable career as a pharmacist was sure to please my family.

On the outside looking in, I was coasting on the road to success. After all, I earned good grades and I had received great accolades. Behind the scenes, I found myself trying hard to convince myself that I enjoyed my classes. I failed miserably in doing so. After all those nights of studying hard, getting good grades, and even receiving great accolades, I started to come to grips with the ugly truth that I did not enjoy what I was studying. After almost two years of studying at this school, I started to recognize that a particular emptiness lingered inside of me. One day during chemistry class, I noticed that my colleagues were far happier than I was. With bright smiles on their faces, they moved around class very passionately, and placed a certain pride into their work. I knew that they were genuinely happy because they enjoyed their majors. They seemed to have a great sense of what they wanted out of life. I, on the other hand, could not say the same.

After two years of studying at PBCC, I no longer walked around the campus with the same zeal and enthusiasm as I did when I first enrolled. On the contrary, I now walked around the campus feeling lost and empty on the inside. I went from listening closely to class lectures to not listening at all. My professors' lectures started to go through one ear and out the other. I was physically present in my classes, but my mind was elsewhere. With that said, it was not long until my grades started to slip and I started to fail my courses. I was starting to realize that my happiness was far more important, than making six figures and pleasing my family. Then, I finally decided to take action and move towards finding this happiness, whatever it was. After a whole two years of studying at PBCC, I finally decided to drop out. The superficial motive of money and my desire to please my family, did not keep me at PBCC.

Dropping out of the pharmacy program was not a real surprise. Studying pharmacy never really did sit right with me. I started studying pharmacy while I was attending Summit. One day when I was the main speaker for a major event called "Youth Day" at Summit Church, a strong feeling came over me that told me that studying pharmacy was not the right direction for me. On this day before I got up to preach, Sister Audrey (the woman who asked me to set a better example for the youth at that lunch that followed church that one day) was the one who introduced me. In the introduction, she said that I was studying pharmacy. As I sat there on the pulpit getting ready to go up and preach for Youth Day, something deep inside me told me, Thierry, you know that a career in pharmacy is not where you belong. However, due to my desire to please my family and make a whole lot of money in the process, I continued my matriculation through college.

While I was still attending Summit Church and Palm Beach Community College, the members of Summit tried their best to lead me down the road of becoming a minister. I could remember talking to Brother Sharpe while I was on the campus of the school one day. He told me that there was something special about me, and this "something special" had nothing to do with pharmacy. This "something special" always had something to do with being a minister of the gospel. He along with many of the other elders of Summit saw something in me that was in deep contrast with what I chose to study at Palm Beach Community College. With all of my power, I pulled away from that direction and submerged myself in my studies towards a pharmacy degree, and pharmacy failed to grant me fulfillment.

When I failed to make the basketball team at Boynton Beach High School years ago, I wondered, What am I going to do with my life now? The answer to this question came back to me void. In contrast, when I dropped out of college, I was clear on what I was going to do next. I said to myself that I would perform spoken-word poetry until I figured out which college major would grant me fulfillment. Spoken-word poetry is not something that I just decided to start doing after I dropped out of PBCC. Behind the scenes, I was performing spoken-word poetry while I was attending Summit. I was also performing spoken-word poetry while I was working towards a pharmacy degree at PBCC. For some reason, I had always gravitated more towards this craft than the calling that God had placed on my life. So the idea of submerging myself in it after dropping out of PBCC, quickly flowed into my mind.

CHAPTER 7
Spoken-Word Poetry

Spoken-word poetry is the art of performance poetry. As the name suggests, spoken-word artists pour their souls out onto a sheet of paper, with the ultimate goal of reciting this poem to an audience. Spoken-word artists often performed at venues such as poetry lounges and coffee shops. But the places that a spoken-word artist can go with their art are not limited to these venues.

You've read about my passion for the game of basketball. When did my interest to write poetry creep onto the stage of my life? Before I moved out of Miami, before I tried out for the Boynton Beach High School basketball team, before I started attending Summit Church, and even before I attended school for pharmacy, I was made aware of my talent to write well. At North Miami Middle School, my Language Arts teacher made me aware of this talent of mine. Handing back a graded writing assignment to me in class one day, he encouraged me in a sincere tone to exercise my writing potential.

Though his counsel made an impression on me, I didn't immediately start to exercise my talent. It was not until I moved on to my freshman year of high school, did I start to exercise this gift of mine, and my motivation was a beautiful high school freshman named Laquisha.

She had a captivating personality, a soft caramel complexion, and her eyes and hourglass body shape seemed to scream out "Seduction." Early one morning, the school bell rang, signaling for all the students in the school to transition to their next class period. As soon as I walked out of my class into the busy hallway of students rushing to class, my eyes fell on Laquisha in the crowd. She wore a pair of tight black pants that left no room for the imagination of a teenage boy. The kind of pants that made you wonder, How was she able to get them on in the first place? I quickly found myself gawking at this young lady's jaw-dropping physique, and I was not the only one who had taken notice. One of my good friends, who was also one of the many students that poured out of their class, also took notice. I mean, how could we not have taken notice? Those skintight pants she wore practically demanded our attention. Immediately after noticing Laquisha's body, both my friend and my eyes locked on each other. We both looked at each other with a look that said, "Do you see what I'm seeing?" In awe and impressed by Laquisha's voluptuous body, both my friend and I loudly exclaimed a prolonged, loud, and overly exaggerated "Daaaaanng!"

In biology class, there were tables so that the students can sit, two students sat at each table. My friend E-Say and I sat at the same table, sitting at the table directly in front of us was the beautiful Laquisha. E-Say was aware of how I felt about her and how afraid I was of telling her how I felt. One day, while in biology class, E-Say suggested that I write her a poem. I quickly rejected the idea. I firmly believed that writing poetry was for sissies. Despite this view of mine, the more I came to grips with the truth that I was too afraid to verbally let Laquisha know how I felt about her, the more attractive the idea of writing her a poem became to me. After gathering all of my thoughts, I wrote her a poem right there in biology class and immediately handed it to her.

Laquisha enjoyed my poem so much, she said she would hold onto it. I watched as arguably the most attractive girl at North Miami Senior High placed my poem neatly inside one of the pockets of her flat folder. To me, this signified that she had accepted my poem into her heart. I was confident that I was making strides towards her heart. In that same class period, Laquisha did something to make me angry. I was so furious that I said a few harsh words to her. If there existed any glimmer of hope of me making strides towards her heart, I knew instantly that they were now gone. Turned off, Laquisha handed my poem back to me. She handed it back almost as quickly as she had accepted it! Needless to say, after this episode, Laquisha did not grant me the opportunity to get to know her better. Nevertheless, the poem that I wrote her ignited a hunger in me. From that point on, I wrote more often using the medium of poetry to help me express my innermost feelings. Though Laquisha did not give me the opportunity to love her, I fell in love with poetry.

Still, the art of spoken-word poetry goes beyond just simply writing a poem. When did the art of spoken-word or performance poetry come into the picture? While living in West Palm Beach, I became good friends with a young man named DeJean. He and I both shared the same passion for writing poetry. Fully aware of this passion of mine, DeJean called me one night while I was at work. I worked as part of the stock crew in a store in West Palm Beach called Albertson's. My main job was to place new incoming products on the store shelves. While working on the shelves one night, I received the call from DeJean. He informed me that there was an open mic event opening for the first time in West Palm Beach that night. In a state of bewilderment I asked him, "What is an open mic?" He said that it was an event where I would be able to perform my poetry for others. The more he spoke about the event, the more excited I became. You would have thought that I had been waiting for a long time for an opportunity to share my poems with others. After DeJean told me the date, time, and location of this open mic, I told him that I would attend. By this time, I had a notebook full of poems that I had written over time. With that said, I was equipped with more than enough poems to recite for the audience members at this open mic event. Just like that, I started performing spoken-word poetry.

Chapter 8
Covering More Ground

After a while of performing spoken-word poetry, I developed a particular habit. I was performing in the same places over and over again, making me a local poet. I grew to fall in love with the same great feedback I received from the same people in the same venues. Having grown content with being just a local poet, often times in the privacy of my bedroom, I would daydream about the feedback I would receive for a poem while I was still in the process of writing it. Content with performing in these same venues, I also gladly made sure that I had the door fee for the venue that I was attending. Every person attending the open mic event had to pay the door fee, and this included the performers. Imagine this, performers were the ones who made the show. Without performers, there would be no show. If anything, the performers should be allowed into the venue for free. Not to mention, I was not being compensated for my performances. I was blinded to the truth that I was stuck in a stagnant place of being just a local poet. I was blinded to the point that I was willing to do anything to quench my desire to perform my poetry for others. This is why I gladly and ignorantly paid my own money to instantly grant me this opportunity. My thoughts were unable to elevate beyond the regular humdrum lifestyle of a local spoken-word artist. Before I dropped out of PBCC, a successful national performer entered my life to help break this stagnant cycle. He would break this cycle by opening the curtain and revealing a beautiful picture of other worlds that had better performance opportunities. The name of this person is Kevon. In the same way that my friend Junior made his entrance into my life a few years ago (when I had no idea of what I wanted to do with my life after basketball), Kevon made his entrance into my life when I was stuck in the stagnant state of being just a local poet.

Years before I met him, Kevon had already devoted his life to educating others. Only in his mid-20's, he was already a successful entrepreneur, activist, actor, and poet. His main focus was to educate others about the dangerous disease of AIDS. He himself did not contract this disease; he was simply passionate about educating others about it. He often educated others about this disease through the craft of acting. Though educating others about sexually transmitted diseases was his passion, he has also educated and empowered others through acting on topics such as black history. Countless schools and organizations eagerly paid him to educate their people. He would then invest this money to promote this business of his, and to travel out of town and out of state to educate others at various high schools and universities. He would push his intellect to the limit, with the goal of advancing his business. Within the deep recesses of his own imagination, Kevon created a concept called Confessional Narratives. Confessional Narratives resembled monologues when they were performed, but had a specific nature about them. Confessional Narratives had five distinct components: acting, motivational speaking, poetry, comedy, and they had to be used to educate others. He often used these pieces to educate others on various topics such as black history, but his main focus was educating others about the dangerous diseases of HIV and AIDS. He also often traveled to other cities and states to teach others. While furthering his agenda to educate others, he pursued a bachelor's degree in theater at a school called Florida Atlantic University. Talk about being driven! Many college students attended school for something that they did not enjoy. Not only were they studying something that they didn't enjoy, but they also waited until they received a degree before they went out into the world and did something with themselves. Kevon was not even remotely in any of these stagnant and depressing categories. He did not wait to earn his degree before taking the world by storm with his educational shows and enriching workshops. Way before he graduated in the theater program a FAU, he was actively putting to use what he had learned thus far to further his business.

When did I meet this successful young entrepreneur? Before I dropped out of Palm Beach Community College, I often times performed my spoken-word poetry at many open mics that were organized on campus. On one open mic night, Kevon walked into the open mic fashionably late. As soon as I saw him, I sensed immediately that there was something different about him. I thought to myself, Who in the world is this guy? It was apparent to me that this was not an ordinary young black man. When he walked in, his presence commanded the room. He dressed in business attire and carried a briefcase. He seemed to be in some way above every young college student that was in attendance on this night. He walked with a strong sense of purpose that said, "I know exactly where I am and where I am going in life." The first thing that I found out about Kevon was that he, like me, was a performer. I found that out when he performed one of his spoken-word pieces at the event on this night. Everyone enjoyed his performance. After the event, it was determined that he and I had the best spoken-word pieces at this event. As a result, we were told to battle it out using our spoken-word pieces as our weapons. I recited my piece, and then he recited his. Kevon had this look of fear and discomfort on his face, as I directed my piece towards him as if I was trying to demolish him right where he stood. At the end of the battle, the audience was asked by the host of the show that night to determine who won this battle. They decided that it was a tie. On this night, Kevon recognized my talent as a performer, and was so impressed that he immediately took me under his wings as his protégé. Just like that, a local spoken-word artist became the disciple of a successful national performer.

Once again, I was not performing in nearly as much places as him, making as much money as he was, and I was not nearly as purpose driven as him. While he was getting paid big bucks to perform nationally, I was paying out of my own pockets to perform locally. I could remember a time when I was performing at an open mic event at Palm Beach Community College. This was around a time that I did not know what it meant to be a professional artist, so I was performing for free. While at this event, I noticed one of the PBCC faculty members handing Kevon a check. He was getting paid to perform poetry! Kevon proved to me that it was possible to perform professionally. This scene also made me more aware of the fact that I was not at the level that Kevon was on. He had accumulated a plethora of knowledge on how to be a professional artist. His mind was full with information on how to earn money as a professional artist. This event boosted his credibility as my mentor, and I was willing to learn more from him. As if his great sense of work ethic and purpose were not enough, he had his very own office on the campus of the school he attended. How many students who attend college can say that they have their very own office on the campus of the school that they attend? Not many. One day he asked me to meet him on the campus of FAU. When I arrived I found that he also had his own secretary! As soon as I walked in his office that day, I noticed her. She was a middle-aged black woman sitting behind a desk with a computer in front of her. Here Kevon was a young black man who was still attending school, having not yet earned his degree and he had an older woman who was probably old enough to be his mother, working under him and checking his emails. When I witnessed the fact that this young mentor of mine had his own office and secretary, it boosted his credibility in my eyes. I saw him as a person who had a lot of great knowledge that he could pass on to a local artist like me that didn't know the first thing about how to venture out as a professional artist.

Kevon's work ethic was impressive. One time I went to go meet with him at his school Florida Atlantic University (FAU). I found him in one of the media rooms using one of the computers. He was effectively using the school's resources to edit the footage of one of his shows. I guess to use this footage to make a DVD to sell at his gigs or to use it as a promotional video to help him sell himself to get his next gig. While he was enrolled at FAU, this driven young man was constantly on the move and on the lookout for resources to push his business forward. He did this while other students were waiting to earn a degree before they decided to do more with their lives. During his matriculation at school, he also created and self-promoted his highly educational shows to students and the faculty at FAU. Kevon moved with purpose and he moved within that purpose relentlessly. So much that he stuck out like a sore thumb amongst the other students that were in his age group. As the mentee of this successful young black man, I gladly walked beside him as he eagerly taught me his ways. I was with him one day while he was self-promoting one of his upcoming shows. This show was going to take place in one of the auditoriums on the campus of FAU (the school that he attended). As I watched him work, it was very apparent that he had a lot of sway on the students on campus. One afternoon as he was promoting one of his upcoming educational one-man shows, he walked up to a group of young women on campus, who were also students, and asked them to help him promote his upcoming show by passing out fliers. It was obvious that they already knew who he was judging by the way that they were open to helping him. It was apparent that they were more than familiar with him, and knew exactly what he was about. While promoting his show, he made sure that he saturated the campus with all of his fliers. I walked beside him like the mentee I was and studied his work ethic as he walked to the mailboxes of the professors of FAU and dropped the fliers in each of their mailboxes. Before Kevon, I never met any other young black man with a relentless work ethic such as his. With that said, I followed him faithfully as his disciple.

As Kevon's protégé, he immediately recognized my stagnancy as a local performer. With urgency, he started to teach me things with the goal of delivering me from this bondage of stagnancy. Kevon was the person who brought to light the truth of this depressing dead-end cycle that I was caught in. In his own very passionate way, he would tell me things like, "If you do not venture out, you will become a 30 year old poet who will still be performing for free in the same venues over and over again." He was right! I knew that he was right, because when he said those words to me, they resonated with me. It forced me to look at myself truthfully under a microscope. When I did, I saw that I was right on track to becoming this figurative 30-year old poet who Kevon warned me about.

As Kevon's protégé, I often tagged along with him when he traveled to his various gigs. Many times he would allow me to perform my spoken-word poetry. In this way, I was able to cover more ground with my poetry. Sometimes these performances were close to home, and other times they were out of state. One special opportunity in particular that Kevon is responsible for is my opportunity to perform at the world famous Apollo Theater in Harlem, New York. Talk about branching out! On May 19, 2007, both Kevon and I flew up to New York to audition for the world famous Apollo Theater Amateur Night. I was 21 years old at the time. When we got there, the audition line curved around the building. It appeared to be that the whole neighborhood wanted to have a shot at being on that Apollo stage. Standing in that line were singers, rappers, dancers, and everything in between. For this particular audition, I was auditioning with one of my original spoken-word pieces. I don't remember which one it was, but I do remember that the judges enjoyed my work so much that they gave me a date to fly back up to New York for Amateur Night. When we were done with our audition, we both flew back home to Florida.

When my date arrived to fly back up to New York for my scheduled performance date, I was excited. When I was younger, I use to watch Apollo performances on television. I never imagined that I'd be performing there one day. When I arrived, all the performers were told to go to a waiting area and to wait on their name to be called. When my name was called, I walked upstairs to the stage, and I performed a poem of mine entitled "The Sky is Falling." This particular piece was about the terrorist attack on the World Trade Center in New York on 9/11/2001. With this piece, I showed sympathy for the people who lost their lives in that attack. Before I walked on stage, the host told the audience that I was from Miami, Florida. It's good that she mentioned where I was from, but there is something about a person coming from another city that makes you have to work a little harder to impress the natives of another city, especially at the world famous Apollo Theatre. Nonetheless, the crowd did not intimidate me. I got on that stage and performed my heart out, but I did not last. The audience started to boo me. For some reason, the audience thought that I was making a mockery of the 9/11 event. The more they booed, the harder I performed, hoping that they would stop booing. They didn't stop. I was escorted off the stage by the sandman. I must admit, that this was a real hurtful experience for me, and I was affected by it for a few days. Nonetheless it was a great experience. If it were not for Kevon, auditioning for the world famous Apollo Theater would not have crossed my mind. Some other places I performed with Kevon are: Drake University (Iowa), Oklahoma State University, Florida International University (Miami), and Bethune Cookman College (Daytona Beach, Florida).

If it were not for Kevon, more than likely I would have continued to perform in the same dead-end venues over and over again mistakenly thinking that's all there was to life. Kevon opened my eyes to help me see other worlds that I could reach as an artist. If it were not for him, I have no doubt in my mind that I would still be content with being a local spoken-word artist with a limited audience. The audiences for my spoken-word poetry increased exponentially because of him. Kevon was also the person who taught me about the value of hard work. Even during those times that it seemed like I was stubborn and didn't want to listen, he remained persistent and tried his best to drill values in me that he himself learned by trial and error. One time he said to me, "I'm sharing these things with you so you don't have to go through the grueling process of trial and error that I had to go through while I was building my business."

As Kevon's protégé, I still had this unsatisfied urge for fulfillment. In my attempt to fill this urge, I was constantly adding titles to my name. I would continue to add titles such as "actor" to my name, without knowing the first thing about the craft of acting. In my mind, if I dabbled in something once or twice I had a right to call myself this thing. This is like a person who has baked a cake once or twice and then using this accomplishment as sufficient grounds to call themselves a "baker." Kevon, on the other hand, had earned the right to call himself an actor. Not only was he in school studying theater, but he was also constantly organizing and acting in his own one-man shows. Kevon was also an activist who was constantly educating others about sexually transmitted diseases like AIDS. He had earned his right to call himself this, because for years before I met him he had devoted his life to educating people about these lethal diseases.

One day Kevon noticed what I was doing, and he was angry and amused at the same time. He said to me that I could not add a title to my name just because I did something once or twice. What he was telling me was that before I added a title to my name, I had to have first earned that right. When he told me this, it struck a nerve, because he was right. What I was doing in essence was saying that I was a baker just because I baked one or two cakes in my whole entire life. This does not make me a baker! Constantly performing spoken-word poetry, the only title that I had truly earned was that of being a "spoken-word artist." Deep inside I knew that I was adding these titles to my name because I was in desperate need of a sense of purpose and fulfillment, and I continued to do this.

Chapter 9
Journalism, Activism, and Acting

I had always been living with my mother, but this would eventually change. Right before I dropped out of Palm Beach Community College, my mother decided to move to Jacksonville, Florida. Since I had always been dependent on my mom to have a roof over my head, this meant that I had to now move out on my own. Before she moved, she helped me find a place. Through one of her friends, she found an apartment in West Palm Beach. A young man named Reed was seeking roommates to fill two rooms in this 3-bedroom apartment. Having been living on his own in this apartment, Reed has had to carry the weight of having to pay the hefty rent of the 3-bedroom apartment. So he was in desperate need of roommates to help him carry this burden. My friend Greg and I became those two people.

I only lived at this place for a short time before I decided to move in with my mother in Jacksonville, Florida. The day I was getting ready to move out of my place, my mother came down to Jacksonville, Florida, to help me pack my things. After we were done placing these things into my Monte Carlo, we both drove four hours to Jacksonville, Florida.

Journalism

After dropping out of Palm Beach Community College in West Palm Beach, I was no longer enrolled in any school. But now after arriving to Jacksonville, Florida, I decided to make a second attempt at getting enrolled in college. On June 2, 2008, I started to attend a school named Florida Community College of Jacksonville. This was one of the several campuses that were located throughout the city of Jacksonville. The campus that I enrolled in was located on the south side of Jacksonville. Therefore, this campus was considered the "south campus" of FCCJ.

Once again, I did not attend college because I felt like God was leading me into it. Just like when I attended PBCC for the first time, I just simply felt like attending college was the thing to do. Once again, instead of depending on God, I depended solely on myself to figure out what my concentration would be in school. Of course I did not choose pharmacy as a major, because this major left me unfulfilled. Also, the amount of money that I would make in a particular career was not the main motivation for the major I chose this time. To figure out what major would best suit me I now asked myself, "Which major would lead to a fulfilling career?" To find the answer to this question, I analyzed my talents. I thought about my talent to write, and said to myself, I enjoy writing, maybe I should try studying journalism! I figured that a career in journalism would grant me the joy that I desired to have.

That Same Empty Feeling

Just like when I started school at Palm Beach Community College, I worked tremendously hard. This hard work did not last long. Not after long of being enrolled at FCCJ, I started to get a strong feeling that I did not belong there. There were times when I would be studying on campus, and a strong feeling would come over me and tell me that I did not belong there. It reached a point where I would be walking around campus, and I would feel this strong empty feeling on the inside of me. I felt dead on the inside like some kind of zombie, and what a horrible feeling it was. This was the same familiar empty feeling I felt right before I dropped out of Palm Beach Community College.

As opposed to the two years it took me to drop out of PBCC, it didn't take anywhere near as much time at FCCJ. I dropped out of FCCJ after a short-lived two months. One morning when I was scheduled to attend one of my classes, I just remained in the comfort of my bed. My mother walked into my room, saw me just lying there, and asked, "You're not going to school?" I replied "No." This marked the second time I have dropped out of college, and just like when I attended PBCC I did not go back.

Activism

As an activist, my mentor, Kevon, brought awareness to others about the dangerous disease AIDS. He himself had created an organization called Aids Awareness Poets. Like him, while living in Jacksonville, Florida, I thought I could find fulfillment in building my own organization and becoming an activist. Once again, instead of looking to God, I often mirrored the things that Kevon did to bring him success, in hopes that these things would also grant me success and fulfillment. There was one problem. I did not know what this organization would be about and exactly what I would be fighting for as an activist. To help me figure this out I went to Kevon, the person who had already built a successful organization.

One night I called Kevon. I shared with him my new endeavor of starting my own organization. With wisdom, he told me the first step to starting my organization was to first pinpoint my passion. He then said that once this passion was found, it would function as the solid foundation to build my organization. Taking the counsel of Kevon, I racked my brain and asked myself, "What exactly is my passion?" This was a recurring question for me on my quest to find fulfillment. When I was living in West Palm Beach, I became fascinated with street gangs. I think this fascination stemmed from the fact that some of my friends became gang members. As a result of this fascination, studying gangs became one of my favorite pastimes. Constantly visiting online sites like YouTube and Google I came to know a lot of information about street gangs. I found out where these gangs originated, the colors they wore, and their gang signs, etc. So when Kevon gave me his counsel of finding something that I was passionate about, I thought to myself, Street gangs. Since this was a topic that I relentlessly studied, I said to myself, This just has to be my passion. The very thing that would grant me the fulfillment that I am seeking.

While in Jacksonville, Florida, I created many anti-gang poems and confessional narratives that educated others about gang violence. Remember, a confessional narrative is a concept that my mentor Kevon created. They resembled monologues, but were a mixture of acting, motivational speaking, poetry, comedy, and had to be used to educate others. This shows the major influence that Kevon has had on me. I decided that my organization would be against violence and gang activity. More specifically, its mission would be to stop the illegal things that gangs did and to prevent kids from becoming gang members.

This so-called mission of mine was not a major drive of mine. In other words, it was not truly my passion to go against gang activity. I was simply attracted to the idea that I could be a leader of my own organization. Here I was thinking about starting an organization against gang activity, and I was not totally against street gangs myself! Before I walked out of Summit Church I considered joining a gang. At that time I felt like joining a gang would grant me the sense of fulfillment that I was searching for. For some reason, my plan to join the gang fell through, but I consciously wore their gang colors, threw up their gang signs, and used their lingo. I was doing all of these things, while I was considering starting an organization against gangs. In other words, I was considering starting an organization against the very thing that I constantly perpetuated. Talk about confusion!

What was going to be the name of my organization? The acronym for my organization spelled out the word "gang." It stood for Generation Against Negativity and Gangs. I spent a lot of my hard earned money to order t-shirts with my organization's name on them. In essence, I spent a couple hundred dollars to buy t-shirts for a cause that I was not totally committed to. The t-shirts were white with lime green lettering. On the front the shirt brilliantly read, "I Am a G.A.N.G Member." On the back of the shirt unpacked the acronym also in lime green lettering: Generation Against Negativity and Gangs. I visited open mic venues, promoted my mission, and performed original works with the goal of combatting violence and gang activity. I held on to my mission until certain events happened that made me re-consider the stand that I claimed to be taking against gangs and violence. One night I visited an open mic event in the city of Jacksonville, Florida. A poet friend of mine named Moses hosted this event. On this particular night, there was a party being held in the room that was adjacent to the room that the open mic was being held in. At this party there were many inner city kids in attendance, and many of them were probably gang affiliated. The contrast of the people that attended both events could be seen in the clothes they wore. The people that attended the open-mic event were dressed to impress, and the young people that attended the party were not dressed so impressively. The young men allowed their pants to sag, and the clothes that the women wore were very revealing.

Mid-way through the poetry event, one of the audience members screamed out, "Someone is shooting outside!" One side of the room had windows that faced the parking lot. Being aware of this, everyone, including myself, immediately hit the ground. At this event, I was selling my poetry CDs. Not taking the situation seriously, very stupidly, I stood up and started to promote my CDs to everyone in the room while everyone laid on the ground. If a stray bullet came through that window, I could have been hit. Then some people yelled at me and told me to get back on the floor, and I did. I could have gotten shot for my stupidity. When everything felt safe again, everyone in the room got up from the ground and got back in their seats. The money that the host, Moses, earned that night was kept in a metal box that sat on a table near the door. When Moses went back to the box, he found that the money was gone. I guess while everyone was on the floor and distracted, one of the kids walked in stole the money out the box and walked out. This event made me question, "Is fighting to keep kids from gangs really something that I want to do?" Something inside me told me that this was not my mission.

Moses was aware of what I claimed to be my mission. I was not sitting too far from the door when one of the young gangsters stole his money. So after he found out that one of these hoodlums took his money, he looked directly at me. The way that Moses looked at me after the kids stole his money spoke volumes. The look he gave me said, "Are you sure you want to still fight to keep young people from joining gangs?" His look also said, "I don't think you are built for or even serious about this mission." If those were truly the words that were running through Moe's mind, I did not for one second argue with his view, because something deep inside me already told me that stopping gang activity was not for me.

There was yet another event that made me question my mission choice. One day my mother was talking to one of her male friends in Miami. His name was Paul, and he used to be my step-dad as a child growing up in Miami. When I used to live at Tiffany Squares in North Miami Beach, his son Junior also lived with us. Junior was much younger than me and was in the house more often than I was. I don't know at what point it was, but I lost contact with Junior. His father on the other hand stayed in contact with my mother.

Years later, through my mother, I would hear sad stories about Junior. Junior's father would relay these stories to my mother. There was one particular story about Junior that stuck in my mind. I heard from my mother that Junior was shot several times while he was at a party. She then said to me the doctors decided to leave the bullets in him. Because the bullets were lodged in such a place in his body that if they were removed, it would be lethal. So the doctors said that they would wait until the bullets came out on their own--whatever that meant. When I would hear these stories, I would think to myself, This is not the Junior I once knew. I hadn't seen Junior for Lord knows how long, so in my mind I still had the same picture of a skinny quiet kid who was forced to remain in the house while I would be outdoors playing all day with my friends. With that said, it was surreal to me that this same Junior was involved in these street stories. Junior's dad loved him so much and I bet that he did not know that his son would grow up to be on the streets. I did not have to ask Junior's father to know that he was heartbroken on how his son had turned out.

Anyways, one day while Paul was on the phone with my mother, I guess he asked her, "What was I doing with my life nowadays?" My mother told him that I started an organization with the goal of keeping young people from joining gangs. Paul then said to her in a hurtful tone, "Does he think that he can stop gang activity?" I knew he was saying this out of his experience with his own son. He--as Junior's father--was still not effective in keeping Junior from the street life. When Paul asked this question, I felt like he was saying, "I'm Junior's father and I was not able to keep him from getting into trouble! Does Thierry think that he will be able to keep kids from gangs, especially based on the fact that he does not know them personally?"

When I heard this from Paul, I was hurt. I was hurt because he was right! Keeping kids from gang activity was not my mission, and my mother agreed with him. She questioned, "Why did you choose to do this with your life?" And I didn't have an answer to this question. I was never involved in a gang, I never killed anyone, and I did not just come out of jail from doing a sentence for robbery or murder. Not after long I ceased to stand for G.A.N.G. I don't know at what point I made this decision, but I do know that it was not too long after I started it. I was frustrated. My whole reason for starting G.A.N.G was to find a sense of purpose and fulfillment, and it did not happen. After spending a couple hundred dollars on my organization's t-shirts, I ended up wearing the shirts myself. How pitiful! I knew the reason for my lack of sales was the fact that I was not truly passionate about preventing young people from joining gangs. Here I was not choosing to lean on God (who knows the plan for my life) and depending on myself to find fulfillment. Pharmacy and journalism did not grant me fulfillment. Now I found that even starting my own organization against gangs, could not grant me this fulfillment either.

Acting

After having tried many things to find fulfillment, I finally decided to go to God to see what He wanted me to do with my life. I knew that if I were to be aligned with what He wanted me to do, I would undoubtedly be fulfilled. Going to God as a final resort was something that I have done before. Like when I got those anxiety attacks while I was attending Palm Beach Community College. After failing to relieve these anxiety attacks on my own, I finally went to God, and He healed me. This was the same case here in Jacksonville. But the thing is God already convicted me of what he wanted me to do before I walked out of Summit. It goes to show that I was trying my best to stay away from this truth.

Not too long after I sent this prayer up, three close friends of mine recommended that I try acting. They all suggested this because they've all experienced my personality. Naturally I am a character. They've all witnessed me imitate people in a joking manner. So to all three of these friends of mine, I would make a great actor! One of these friends of mine was Michael. I met Michael when I had just moved to Jacksonville, Florida. He was my next-door neighbor. One day I accompanied Michael while he was doing a job search online at a restaurant called Panera Bread. I was acting like a character at the time and laughing hysterically at my impression, Michael said to me, "You should try acting, man!" The second instance that involved one of my friends telling me that I should try acting was one day while I was on the phone with my good friend Mick (who lived in Palm Beach). He asked me, "You ever think about acting?" The third instance involved one of my lady friends (who lived in Palm Beach). After the third person confirmed that I should try acting, I said to myself, This is the sign that I was looking for. God wants me to be an actor. This sign to me was profound enough for it not to be a sign from the Almighty God. This sign was profound for the following reason. These three friends did not have some kind of mutual agreement to tell me to go into acting. I knew that they did not have a mutual agreement because two of these friends did not know the third, which was my friend Michael. With that said, they could not have gotten together to make a mutual agreement to tell me to pursue acting. For this very reason I took this as the sign from God that I was searching for that revealed to me what he wanted me to do with my life. In desperate need for fulfillment, I jumped into acting with both feet.

Acting (or at least what I thought was acting) was something that I was already dabbling in. In my confessional narratives, I was "acting." The person who was responsible once again for me being interested in acting was Kevon. When I saw him perform his original confessional narratives, I said to myself, I could do that! What my friends were suggesting was not that I start acting, but to submerge myself deeper into the craft. The craft of acting is not something that I ever dwelled on to the point that it became my dream to be on the big screen or to act on Broadway, until these friends ignited a new fire within me. In Jacksonville I became exceedingly desperate to find fulfillment. So as a result of my need, I was willing to try anything to find it, such as yielding and listening to any suggestion that came along such as going into acting. I was in a dark place and I needed a way out.

Desperate for fulfillment and hoping acting would grant me this fulfillment, I immediately started doing research on local talent agencies in Jacksonville. Feeling extremely empty on the inside, I aimed to leave no rock unturned, until I uncovered something that granted me fulfillment. I would drive to them and check them out. I visited many acting agencies, and most of them were frauds. There was always something that did not seem authentic about them when I would visit them. To me they were scamming people just to make money. To me they made many promises but they would not deliver any of the things they said they would deliver. They asked you for all this money to get headshots and acting classes, but would not deliver. To me the amount of money that they were asking for was a red light, so I walked away. This continued with every acting agency that I attended, until I finally ran into one that seemed promising. It was an acting agency that offered classes to people who were interested in learning how to act. While there, they handed me a curriculum and told me the cost of the classes. The price of the classes was a couple thousand. To me this was the real deal!

With a need to please my mom, I rushed home to show her my plans. When I arrived home, I went to her room where she was laying in her bed. I shared with her the curriculum and I told her all about the program. I was excited to share with her the opportunity that I just uncovered. I knew that my mother had no idea of what I was doing with my life, and I didn't like that feeling. It was a horrible feeling to think that my mom thought that I was stagnant. I felt the need to comfort her by showing her that I did have a plan for my life. Once again, I was always trying to please my mother instead of pleasing God. This reminded me of the time I denied the offer of the church elders for me to study theology. The very thought of how my mother would feel about the decision played a major role in the decision that I made. This also reminded me of the time that I initially made my decision to study nursing after high school. To please my mother, I immediately told her of my decision to study nursing.

I never did settle with this acting agency because something made me question its authenticity. I continued to toil to find that one agency that seemed promising. One day I found out about another acting agency that was in Jacksonville, Florida. On this day, there was an agent there visiting from New York to recruit new models and actors. This was very enticing to me. I thought to myself, This is an agent from New York, this agency has got to be the real deal. Because most people knew that New York City is one of the meccas for actors and actresses. I arrived there one bright day in Jacksonville, Florida. This particular agency was located in one of those tall beautiful business buildings. When I got there, I caught an elevator to one of the top floors. When I arrived upstairs, I found that most of the talents that were there were little children. Here I was an adult male sitting in a room full of children accompanied by their parents. Each and every one of us was told to wait in this room until our names were called. When we were called, we were to then go into a room where this agent was waiting and to audition for her. After a while I was finally called in. I walked in to find a young white lady who looked to be in her late 20s. Her name was Aviva. She was an International Talent Manager for an agency called MMG, which stood for Model Management Group.

Right in that room, I auditioned for her and she said she enjoyed me and immediately signed me to her agency. Afterwards they provided me with an online database where I could apply for various acting gigs. To my dismay, when I visited the website, I found that most of the good gigs were either in New York or California. There were no good gigs in Jacksonville, or all of Florida for that matter.

Not finding any good acting gigs in Jacksonville, Florida, frustrated me. It frustrated me to the point I felt like I had to move to a city like New York to find great acting opportunities. Did I move to New York? The answer is no. The reason I did not decide to move to New York was because I knew that the cost of living was too high there. Besides, due to a lack of funds, I did not have enough money to get my own place. So the next best place that I could think of was Philadelphia, Pennsylvania. By this time my cousin Garincha had been living in Philadelphia for years. He had even started his own dance studio there. I decided that I would move in with him until I was able get my own place. Living with him in Philly would be ideal, for I would only be two hours from New York. If push came to shove, I could just catch a bus or train to New York to do gigs there. When I found out that my cousin was living with his girlfriend, moving in with him was no longer an option. Luckily, I had an aunt and uncle that had a house in Lansdowne, Pennsylvania. Lansdowne was located just outside of Philadelphia. One day my mother called my aunt (her sister) and uncle and informed them that I decided to move to Pennsylvania, and asked them if I could stay in their house until I was able to get on my own two feet. They agreed to this. Early one morning, after packing a few of my belongings into my car, my mom and I drove thirteen hours from Jacksonville, Florida to Lansdowne, Pennsylvania.

Chapter 10
Film and Stage Plays

In May of 2009, at the age of 23, I moved to Pennsylvania. Moving out of the state of Florida marked a major pivotal point in my life. It was the first time that I would be living in another state, after having lived in Florida for most of my life. As I drove through Philadelphia on my way to Lansdowne, Pennsylvania, the huge old skyscrapers that aligned themselves along the streets let me know that I was far from my home state of Florida. I drove until I finally arrived to my aunt and uncle's house. This house was located in a suburban neighborhood in Lansdowne, Pennsylvania. This was my first home in the state of Pennsylvania.

Upon arriving to Pennsylvania, I had already made up my mind that I was going to be successful. I worked hard when I moved from West Palm Beach to Jacksonville, Florida, but I pushed myself even harder to find fulfillment when I moved to Pennsylvania. Many people knew me as a performer in Florida. I knew that this was not the same case in the state of Pennsylvania. Therefore, I knew that I had to work hard so that this can become a reality. I remember one of Kevon's counsels to me. He said to me one time, "If you want people to know who you are, you have to perform every day." With these words echoing in my mind, I didn't waste any time once I made it to Pennsylvania. I hit the ground running. I said to myself that I did not move all the way to the state of Pennsylvania just to fail. My mother (who drove up to Pennsylvania with me) was very excited about my goal to be an actor. As a matter of fact, when we just arrived to Lansdowne, she said to me, "When you are successful, I want you to buy me a Jeep Wrangler." This request of hers was much deeper than buying her a Jeep Wrangler. What she was truly demanding of me was to be successful so that I could take care of her in the future. Being that my mother had a strong influence on me that is what I sought to achieve. Once again, I had set my mind to please her instead of God. The following was my equation for success upon moving to Pennsylvania: "I will get involved in as many projects as I can until one of them grants me the success and fulfillment that I desire to have."

Film

Now that I was living in Pennsylvania, I was only two hours driving distance from New York. The city of New York was where some of those major acting opportunities were located on the database that the talent agent, Aviva, provided me with before I moved out of Jacksonville. Upon moving to Lansdowne, my first order of business was to submit my name for these big opportunities. Persistently, I would submit my name over and over again, but I was never given the opportunity to audition for any of the roles. But one day there was a glimmer of hope. I had finally received an opportunity to audition for a film opportunity with MMG in New York. After being sent a short script, I quickly memorized it. When the day arrived for me to audition for MMG, I caught a bus to New York, and gave my all during the audition. I never received a call back. I immediately knew that I was not chosen for the role. Soon, I viewed the MMG talent agency as a lost cause and I stopped submitting for their acting opportunities. Though I was unsuccessful with MMG, my ambition to be successful would not allow me to quit. Through networking with a woman I met at an open mic venue in North Philadelphia called Patterson's Palace, I received a major film opportunity. Her name was Cassandra, and she had her own talent agency. I auditioned for this film in November of 2009. This audition took place in a restaurant in Lansdowne. This place was only minutes from my aunt and uncle's home. Once I arrived to the restaurant, I saw two white men sitting behind a long table. One of the men was the director of the film. Once I arrived and stood before them, they asked me to audition once I was ready. Since I didn't know any monologues from published stage plays at the time, I simply auditioned some Confessional Narratives that I had written. After auditioning for this film, I was treated as though I had received the role. I along with some other people who had auditioned were invited to the cast meetings. In these cast meetings we also rehearsed for the film. I thought to myself, I'm rehearsing with the rest of the cast. I've got the role! The director would say things in the meeting to heighten my excitement. "I know great actors and other people in high places," he would boast. I said to myself, "This is it! I haven't been in Pennsylvania long and I'm already a part of a great film project! This feeling would quickly change, just like when I had to learn "Options" for the Boynton Beach High JV basketball team years ago.

One night, for whatever reason, while the cast meeting was still going on, I abruptly walked out and went back home. After that night, while home at my aunt and uncle's house, I received an incoming call on my cell phone. It was from one of the men who were making the film. Very calmly he told me that I was being cut from the cast. He said the reason for this was because the director frowned on the fact that I walked out of the cast meeting before it was over. I was hurt. I fought hard to make a good argument on why I had to walk out of the cast meeting. But no matter how much I tried to plead my case, my words did not penetrate. Just like that, I was no longer a part of the cast of this major film. This great opportunity slipped from my grasp, almost as quickly as it came.

After getting off the phone with the director's assistant, I laid on a kiddie bed in a dark room that was reserved for my aunt's grandchildren. As I laid there, tears rolled down my face just like the night I sat in my mother's car after I didn't make the Boynton Beach JV basketball team. My hopes were dashed. As tears proceeded to run down my face, I thought, I just moved hundreds of miles from Florida, and I don't truly know why I am here and where I'm going. I continued to push forward. My determination to be successful continued to burn within me like an everlasting flaming torch.

Not too long after I moved to Pennsylvania, I met a young woman named Malaina. Upon meeting her, she told me that she was a part of a theater ensemble called Destiny Productions. I saw my connection with Malaina as an asset to help me become a successful actor.

On November 15, 2010, about a year after I failed to land that film role at that restaurant in Lansdowne, Pennsylvania, Malaina emailed me an acting opportunity in an independent film. In the email, I found that this film was entitled "Revelation Blue," and was going to be broadcasted on television and the Internet. It was also being directed by one of the top dogs of film, Tony Lankford. He was a very well known director in the city of Philadelphia. With that said, I was quickly drawn into this opportunity. I thought to myself, Lundy, this is a big film opportunity. You can't let this one slip away.

On the bottom of the email it read, "…Write what you could you bring to this production." I saw this statement as a life and death situation. Depending on how I answer it, I can either be considered for the role or not. So I took my time in crafting my answers. I responded, "I will make people hate me, love me, sympathize for me, cry, and fear me. I will do whatever it takes to satisfy the objectives of the character. I will bring the character to life!"

When I was finally content with what I had written, I sent the email. The director and his wife were impressed with my answers and wanted to meet with me. Sitting with the director and his wife in a small coffee shop in South Philadelphia, I tried my best not to mess this opportunity up. Very carefully I said to them, "I'm going to work very hard to build the character to make him as believable as possible." They liked me and chose me for the role of the antagonist of the film. The name of this character was Jonathon, who was a crooked preacher.

Not long after that meeting, they sent me the script for the film. In the privacy of my bedroom I read my script over and over again until my lines were committed to memory. While reading the script I also tried to find clues on who exactly my character was. I was hungry to do my best in this big role. My hard work was evident in the way that the other cast members looked at me on the first day of filming. The first day of filming took place in an old-fashioned looking church in Center City Philadelphia. In one scene, while I was preaching to the congregation, I could remember looking at the face of one of the extras sitting in the pews. As I preached, he had a look of admiration on his face for the great job that I was doing with my role. I sensed that this gentleman was saying to himself, Wow! This man knows how to act!

Revelation Blue was the biggest film project I got involved in since I moved to Pennsylvania. Just when I thought being broadcasted on television was the pinnacle that this independent film would reach, it has also won several domestic and international awards. These awards include but are not limited to the Silver Award for Best TV Series, Second Place Best Narrative Film, and the Diploma of Excellence.

"Not long after I moved to Philly, I met some people, young ladies who were part of a group called destiny productions. Through them I got a lead to a film production that was called "Revelation Blue." This was my first real film experience, and the director, Tony Lankford, was wonderful to work with. Since then, the film has won three awards, both domestic and international. I played the role of the antagonist in the film, Jonathon. Every now and then I see the wife of the director, and she expresses to me how great of a job I did on film. And she says that I am a good actor. Maybe I am destined to be a "great actor."

-December 22, 2012

Stage Plays

Determined to be successful, I was also simultaneously seeking acting opportunities in stage plays. The first published stage play I've ever acted in was Topdog Underdog. I received this opportunity through a man who was born and raised in Philadelphia named Carlo. I met him not too long after I moved to Pennsylvania. I met him at a place in Philadelphia that some artists called "The Sanctuary." This place was essentially a spacious apartment where various artists in the city of Philadelphia would come, hang out, and be themselves. Many of these artists I met on the Philadelphia spoken-word scene. As opposed to a church sanctuary, "The Sanctuary" was a place that artists would come to party, drink alcoholic beverages, and smoke weed. Carlo was a tall, 30-year-old, light-skinned man who was born and raised in Philadelphia. What stood out most about him was his strong passion for the craft of acting. When he was not auditioning, he was memorizing lines for a role or reading highly respected pieces of literary work. When he was not auditioning or memorizing a script, he would study great actors by watching movies. If he was not doing any of these things, he was getting trained in the craft of acting. He would take frequent 2-hour bus trips to New York to meet with his acting coach.

Another thing about Carlo that was very apparent was his relentless drive to make it in the acting business. Not having a traditional 9 to 5 job, he would pack his backpack with countless hip-hop mix tapes he made himself, then head to a busy street in South Philadelphia called South Street to sell these mix tapes. He would then use that money to fund his passion for acting. When

Carlo and I both found out we had a mutual interest in acting, we became good friends.

One night while walking through downtown Philadelphia, I ran into this highly driven man who always seemed to be on the move. Filled with enthusiasm, he said to me, "I want you to act alongside me in a play called Topdog Underdog." This was a well known two-character stage play written by a famous black female playwright named Suzan Lori Parks. At the time, I never heard of the play or the playwright for that matter, because I was relatively new to this acting thing, but Carlo, being as passionate about acting as he was, knew all about the play and the playwright. Nothing about Carlo said that he was not serious about this idea. As I stood there and listened to him I could hear the passion bubbling in every word he said. I was excited about this opportunity and agreed to act alongside him this play that I never heard of. Wasting no time, he said, "There is one copy at the Barnes & Noble bookstore and another at a another bookstore I know." This statement of his showed me that this passionate actor had already done his research prior to this abrupt meeting in downtown Philadelphia. Wasting no time, that same night we both visited both bookstores and bought two copies of Topdog Underdog.

This production of Topdog Underdog was solely put on by Carlo and I. One day while I was home, I received a call from Carlo. Very ambitiously he said, "I don't see any reason why we should not be able to memorize this play in a month." When he said this, I was slightly shaken up by the thought of having to memorize this two-man play in a month. After all, the book that the play was in was about half an inch thick, and it only had two characters! This meant that each character in this play had a whole lot of lines. As Carlo made this bold declaration, I wearingly flipped through the pages of my copy of the play. As I flipped through the pages, I thought to myself, Carlo is really pushing the envelope on this one. Nevertheless, I took on his challenge.

Carlo and I set up a rehearsal schedule where we rehearsed several nights a week in the basement of his family's home in west Philadelphia. Hungry for success, I committed myself to these rehearsals. Right there in his basement, Carlo and I would rehearse for several hours, as we drilled each other on the lines. Determined to learn the lines to the play, one page of memorized lines quickly turned into two, then two pages turned into three, and so on and so forth, until I had the whole play memorized.

We put up this production at a small store on South Street called Pearl of Africa. This store had two floors. The play was on the second floor. There was enough space on the second floor to not only set up chairs for the audience, but to also set up the stage area. To show you how Carlo's passion for acting far exceeded mine, he readily volunteered to set up the whole world of the play. He was the one who rounded up all the stage props that were needed to create all the scenes in the play. He was also the one who hired all the stagehands that we needed. These were the people that would be in charge of lighting, sound and other things to make sure that the run of the play was successful. In making sure that this production of Topdog Underdog goes well, Carlo moved with unmatched drive and purpose. Me on the other hand, I did not move with the same sense of purpose as Carlo did. I just kind of went with the flow of things. We ran the play from June 16-18 and also 23-25. Many of the audience members let me know how much they enjoyed my performance in my role as Booth.

One day I found out about another opportunity to act in a stage play entitled Shaking the Truth Loose. The auditions were held in Philadelphia. The actors that were interested in this opportunity were called into a spacious room one by one. Already in the room waiting to see each actor, were Tiffany (the writer and director of the play) and her significant other. Tiffany was a young, light-skinned, wide-eyed black woman who was very excited, for this was the first stage play production that she was putting up. She and her significant other sat behind a long table as the actors who were auditioning came into the room one by one.

Before each actor went before Tiffany (and the other people who were a part of this panel), they were given sides to the play according to the role that they were auditioning for. It was finally my turn to audition. In the imaginary scene, my stage wife was cheating on me, and the scene starts off with her coming home late one night. Already in the house she is walking into, I'm sitting on a chair waiting quietly for her to come home. When she walked in to find me waiting on her, she was surprised. My character in the scene suspected that she had been cheating on him. As I questioned her about her coming home late, my eyes quickly swelled up with tears. The real emotions of sadness and anger ran through my body like electricity through a wire. These emotions were pulsating through my body, and the panel saw how alive I was with emotion and was impressed by my performance. Needless to say, I received a call back from the playwright. She informed me that I was chosen for the role of Curtis, the antagonist of the play.

When I was brought on as one of the actors in the stage play Shaking the Truth Loose, I was very excited and determined to bring my character to life. I pushed my body to be at every rehearsal. At the time of rehearsals, I was working an 8-hour shift as a security guard at the Campbell's Soup headquarters in Camden, New Jersey. After working this 8-hour shift, I would walk to the Patco train station (which was a train that went from New Jersey into Philadelphia). After walking 20 minutes to the train station, I would then catch the Patco train into Philadelphia. Once I arrived to Philadelphia, I then boarded the El Train towards the 69th Street Station. I would then get off on a stop (such as 30th St) that would allow me to catch the 10 trolley towards 63rd Street, which was the street I lived on. When I arrived home, I would quickly change out of my security uniform, before continuing my journey to the Shaking the Truth Loose rehearsals. From my home, I went to another train station that was a few blocks from my home. Once on the train, it was several stops until I finally arrived to Bryn Mawr, where the rehearsals were being held. While at rehearsals I worked tremendously hard to bring my character to life. To me, being a part of this stage play project was a big deal. For it was part of the Philadelphia Urban Theatre Festival. This was an annual event where very well known and not so well known playwrights were given the opportunity to showcase their projects. This year's festival was held in one of the regional theaters in Center City Philadelphia called Adrienne Theatre.

When the opening of the play arrived, I was more than ready. I had with me a composition notebook that was filled with my character's bio. In this bio, I painstakingly created a background story for my character and described in great detail the relationship I had with all the other actors I was acting alongside. On the night before I made my first appearance on stage, I continually looked over the bio like a mad scientist that was trying to make a monster come to life. With my antagonistic character, I had to become a monster. A monster that I was trying hard to make come to life. I read the bio of my character over and over again, until I was content that I was now the character. When it was almost my cue to make my first entrance on stage, keeping my character's backstory in mind, I slowly walked up the steps towards the stage.

As I walked, I convinced myself that I was no longer Thierry Lundy, but Curtis, the bad guy of the play. As I stood behind the stage curtains getting ready to make my entrance, I felt so in tune with the character. I worked so hard on the role that I lost myself in it. While in this zoned out mode, the writer and director of the play, Tiffany, walked up to me. She immediately sensed how deeply immersed I was into my character. When she walked up to me, she looked as if she was about to say something to me, but then chose not to. Looking at me from head to toe, she slowly backed down like a scared dog with its tail between its legs. This reaction of hers told me that I truly worked hard on bringing my character to life.

That night, I played my role well. Having worked hard to create a believable character, the audience quickly learned to hate me as the antagonist in the play. After one of the runs of the play I saw two women standing off to the distance staring directly at me with a look of contempt and I knew why they were looking at me in this way. In the imaginary world of the play, my character, Curtis, physically abused a female character. These two women just stood off in the distance and stared at me with a look that said, "I'm not too sure if he is this abusive in real life, but I'm not going to be the one to find out." I did so well in the play that they weren't sure how much of this bad character was a part of who I was in real life. This reaction of theirs made me proud as an actor, and testified of how hard I worked on the role.

Hungry for success, there was yet another stage play opportunity that I took very seriously. Through Tiffany Smith, I aligned myself with a well-known playwright in Philadelphia named Rick. He was a middle-aged black man from south Philadelphia. Though he only had a high school diploma, he didn't let that stop him. By the time I met Rick Watson, he had already been successful in putting on his plays and building a large fan base. He was so successful on the Philadelphia Theater circuit that he was deemed as the Tyler Perry of Philadelphia. And if you know anything about Tyler Perry, you would know that he is a very successful African-American playwright who made it to the big times. Being compared to Tyler Perry shows you that Rick was a very highly esteemed playwright.

When I met Rick Watson for the first time, he expressed to me how much he enjoyed my performance as the antagonist Curtis in Tiffany's Shaking the Truth Loose stage play. Needless to say, I was quickly accepted into the circle of this successful playwright, and I did not take this opportunity for granted.

One day while I was home, I received a call from Rick. Very excitingly, he said, "I'm going to be putting up a play called Momma Knows Best, and I want you to be in it." He then said, "I have a crack head character named Kurt, and I think that you would do a great job with the role." As Rick spoke, I remained silent and listened carefully as I pressed my cell phone tightly against my ear. After all, I was not on the phone with just any person. I was on the phone with the "Tyler Perry of Philadelphia!" When Rick offered me the role, I quickly accepted. "I would love to do the role," I told him.

Just like my Curtis character in Shaking the Truth Loose, I worked extremely hard to bring my Curtis character to life in Rick's play. I wanted my character to look as destitute as possible. With that said, I made the choice that my character would have two missing front teeth. To play this off, I placed a black film over my two front teeth. To make him look like he was really down and out on the streets, I wore a very soiled white shirt, two shoes that did not match, a pair of jeans (that were ripped and also soiled), and to hold up these jeans, I did not use a conventional belt, but a long computer power cord. For my character's physicality, I studied a bum walking through center city Philadelphia one night. I watched as this destitute bum slowly walked passed me. The most prominent characteristics that I noticed about this bum was his posture and the particular way that he was walking. With both his arms hanging to his side, this bum's head was hung so low that it seemed like his chin was touching is chest. As he walked, his feet did not come off the ground like normal persons feet did when they walked. They just stuck to the ground and just kind of shuffled along. I studied that bum and added his characteristics to Kurt, my crack head role.

The play was put on at a well-known theater in south Philadelphia called the Arts Bank. Back stage, when I dressed up as my character on the night of the show, the other cast members were entertained by my portrayal of Kurt the crack head. They found it very difficult to contain their laughter as I walked around backstage with this new persona.

When it was almost time to make my first entrance on stage, I stood behind a door that led to the stage. As I stood there, I felt deeply immersed in my crack head character, Kurt. This reminded me of the time I was getting ready to make my entrance on stage in the Shaking the Truth Loose stage play. Once again, due to painstaking hard work, I successfully convinced myself that I was no longer Thierry Lundy but another character, a crack head character named Kurt. When it was my cue, I ran through the door onto the stage where I was met by bright lights and thundering laughter from the crowd. This was a Philadelphia crowd, so they have seen crack heads before. So as soon as they saw me they immediately knew what they were looking at—a very good portrayal of a crack head. The audience could not contain their laughter. From that point on, I took the audience on a roller coaster ride called "Kurt the Funny and Off the Wall Crack Head Character."

After the performance, the whole cast of the play lined up on the stage before the audience. As we all stood there, Rick introduced each actor to the audience. With applause, the audience showed each actor their appreciation as they were introduced. Then it was finally my turn to be introduced. Very loudly over the mic, Rick said "Ladies and gentleman, Thierry Lundy!" The theater exploded with applause and laughter. The applause that they gave me was much greater than the one they gave the other actors. This showed me that they too appreciated my hard work on building the character. This was hard work that was driven by my desire for success and fulfillment.

Chapter 11
My One-Man Shows

On top of acting in film and stage plays, I was simultaneously creating my own one-man shows. In these shows, I depended solely on my imagination to create works of art that people never saw before. To me, this was a foolproof plan to grant me success and fulfillment. Moving quickly, two months after I moved to Pennsylvania, I started organizing my "Faceless" one-man show.

As the title of the show suggests, part of my concept for the show was to wear a mask throughout the performance. But where was I going to find the perfect mask for my show?

At the end of the "Journalism, Activism, and Acting" chapter, I mentioned that my cousin Garincha had been living in Philadelphia for years. I also mentioned that he had even built his own dance studio here. "Take the Lead" dance studio was the name of it. It was a very intimate studio that was located on the first floor of an apartment building, and was positioned on the corner of a block. Once you walked in, it had hardwood floors, and along one of the walls of the studio was a huge mirror. Here my cousin passionately taught ballroom and Latin dancing. Towards the back of the studio was a break room. My cousin being an artist at heart often dabbled with theater concepts and had countless props in this break room. This break room did not only have props, but also great costumes. On a search for the perfect mask, one day I walked into this break room and found a white mask hanging off an antique coat hanger. As soon as I laid my eyes on it, I said to myself, This mask will be perfect for my show.

When I got the mask, I thought to myself I don't just want to wear a mask just to wear one. It has to have some kind of significance. Then I said to myself I'm going to paint the mask. But what color is it going to be? After researching several colors, I found that the color bright yellow brightened up people's moods. Then I said to myself, This is what I'm trying to achieve with my show. I want people to be happy as a result. One day I visited a hardware store in Lansdowne, Pennsylvania, which was not too far from my aunt and uncle's home, and I bought a can of bright glossy yellow spray paint. After arriving back home, I spray painted the mask until I was content with its appearance. Admiring the finished product, I said to myself, Perfect.

Simply wearing a yellow mask during my show was not enough to help me find the success and fulfillment I was seeking in the one-man show arena. I had to take it a step further. I asked myself, Is it possible to copyright my idea of wearing a yellow mask during a performance? There was a theater buff who worked in my cousin's dance studio and her name was Morganna. This was the person I felt like would have the answer to my question. Amused and practically laughing at this notion of mine, Morganna said, "No, you cannot do that." I was disappointed. I felt like my becoming-successful-quick scheme had failed. After revealing my concept to my cousin, he too was amused. Not impressed, he said, "You have way too much time on your hands." Reading between the lines, he was truly saying, "That is a ridiculous idea!" His statement was a painful stab to my ego. I thought to myself, "He is right, I do have way too much time on my hands." I also thought to myself "Thierry, you do not truly know where you want to go in life. You're just creating these concepts out of a desperate place hoping that they will catapult you towards success."

As a part of my "Faceless" one-man show, desperate for success and fulfillment, I dug deeper into the recesses of my imagination. I said to myself I'm going to create a character that is an actual Snickers chocolate bar. I figured that no one has ever seen anything like that before. Once again, I held onto my belief that a never before seen concept equals success and fulfillment. This portion of my one-man show was entitled "What Goes up, Must Come down."

To make the Snickers bar a believable character, I did extensive research on this candy bar and the company that created it. I also did this research to mold this show into something no one has ever seen before. After all, this was a foolproof plan for success. In this portion of my "Faceless" one man show, this Snickers chocolate bar spoke from within one of those vending machines with the transparent glass on the front of it. This was the type of vending machine that allowed customers to see the candies within the machine. Since I was now personifying a candy bar, the transparency of the glass also allowed the Snickers bar to see the customer. During the whole show the Snickers bar has an ongoing argument on why he is the best candy in the vending machine. Going off of this argument, he also claims to be the only candy bar in the machine that will be purchased. He would boast, "And in the Right Corner, with annual global sales of $2 billion dollars, making him the best-selling chocolate bar of all-time. Decked out in the brown package with red, white, and blue trim. At a combined weight of 3.29 ounces, putting him in a higher weight class then Twix, Skittles, and all three Musketeers!"

This arrogant Snickers bar is so busy bragging about how he is the greatest candy bar that's ever been created that it never dawns on him that in being purchased, he would meet the gruesome fate of being devoured. Blinded to this inevitability, the bulk of this portion of my one-man show involves this Snickers bar relentlessly talking down to and ridiculing the other snacks that are in the vending machine along with him, as if they were inferior to him.

Towards the end of the show while a person is standing at the vending machine deciding what they should purchase, the Snickers bar says his own slogan, "Hungry? Why wait?" After saying this statement, it finally hits him that he would be eaten once purchased. His attitude quickly changes. He now had a new agenda. Instead of teasing the other brands of candy, he starts to promote them. He says, "No don't choose me, pick…um…two…Almond Joy doesn't have anything to lose…No one likes him…or choose five…Baby Ruth already got all the fame he could get…or three for Twix…they're practically Siamese twins, I'm sure they are sick of each other." Unsuccessful in his attempt, the customer decides to choose him. While falling he tries to persuade the customer to purchase the Skittles candy instead of him, by screaming out the Skittles slogan "Taste the rainbow!" With this show, my goal was to show the audience how arrogance can blind them to the truth. More than that, my goal was to find success and fulfillment.

Continuing to push my imagination to the limit, I created another character for another one-man show I created entitled "Follow Your Dreams." I received the inspiration to create this one-man show one night while I was at my cousin's dance studio. On Friday nights at his dance studio, my cousin would hold these highly energetic salsa parties. One night while standing in the midst of passionate dancers dancing to blaring Latin music, a Latin dance instructor named Antonio Antonio popped on my mind.

To add humor to the character, I intentionally made his last name the same as his first. The question now was, "What would be the appearance of this Latin man?" To help my imagination, I visited a costume store in Philadelphia. As I looked around the costume store I received a lot of inspiration on what would be the appearance of Antonio Antonio. Walking through the store, I picked up a huge fake diamond ring, a fake gold bracelet, and a fake gold necklace. I also picked out a long black curly wig and a thick handlebar mustache. Determined to bring this character to life, this dance instructor also had to know how to dance. I decided that his go to dance would be the salsa. Since this was a one-man show, I would not be able to have a dance partner, so I asked my cousin, "Are there some dance moves I could do without a partner?" He responded, "Yes, I could teach you some solo salsa steps." At his home in west Philadelphia, my cousin took me through the steps of this character of mine. I diligently practiced the steps. Basic step-basic step. Now, side-step… side-step. Now…step…step…and crossover and spin. Using my imagination, I successfully created the Latin dance instructor, Antonio Antonio.

Another one man show I created was entitled "Roscoe the Roach's Story." This show was based off of one of my well-known spoken-word poems entitled "Why Must They Die?" This poem has a war theme where I describe in vivid detail how I plan on exterminating roaches.

Often times when I reached the end of this poem, I acted the part of the roach that I was killing. So right on stage I would transition from my character to the roach's character and play his part. As it turns out, the roach in this poem has survived my attack, and has now come back to tell his side of the story in my "Roscoe the Roach's Story" one-man show.

Roscoe's favorite saying was "Roscoe is standing now!" With this statement, he was making the declaration that he was not going to allow life to pick on him anymore. Wielding a toothpick, he showed the audience that he would now stand up and fight back. Every now and then he would pounce around and wield this toothpick with aggression as a warning for anyone who thinks about picking on him.

I placed a lot of thought into my one-man shows. I pushed my creativity and imagination as if they were the only things working for me. Though many people attended my shows, I still felt empty on the inside.

Chapter 12
Acting School

Scarred by the previous bad experiences I had with college, I pushed the whole notion of going back to college to the back of my mind. But after I moved to Pennsylvania, certain events transpired to make me consider attending school again. One of the main catalysts that convinced me that I had to attend school to get acting training was the fact that I failed to land many acting roles. On top of this, every time I told my new Philadelphia friends, "I moved from Florida to pursue acting." They would ask, "Did you go to school for it?" When they would say this, I would hear, "If you want to be a successful actor, it is imperative that you attend college again to get trained in the craft." This was the most irritating suggestion ever. Nevertheless they had successfully planted a seed that started to convince me more and more that I needed acting training. But I was still hesitant in taking that leap of attending college for the third time!

One night, at an open-mic venue in north Philadelphia, I received another counsel that I needed acting training. After using solely my raw talent (which I felt like was sufficient enough for me to make it in the acting business) to perform a monologue that I wrote myself, a black man named Lee pulled me to the side as soon as I walked off the stage. He said to me, "You are talented, but you need acting training." Once again, here was another person suggesting that I attend college again, and this idea made me sick to my stomach. As Lee spoke, his words became more and more obscured as he continued on. Lee was a trained actor who graduated with his bachelor's degree at a school in south Philadelphia called the University of the Arts. Right there as I stood with him in this dimly lit open mic venue, Lee continued by saying, "There is an audition coming up for the school soon, you should audition."

After Lee's counsel, the feeling of needing acting school only got stronger. I realized more and more that acting was not a superficial craft that you could just jump into and do extremely well at it. I realized that it was a craft that required for you to attain certain skills for you to be great at it. Even after Lee gave me this counsel of his, it took me quite some time for me to come to grips with the idea of having to attend college for the third time. After spending much time in reflection, I decided that I would audition for the acting program at University of the Arts. This was in the spring of the year 2010.

The University of the Arts took up several blocks on a major street in Philadelphia called Broad Street. Broad Street ran north and south. As the name of this street suggests, the road stretched across a very broad area of the city of Philadelphia. Philly's City Hall is what separated the north side of Broad Street from the south side of Broad Street. When you were on one side of City Hall, you were on the north side of Broad Street. When you were on the other you were now on the south side of Broad Street. University of the Arts was located on the south side of Broad Street. On this street were theaters that the school owned. Also on this street were its library, administration offices, and the Terra Building (which had several art departments such as dance and theater.) The theater school itself took up a couple floors. Auditions were being held in one of the rooms on one of the theater floors. When I arrived, I found that the room was already filled with people who were auditioning for the UArts highly accredited theater program. This room was filled with many teenagers interested in the acting or the playwright program.

For the audition it was required that I prepare two contrasting monologues. Thanks to my friend Carlo (who was more passionate about acting then I was) I was able to have two monologues prepared for my audition. Because of Carlo and his impressive hunger to act, I acted in my first published play entitled Topdog Underdog by the well-known playwright Suzan Lori Parks. I acted in this play a little time before I auditioned for UArts. This was a two-character play about two brothers named Booth and Lincoln. From this play, I memorized a monologue by the character Booth, to prepare for the audition. Carlo also had a library full of plays at his house, and he said that I could choose my second contrasting monologue from it.

On audition day, many young people waited patiently for their turn to audition inside one of the rooms of the school. Young adults came from all across the nation (even from California, which is known as a mecca for actors) just to be at this school in Philadelphia. When my turn had arrived for me to audition, I walked into a large and almost empty studio room that was used for acting classes. The only thing that was in it was a long table and a couple chairs placed behind it. Sitting in one of these chairs was a white middle-aged man. He was one of the professors in the acting program.

While I stood there before him in the middle of this space, he told me whenever I was ready to start I can begin my performance. As I performed both monologues, I felt deeply submerged into the characters. After I was done performing, I was told to go back to the waiting room. It was in the room that everyone that auditioned would find out if they made the callback list or not. After all the auditions were over, someone came by and put the callback list on the door. I glanced at the list, and my name was on it! I was excited. This meant that the professor liked my audition. It also meant that I was to go back into the room where the auditions were being held, and to audition one more time.

When I walked into the room again, there was not one but now two white men sitting behind the long table. One of them was simply a professor in the acting program, and the other was a professor and the head of the acting program at University of the Arts. They requested that I audition for them again. Without any hesitation, I did. One of the monologues was not a comedic monologue, but they asked me to recite it in a comedic tone. I knew that they were trying to get a sense of my talent. This was a difficult task for me. When I was done in the call back audition, they told me that I would receive a letter in the mail that told me if I got accepted into the acting program or not.

Two weeks went by and I still did not receive a letter in the mail telling me if I made the acting program or not. Growing impatient, I called the school and they told me that they had the letter but that they could not tell me if I was accepted into the acting program over the phone. They told me that I would have to come in to find out if I made it into the acting program. So I did. When I arrived to the school, the people who had the letter were located in a separate building that was not too far from the Terra Building. This was the UArts administration building. When I walked into the office where they were located, the woman walked up to me with the letter in her hand, but she was preoccupied with something at the time, but the letter was in her hand. It was not in an envelope so that made it possible for me to see words that were on the letter. Anxious to see the answer, I made an effort to see the verdict before she even handed the paper to me. The first word I saw told me everything that I needed to know. This first word was "Congratulations." A smile grew on my face, because I knew that I was accepted as a new student at the prestigious University of the Arts.

When the fall of 2010 had arrived, one of my advisors said to me, "Before you are able to begin school, you will have to pay the balance of $1,000." Not having a grand just laying around, I was a little discouraged. Aware of the fact that I did not have this money, she said, "I suggest you use this year to work on raising these funds, and to start school the following year." I agreed to this.

Around this time, I was involved with a Theater Ensemble in west Philadelphia at a theater called Bushfire. What I would like to call a guru of acting was the director here. He was an elderly black man who stood about 6 ft. 3. He often times wore a beret that sat on top of his greyish white afro. His name was Al Simpkins. At bushfire, Al taught me a lot about the craft of acting. What he often stressed was the importance of becoming a trained actor. In his calm, but serious demeanor, he would say, "If you want to be great in the craft of acting, you have to get trained."

The day I told Al Simpkins that I was accepted into University of the Arts, he was especially happy for me. One day after I found out that I would not be able to start school until the fall of 2011, Al asked me, "Did you start school yet?" I answered, "No." Alarmed by my answer, his eyes widened. The look on his face said, "Why in the world didn't you start yet?" Though I enrolled at UArts there was still a part of me that hoped to get my acting training elsewhere (such as Bushfire Theater) without having to go back to college for a long four years. I was still trying to avoid college. But the concerned look on Al Simpkins face made me feel guilty for not having started at UArts in the fall of 2010. I told him, "I will not be able to start in 2010, because I do not have the money to do so." Like he often did, he made his point on the importance of getting acting training. Then he confidently commanded, "Go back to the school, and tell them that you would like to defer your enrollment until the spring of 2011." With a sense of urgency, I did exactly as this acting guru commanded me.

"I would like to begin in the spring of 2011," I told one of the faculty members in the acting program. They responded, "I'm sorry, but because of how the acting program is set up, you'll have to start your classes in the fall." So this is what I did. In the fall of 2011, I started classes at University of the Arts.

That Empty Feeling Again

At UArts, I was there physically but not mentally. This reminded me of the time that I attended Palm Beach Community College. My colleagues in my chemistry class seemed to be more passionate than I was about what they were studying. I felt the same way at University of the Arts. Talk about having a deja vu moment! My teenage colleagues at UArts were more passionate about acting than I. It seemed like they've had a deep passion for theater and acting ever since they were kids. They would speak about the famous actors they admired or the stage plays that they loved. While talking about a famous actress that I did not know, one of my classmates would exclaim, "Oh my God, I love her so much!" And when they would mention a particular play, they spoke with a particular assertiveness. Sensing the extensive knowledge that they had on the topic, I had question marks hovering over my head. I would think to myself, Who is that? or What stage play is that? It was obvious that their aspiration to become great actors and actresses was something that they did not just conjure up yesterday. I, on the other hand, did not speak passionately about acting in the same way that they did. As a matter of fact, I remained silent most of the time in my own little bubble. I felt as if I was just taking up space in the class. No doubt I had a talent for acting, and many times my talent surpassed that of my colleagues. But I still felt like I was not supposed to be sharing the same space as them. A person who I felt deserved my spot at UArts was my good friend Carlo.

After my freshman year at UArts, I felt like my time at UArts had expired like an hourglass whose sands have run very low. No matter how much this internal battle waged, my ambition was overridden by how I truly felt on the inside. I decided to move on to my sophomore year. Still, I had tremendous difficulty of getting acclimated in school. Once again, this difficulty reminded me of when I used to attend Palm Beach Community College in West Palm Beach. In the same way that my grades started to slip at PBCC, my grades also started to go downhill at UArts. My grades became so terrible that I started receiving deficiency notices. These notices sent the message to the students that, "You are in danger of failing this class." I received these "failure notices" in more than one class. One of these classes was script analysis. While sitting passively in class on day in a way that said, "I don't feel like being here," my professor said to me, "Your grades are bad. What I want to know is, why are you still here?" He was right. What he was saying with this statement of his was, "Your grades have gotten so low that it is not possible for you to recover. Being that you will not be able to recover, why are you wasting your time by continuing to attend classes?"

In March 2013, I went on my weeklong spring break from school, and I never went back to UArts. This marked the third time that I've dropped out of college.

Chapter 13
Stand-Up Comedy

Even though I was studying acting at the highly accredited University of the Arts, I was still unfulfilled. So much that while I was still enrolled in the acting program there, I simultaneously took it upon my own self to try other things with the hope that they would dissipate this strong feeling of emptiness that I felt on the inside. To find this thing, I used a familiar process. It was the same process I used years back when I was trying to figure out which major was right for me at Florida Community College of Jacksonville. This process involved me analyzing my gifts and talents. To me, if I pursued something that aligned with my gifts, then that thing would grant me the fulfillment that I desperately craved for. To begin this process, I started with a truth about myself. I said to myself, People think I'm a funny guy. Maybe a career in stand-up comedy would provide me with the fulfillment that I desire to have. I jumped into stand-up comedy with both feet. I quickly created a stand-up comedy routine based off some memorable experiences that I had on Philadelphia's public transportation system.

One of my jokes was about a run-in I had with a "Crazy" white man on the Philadelphia Septa Bus. Maybe saying he was crazy is a little too extreme and not fair, but his actions told me that he definitely had a couple screws loose. While I was on the way home from an event late one night, I caught a bus near center city Philadelphia. After boarding the bus, I found that there was only one available seat left, and it was right next to this white gentleman who appeared not to be so right in the head. He was slim, and he was wearing a yellow raincoat and a pair of huge prescription glasses that had very thick lenses. The lenses were so thick that they magnified his eyes to a disproportionate size, adding to his already weird aura. Well, I was so tired that night that I quickly fought off my first impression of him so that I could find rest in this last available seat on the bus. In other words, I made the decision to take my chances.

A few moments after I sat next to him, he turned his head slowly, looked at me and said, "I like your blazer." Somewhat uncomfortable, I responded, "Thank You!" After he heard my response, he immediately turned back around. It didn't seem like ten seconds went by before he turned around again and looked at me. His mind remained on the same subject--my brown tweed blazer. He said to me with a very slow and drawn out speech, "I could not wear something like that, it would make my skin itch." My blazer was tweed, so I understood why it could cause someone's skin to itch if a person were to wear it directly onto his or her skin. Despite this man's weird demeanor, huge glasses, drawn out speech, and random questions and statements, I still did not make up my mind on whether he was crazy or not. After his statement about my blazer I looked at him and in a matter of fact tone, I said, "It would not make your skin itch if you wore something underneath it, like I am." Not sure if he registered my response at all, he then turned back around and looked forward. After a few moments, he turned right back around for the third consecutive time. This time, he made a statement that sent chills running down my spine. In a slow drawn out monotone he said, "You know what, I don't even know where I'm going right now. The only reason why I caught this bus was because it came." I immediately bolted up as if my seat was extremely hot and I found another seat on the bus that was far from him. I finally came to the conclusion that this man was crazy.

There was yet another situation that I experienced while riding on Philadelphia's public transportation system that became a part of my comedic routine. Unlike the first gentleman I mentioned to you, this crazy man appeared to be normal. This man sat quietly and cleaned his nails. He didn't say a word; he just sat there quietly and cleaned his nails.

Then without warning this seemingly normal man got up and proceeded to yell at a very heavy set man who sat at the back of the bus. This caught me off guard, but I still was not alarmed. I was already used to seeing interesting characters on the Philadelphia public transportation system. It had become a norm for me and I guess for everyone else that was on the bus that night because everyone was even calmer than I was. So now we were all witnessing this man yelling at someone that was sitting at the back of the bus. Very loudly he yelled, "Come on, fat boy! I can take you on! Come on, fat boy!" As he screamed these words, I turned my head to the direction that he was looking, and indeed there was a very heavyset man sitting at the back of the bus minding his own business. Being that the man was obviously minding his own business, I asked myself, What did the fat man do to him? Maybe they got into an altercation long before I was even present in this scene. Who knows? All I know is that I was now witnessing this man challenging that fat man in the back of the bus to a fight. What made the situation so comical was the fact that the man in the back of the bus did not say anything while he was being yelled at by this other man. He just sat there with a smirk on his face. The man continued to scream at the fat man. Never approaching the fat man, he continued to scream the words, "Come on, fat boy, I will take you on! Come on," and quickly moved to the front of the bus as he said the words. As he walked to the front of the bus, he continued to challenge the fat man to a fight. When he got to the front of the bus, the bus driver simply let him off at the next stop and shut the doors. As the bus driver pulled off, I looked out of the window out of curiosity. The man continued to invite the fat man to a fight. I could not hear his words as well as I did when he was in the bus, but reading his lips he repeated the same words over and over again: "Come on, fat boy, I can take you on, come on, fat boy!" I laughed to myself.

A third joke that I had was about how in sync that Philadelphia people's bodies were with time. I was on one of the Septa Trains one day and I noticed that one of the passengers was asleep. I said to myself, This person is going to miss their stop! It did not happen this way. Keep in mind that this person was in deep sleep. When this person's stop came up, they quickly got up, grabbed their briefcase by the handle, and walked off on their exact stop. This person did not miss a beat, as if they were not sleeping at all. This blew my mind. One, this person was fast asleep so there is no way that they heard their stop announced. Two, they did not have their hands on their briefcase, but still managed to place their hands directly on the briefcase handle without even glancing at it. I've never seen anything like it. It was very impressive and funny at the same time.

One of the first places that I performed my comedic routine was a small restaurant in south Philadelphia called "The Blue Banana." It was located on a street called South Street. As I write about this experience, I think about how embarrassing this was. I've already told some of the people that were in attendance that night that I was pursuing acting and here I was standing in front of them doing this experiment trying to discover if stand-up comedy was the thing for me. Here I was, having moved hundreds of miles from Florida to Pennsylvania, and I didn't truly know what I was there for! I was trying out different things hoping that I would hit the jackpot and one of these things would grant me true happiness.

While I performed my stand-up comedy routine, I felt like a fish out of water. I still continued to tell my jokes. It seemed like they enjoyed me. One of the jokes that I performed was about how in sync the Philadelphia natives bodies were with time. There were a couple people who laughed at that joke. Another place I tried my stand-up comedy routine was one night when I took a trip to a venue in Harlem, New York. This was one of my best stand-up comedy performances. Everyone died laughing in their seats. They were practically falling to the floor laughing at my jokes. That night as I stood on stage and delivered my jokes, everything was organic. I felt like I was in my element. One of the jokes they enjoyed was the one about the crazy white man I sat next to on the Philadelphia Septa Bus. The host of the show laughed to the point that her eyes started to tear up. Needless to say, I felt like a million bucks after that performance.

Then I figured I'd go to the Laugh House, to learn how to be the best stand up comedian I could be. The laugh house was a very renowned comedy club in Philadelphia that many famous comedians have been known to perform in. Comedy classes were held here. On the night the class was being held, I walked in and I was one of the first students there. As time passed, more students started to trickle into the classroom. Not long after all the students arrived, a tall, dark skinned man came walking into the room wearing a smile that he wore often. The reason why I knew that he wore this smile often was because I saw him before. I recognized this comedian from television. I remember seeing him on a comedy show that I used to watch when I was younger. This black man's name was Turae, and he was the famous comedian that would be teaching us how to be competent stand up comedians.

One by one Turae had us do our comedic routines on the stage. He did it to see what we had to work on. For me, stand-up comedy was more difficult than spoken word. While I stood up there and delivered my jokes, I felt awkward. I felt like I didn't deliver my jokes well. I felt like the young men who were in attendance did not get my jokes, and it was a bad feeling. When I sat back down, something was eating at me and telling me, "Stand-up comedy is not for you." I yielded to the voice and never went back to that class or did another stand-up routine.

Section 4
Sinking

"And every one that heareth these sayings of mine, and doeth them not, shall be likened unto a foolish man, which built his house upon the sand: And the rain descended, and the floods came, and the winds blew, and beat upon that house; and it fell: and great was the fall of it."

Matthew 7:26-27

Chapter 14
Ravaged by the World

Placing my Faith in Men

In section 3, you, reader, have gotten a sense of my relentless search for fulfillment after I walked out of Summit Church. While searching for this fulfillment, I was simultaneously and unknowingly conforming to the dark ways of this world. I found myself placing all my faith in men instead of God. This is against the Bible! The book of Exodus 20:3 reads: "Thou shalt have no other gods before me." One person I idolized was my first mentor, Kevon.

I saw my mentor Kevon as the person who could lead me to the promise land of success and fulfillment. I was so hungry for success that I was more than willing to commute one hour from West Palm Beach (where I lived) to Kevon's home in Ft. Lauderdale. Even if he wanted to have a small ten-minute meeting with me, without hesitation I would have depleted an hour worth of fuel to have this meeting, without him compensating me for the fuel. I was not nearly as ambitious for my Father in Heaven.

Even when all the signs pointed in the direction of him using me for his personal advancement, I still remained a faithful disciple of his. Many times I just brushed off this whole notion of him using me as a figment of my own imagination. One day, while driving back home to West Palm Beach, I received a call from Kevon. He asked me to pick up a group of his female friends from an airport in Ft. Lauderdale and to give them a ride to their hotel in Miami. When I heard this request of his, I could feel a reluctance rising up within me. After all, I was close to home when he called me. With that said, he was requesting of me to turn around and drive forty-five minutes in the opposite direction, pick up the girls, and continue another half an hour or so to Miami. Though I could feel this hesitation flaring up within me, I reminded myself that this was the nationally known Kevon. Not wanting to risk burning the bridge between him and me, I followed his abrupt request.

There was yet another instance where I felt like Kevon was using me to further his business. This event took place after I moved to Jacksonville, Florida, from West Palm Beach. Jacksonville was a long, four-hour drive from West Palm Beach. One particular time, Kevon was doing one of his shows at his school Florida Atlantic University (which was not too far from West Palm Beach), and wanted me to perform my spoken-word at his show, and said that he would pay me for the show. Of course I agreed to do the show, and made that long drive down to Palm Beach County.

After my performance, Kevon paid me like he promised. But he only gave me a measly $20. I was hurt. I felt used. I thought to myself, I just drove 4 hours to come perform at your show and the most you could do is compensate me with $20 for my services! One of my poet friends, Mike, was also in attendance at the show and he was disgusted at the amount I was paid. While I was in the parking lot of Florida Atlantic University, speaking with Mike, I told him how much Kevon compensated me for the performance and he was to say the least, blown away. When I saw how thrown aback Mike was, it made me feel even worse. I felt like an idiot for having driven such a long distance from Jacksonville to perform for $20. It was apparent to me that Kevon took advantage of me, like I've suspected time and time again. But because I viewed him as a valuable contact who can take me places as a performer, I found it very difficult to turn him down.

When we place our faith in men, it's like we are standing on quicksand. The foundation is not solid. Eventually, my foundation of Kevon gave way like the ground being ripped from beneath me. While living in Jacksonville, Kevon invited me to perform at a show that was in another state. He told me to purchase my own plane ticket to get to this show. And I was not being compensated for this show. This meant that I would not get the money back that I was spending to get to the show. The idea of me not getting paid for the show made me very weary. I spent a few days battling back and forth of whether or not I should go through with it and buy my own plane ticket. After much deliberation, I finally made the decision that I would not attend the show.

Kevon called me a few days before the show with a sense of excitement in his voice. He was excited because he had already accepted the idea that

I would attend the show. While I was on the phone with him, I broke the news to him that I was not attending. He was furious! As he yelled on the phone, I trembled with fear. It was obvious that Kevon was extremely disappointed with this decision of mine. So disappointed that I feared that I would lose one of my most valuable contacts, which was Kevon. Very angrily he said, "I will never work with you again!" When those words entered my ears, I was heartbroken and totally crushed. Just like that Kevon and I broke ties. Instead of placing my hope in God and trusting in his plans for my life, I placed my hope in a man named Kevon. This proved itself to be a bad investment, because unlike God, men are not always faithful. Men will let us down, but God will never let us down. The Bible says, "Be strong and of good courage, fear not, nor be afraid of them: for the Lord thy God, he it is that doth go with thee; he will not fail thee, nor forsake thee." Deuteronomy 31:6

Another man who I placed my faith in while out of the church was Dr. Henderson. I met him not too long after I moved to Pennsylvania from Jacksonville, Florida. When I just moved to Pennsylvania, I landed a role in a stage play entitled No Gang War in '74. Dr. Henderson was the director of this play. This is how I met him. Just like Kevon, he took me under his wings as his mentee.

Dr. Henderson was not only a literary doctor, but also a performer. He had a plethora of knowledge to share on everything from writing effectively to how to make money as an artist. With that said, I listened closely to the things he taught me in the same way that I listened closely to the things that Kevon taught me. As a result of being connected with Dr. Henderson I've had many opportunities to perform my spoken-word poetry for new crowds. I placed my total faith in Dr. Henderson, in the same way that I placed my total faith in Kevon.

When I made the decision to drop out of the University of the Arts, my relationship with Dr. Henderson started to go sour. Being that he was an advocate for education, it was obvious that I lost a lot of respect from him. One day I was scheduled to perform at one of Dr. Henderson's events in west Philadelphia. While he was on the podium talking about his friend (who had attained a doctorate degree), he said to the crowd with a prideful tone, "All the people I associate myself with have degrees." When I heard this, I was hurt. I knew that it was a direct attack on me, for I was the one who was degreeless and had just dropped out of college.

Like Kevon, there came a time when this man who I have placed my faith in, broke ties with me. Through him, a friend of his commissioned me to edit and put together a book for her. I didn't put the book together correctly. After finding out about my error, Dr. Henderson called me one night while I was at an open mic event in New Jersey. Like Kevon, he was angry with me, and no longer wanted to associate himself with me.

Though he had taught me a lot of useful information, and though he led me into a lot more arenas to perform my poetry, Dr. Henderson was still a man, and once again, I made the error of placing my total faith in him instead of God. In a sense, I allowed Dr. Henderson to become my shepherd. And once again, it proved itself to be a bad investment.

Destroying the Temple

Drinking

While in the world I also developed a drinking habit. I could remember one particular time that I got drunk while I worked as a security guard at Campbell Soup's Headquarters in Camden, New Jersey. One day while some of the employees had downtime, a couple of my co-workers decided that they would buy a few cans of Four Loco, which was a very potent malt liquor. These co-workers of mine bragged about how much they can hold their liquor. I too, boasted of how much I could drink without getting drunk.

When we bought a couple cans of the much talked about potent Four Loco, I drank to my heart's content. This proved not to be one of the best decisions I've ever made. After a few plastic cups full of this potent Four Loco drink, I started to feel very inebriated. Then these co-workers of mine decided to get in a car and drive around Camden, New Jersey. I got into the car with them, and the motion of the car made my condition even worse. Periodically, my co-workers would look back at me like paramedics checking on the condition of a patient. But instead of helping me, they only laughed obnoxiously. I knew that they were amused at the fact that I could not hold my drink like I bragged earlier. As we drove along, periodically I felt as if I were about to throw up. While the car was in motion, I would open the door to empty my stomach, but nothing would come up. I would just spit and drool like a baby. My coworkers then looked over to me and said, "He's not throwing up! He's just spitting!" Then they commanded me, "Keep the door shut!" My senses were impaired. I could remember looking out the car window, and the world looked like an image on a canvas of wet paint that someone smeared with their hands.

I could remember going to a bar with my good friend Paul Frosty in Upper Darby, Pennsylvania. One of Paul's friends worked as a bartender at this particular bar. He allowed us to drink whatever we wanted to drink on the house. What a mistake! Just like when I got sloppy drunk in Camden, New Jersey, it reached a point where I became so intoxicated that my surroundings became blurry. I could remember making my way to the bar's restroom in my attempt to empty my stomach of whatever was in it, but nothing would come up. Feeling horrible, I sat on the floor against one of the walls of the restroom feeling sorry for myself, and I thought to myself, I should not have drank so much. When we left the bar, my friend Paul and I got into a black car. The next morning, I found myself along with Paul sitting on someone's front porch in south Philadelphia. I did not remember the drive there, I don't know who was driving, and I don't know whose porch we were sleeping on during the night. It was all a blur. To think, we fell asleep outdoors on the front steps to someone's else's home during the night. What a dangerous and negligent way to behave, and a few drinks caused it all.

Smoking Cigarettes

While in the world, I picked up the dangerous habit of smoking cigarettes. This is something I declared I would never do. When I had just moved to Philadelphia, I found that my cousin Garincha smoked cigarettes. I could remember educating him on the danger of smoking them. "Those things will give you cancer," I would say to him. Now here I was years after walking out of the church and I was now indulging in the same thing I warned him about.

After my first pull, I ran with cigarettes, as if they were a baton in the Olympic relay race. The first pack of cigarettes I ever bought were a pack of Newports. I could remember the first pull that I took of one. The smoke felt like an icy vapor as it traveled down to my lungs. As time went on, this icy vapor became less satisfying. It got to the point where just one cigarette was not enough. I quickly went from smoking a few cigarettes a day to smoking almost a pack a day! While sitting in my room one day, I could remember looking over at my ashtray that sat on the dresser. The cigarette butts that were piled high in it resembled a small mountain sitting on top of a foundation of grey ashes.

When I didn't have enough money to buy myself a pack of cigarettes, I would do anything to get my next pull. If I saw someone smoking a cigarette, I would ask this person if I could bum one. Just like that bum, I found myself digging for unfinished cigarettes in ashtrays that were placed on top of those small public trashcans. Many times the person who was smoking the cigarette was not able to smoke the whole cigarette, so there would still be tobacco left in them. Finding these unfinished cigarettes was like hitting the jackpot. Time and time again I was seeking that feeling of relaxation that I got every time I took a pull of a cigarette. In a sense, I was looking for rest in cigarettes instead of Jesus. In the gospels, Jesus says to us,

> *"Come unto me, all ye that labour and are heavy laden, and I will give you rest."*
>
> –Matthew 11:28

I Want to Join the Bloods...Again

I moved to Philadelphia in the year 2009, it is now April of 2012. By this time, I have acted in many stage plays, my own one-man shows, and performed my spoken-word poetry in many places. Also, due to all of this performing, I have gained a lot of prestige. Still after all of this "success," I was deeply depressed. In an attempt to find happiness, I considered joining a street gang. This gang was the Bloods. This was the same exact gang that I tried to get involved in years ago before I walked out of the church.

Mark was the one that initially invited me into this gang, and years later I viewed my friendship with Mark as a bridge to joining the gang, if I ever should decide to join it later. One night while sitting in my home in Philadelphia, I messaged my friend Mark on an online social network called Facebook.

I typed, "I want to come home." When I typed this to him, I could sense his confusion when he typed back, "You mean home as in Palm Beach? Or home as in Blood?" I responded, "Blood." And after he tried his best to deter me from joining the gang, he said, "Let me know what you decide." I immediately typed back, "I've decided. I want in."

Mark never responded back. This reminded me of the time when Mark was ready to take me through the preliminaries of joining the gang years ago at Summit church. He was ready to get me in the gang, but it never happened. Just like then, I believe that here in the year 2012 that it was divine providence that kept Mark and I from going through with the whole idea of getting me initiated into such a dead end dangerous lifestyle as a gang member. The depression I felt is reflected in the following poem that I wrote while living in Philadelphia.

"All Black"

My dark days are black.
They are not colorful,
They are not covered in
vibrant colors like yellow, pink, or purple.

They are ALL BLACK.

These black days torture me and beat me,
until I'm left battered in black blood,
in a black room, on a black bed,
and staring into blackness.

And the black cloud that hovers over my black body is letting
down black rain in a storm that never seems to end on these dark nights.

My dark days are BLACK! ALL BLACK!

Black emotions run through me,
Black images pester me,
Black ropes bound me,
Black walls close in on me,
and black hope spits on me.

On these days I'm submerged in
black anger, black doubts, black pain,
black drive, black stillness,
and black movement.

My dark days are ALL BLACK!
Therefore, they are not like a bag of Skittles.
Unless, the bag is black,
and the word "Skittles" can't be seen because it's spelled in all black,
and all the candy is black,
and when you rip open the black bag,
sprinkle the black candy into your black hands
and take a bite out of it, a black thick liquid oozes out.

My dark days are slimy, ugly, bitter, salty, sour, pungent, and Stink.
They don't believe in taking showers.

You can't share anything with them,
because they don't believe in "This is ours."

You can't plug your cell phone into one of the outlets,
because they want all the power.

You can't invite them to dinner,
because they fart loudly, and pick their teeth with their finger nails.

You can't ask them to help you with your final paper,
because they are too impatient to sort out details.

You can't ask them to hold your heart,
because they would rather have it broken.

You can't put them in the arcade,
because they would take all your tokens.

You can't get away from danger,
because they are pinning you down.

They are taking away all the muscles that you use to smile,
just so they could always see you frown.

When you are around them,
You can't do anything but cry.

My dark days are like an innocent black child with a new coloring book,
That has just been given a 100-count black box of Crayolas.

He peels back the black seal, and cracks the black box open
with anticipation to start adding all these different kinds of
colors to his blank pictures only to find that his only color option is…black.

Chapter 15
Struggling

Reader, in the previous chapter you've gotten a sense of how after leaving Summit Church, and going out into the world, how I was simultaneously submerging myself in the dark ways of this world. On top of this, I often times struggled financially. More specifically, it always reached a point where I struggled to keep up with my rent every time I moved out on my own. In the "Journalism, Activism, and Acting" chapter you read that I had to move out on my own, when my mother decided to move out of West Palm Beach to Jacksonville, Florida. I moved out into a 3-bedroom apartment in West Palm Beach with a young black man named Reed and my friend Greg. The total rent of this apartment was split among the three of us, making it so that we each only had to pay $300 dollars as our share of the rent. Initially, I did a great job in keeping up with the rent. Being that I was occupying two jobs while living in this apartment, this was not a difficult task. I worked as a security guard for a security company called Titan International and a work-study position on the campus of Palm Beach Community College. One day I lost one of these jobs, and that is when everything went downhill.

One day when the rent was due, I could remember secretly pulling my roommate Reed (who collected the rent money from us each month) into my room. Embarrassed that I could not hold my own, and somewhat afraid of how he might react to my proposal, I said to him in a hushed tone, "I'm short on the rent, and I will get it to you as soon as possible." I was relieved when he agreed to this proposal of mine. This was only the beginning of troubles. There came a time where I did not have the rent at all. Desperately in need of help, I sought out one of the elders of Summit Church for assistance. I sought out this particular person in the same way that an ill person visits the hospital to seek a doctor. In this case, the doctor was Sister Antoinette, and the hospital was the hair salon that she owned. After sharing my predicament with her, she happily gave me the funds that I needed to pay that month's rent. This was just a temporary relief for me. My rent troubles continued like a nightmare that just did not want to go away.

While living in this apartment, also due to a lack of money, I often had a difficult time eating regularly. One day, desperate for food, I decided to pawn my valuable acoustic guitar for a measly thirty dollars. I felt like a destitute crack head selling an expensive piece of jewelry for only a few bucks. When I pawned my guitar, I knew that it was not a fair trade at all. With the money I bought hot bread and a drink at a nearby Haitian restaurant of which I shared with my roommate Greg. After a while, I became sick and tired of this rough existence. I finally decided to throw in the towel. I moved in with my mother in Jacksonville, Florida. So you see, I did not just move to Jacksonville, Florida, just to move there. I moved there because I fell on hard times, and moving in with my mother functioned like a pair of crutches, until I was able to get back on my feet.

The second instance where I had difficulty keeping up with my rent was when I moved into a 3-story house in west Philadelphia, Pennsylvania. I moved into this place after I wore out my welcome at my aunt and uncle's house in Lansdowne, Pennsylvania. The people who helped me find this place were Mentor and Leegardy. They were a father and daughter duo who were good friends of my aunt and uncle. Mentor was an elderly Haitian man and Leegardy was his 30-year-old daughter who often times helped my elderly Haiti born aunt and uncle with anything that they needed. Sometimes when my aunt and uncle were out of town, Mentor would come to the house to check on it. Mentor and Leegary both lived together in a townhouse that was located in a city called Upper Darby. This city was located just outside of Lansdowne, Pennsylvania, which explains why they were so readily available to help my aunt and uncle with anything that they needed. They also helped me find my own place, when it was time for me to move out of my aunt and uncle's house.

Finding me this place was not a difficult task for Mentor and Leegardy, for the landlord was a good friend of theirs. When you first walked into this 3-story house there was a living room area. There were also two dingy couches that were adjacent to each other. To the left there was a table that signified that you were now in the dining room area. Directly behind the table there was a door that led to the landlord's bedroom. Now between the living room and the landlord's bedroom, there was a staircase that led to the second and third floors of the house, which had rooms that this landlord rented out to make her living. On the second floor, there were three bedrooms. On the third floor, there were also three bedrooms, a bathroom, and a kitchen. When I first moved in, I lived in a small room on the second floor. The amount of rent for this room was $300 a month. This room was the smallest room in the house. It was so small that my bed took up almost half of the room. It seemed like as soon as I would open the door to the room, my bed would be staring me right in the face. The size of this room reminded me of a jail cell, and for a short time it was the room that I called home.

After a while I got sick and tired of feeling cramped. I needed more room to breathe and move! There was another room that was located on the third floor of this 3-story house that was vacant. This room was more spacious. It was about four times the size of the jail cell that I was sleeping in initially. It was also furnished with a bigger bed, two dressers, and a lazy boy chair. One day, I asked the landlord if I could rent out this big room on the third floor. She then informed me, "It is going to cost you and extra $75 a month." This meant that I would now be responsible for paying $375 instead of the $300.

After moving into this room, I did not have any difficulties keeping up with the rent. At the time, I was working a job as a security guard and making about $1,200 a month. After a while of living in this room, I lost my job. Once again, just like when I moved out on my own for the first time in West Palm Beach, it reached a point where I struggled to keep up with my rent. It reached a point where I went a few months without paying my rent! This was an all-time record. Eventually, my landlord's patience ran low.

One morning, I was abruptly awakened by an urgent knock on my room door. I woke up and cracked the door a little bit. It was my landlord. Being that my landlord did not visit my room often and the simple fact that I know that I had not paid my rent in months, I immediately knew what her visit was in regards to. To support this claim of mine, on this morning I noticed that she had back up. Standing several feet behind her with his big arms tightly crossed on his huge chest, was a very intimidating, tall black man who looked like he meant business. It was almost as if this man did not have the ability to smile. This morning was not the first time that I've seen him. After going months without paying my rent, this huge man seemed to come out of nowhere when he moved into one of the rooms on the third floor (which is the floor that my room was on). One day when I walked out of the house, this big man was being escorted down the sidewalk with the landlord's husband (who didn't live in the same place as the landlord). The landlord's husband rarely made visits to the house. I believed that it was the husband's job to help remove tenants who had neglected to pay their rent. With that said, I was convinced that my landlord commissioned this man to remove me from my room by force if the need should arise. Living at this west Philadelphia home was the second time I was living on my own, and also the second time I failed to keep up with my rent. That morning, the landlord commanded me to pack up my things and to get out of the room.

Before the landlord visited my room that morning, I was totally aware that I had not paid my rent in months, so I knew that the day of my eviction was nigh. With that said, I had been shopping around for other places to live. On the Philadelphia spoken-word poetry scene, I made a lot of friends. I told one of these friends that I was in desperate need for a place to live. She then told me that she had a friend that had a room available for rent in her house. I jumped on this opportunity, and went to go check the place out as soon as possible. After doing this, I told the woman that was renting this room out that I was interested, and she told me as soon as I came up with the deposit money I would be able to move in. It took me a lot of time to scrape up the initial deposit. It took so long that this woman grew weary.

Now, the day that my landlord requested that I get out of the room, I complied with her wishes and packed all of my things, thinking that I had another place to live. I called the woman who was renting out a room in her house, to tell her that I was ready to move in. She said to me, "I'm growing weary. Are you sure that you will be able to keep up with the rent if I allow you to move in?" I told her I would, but she did not buy my words. Now here I was with all of my things packed in a house where the people wanted me to get out as soon as possible, and I didn't have anywhere else to go.

I then decided that I would take a trip to Mentor and Leegardy's house in Upper Darby, Pennsylvania, to see if I could live in their house until I got back on my feet. It was nighttime now, and I walked down the street about two blocks from the house to a bus stop to wait for a bus whose destination was Upper Darby. As I stood on the corner, a familiar blue pickup truck drove up the street and stopped at the red light. It was a friend of mine who I met through my mentor, Dr. Henderson. Seeing me standing there she asked me, "Is everything okay?" I told her about my situation. She then offered to help transport all of my belongings from the house to Mentor and Leegardy's house in Upper Darby. Talk about being on time! I did not have the slightest idea of how I was going to move all of my belongings from the house to Mentor's house in Upper Darby. I got in her truck and she drove me back to the house to get my belongings. We packed all of my things into the back of the truck, and we were on our way to Upper Darby.

There were still a couple problems. One, I was not even sure if Mentor and Leegardy were home. Two, I wasn't even sure if they would allow me to stay in their home until I got back on my feet. When I arrived to their house, I walked to the door and knocked, hoping that someone was home. After a few moments, Mentor answered the door. I was relieved. I shared my difficult situation with him, and he told me that I could bring my things in. His home was a townhouse that also had a basement area. He helped me place all of my belongings in the basement.

Mentor's townhouse had a total of three bedrooms, which were all on the second floor. Mentor slept in one room and his daughter slept in another. The extra room functioned as a guest room, and this is where I made my home for the time being. One night I invited my friend Kina to come to the house. I did this without Mentor's permission. In doing this, Mentor felt like I was disrespecting him and his house, and requested that I get out of his house immediately.

Out of a desperate place, I quickly looked up a few places online on a website called Craigslist. I found a place that was cheap enough and it was located in an urban neighborhood in north Philadelphia. The gentleman who was renting the room out to me offered to help me get my things from Mentor's house one night. He had his friend with him, who was a white man who had a truck. I didn't have the money to pay this man. The gentleman who was renting out the room in north Philadelphia, told me to just simply give this man some money whenever I had it. I never did have the money to pay him. Anyways, they came one night to Mentor's house, parked along back near the back door that led to the basement (where all of my things were) and they helped me load all of my things into the truck. I could sense Mentor's relief that I was finally moving out of his house. I had become a burden and I knew that he was thinking to himself, Good riddance. Before I left his house, I told him thank you for allowing me to live there for the moment and in Creole he said, "No problem, anytime."

It is early in the year 2013 (a little less than four years since I've been living in Pennsylvania), and my new living arrangement in north Philadelphia was by far, the most uncomfortable place I've lived in since I walked out of Summit Church. I would rather have been in the tiny room that I lived in before as opposed to this room. When you first walked in, the hallway was very narrow. It was no more than the width of the door. I knew this because when I would open the door, the door would not even open to a 90 degree angle, almost as soon as you opened the door, it would hit the wall that was behind it, and I would have to turn my body to the side so that I could squeeze my body through the door way into the narrow hallway. When you first walk into the apartment, there was a pungent smell that was always in the air. I think this smell was the cause of constant spilled drinks on the carpet. The kitchen was to say the least dirty and unsanitary. There were dirty dishes everywhere, and like the hallway, there was a thick pungent smell in there, too. To the right when you first walked in, there was a room. The couple (who were my roommates and the ones that posted the availability of the room on Craigslist) occupied this room along with their two children, who were a little boy and girl. On the other end of the hallway was my sorry excuse for a room. To me, it was unfit for a human being, such as myself, to live. I would not even wish this room upon an animal. It was small and built like a jail cell. The room was so cramped that all of my clothes were piled high in one corner against my mini refrigerator that was against one of the walls. This room often times became unbearably hot. It felt like I was occupying a furnace. It was more humid than a sauna. The reasons for this was the window that was not easy to open, and the fact that there was no AC vent. The closet was not big at all. It was about the width of its door, which was not a fancy sliding door. It was just a regular door. Since I did not have an ironing board, I had to iron my clothes on my bed, which was simply a bed sheet spread across the floor. This reality added onto my nightmare. Many mornings, my roommates' two children would run up and down the hallway, which was directly on the other side of my room door. Since my bed was the ground itself I could not only hear, but also feel every vibration that their little feet made when they hit the ground. I would be awakened not by an alarm clock, but by the rapid pounding sound of little feet hitting the ground in the hallway directly on the other side of my room door. It's remarkable to me how people so small can cause such a disturbance with their tiny bodies. This north Philadelphia home was by far one of the worst conditions I ever lived in since the day I walked out of Summit Church. It is now the year 2013, and little did I know, but this would be one of the most eventful years of my life.

SECTION 5
Found

"How think ye? if a man have an hundred sheep, and one of them be gone astray, doth he not leave the ninety and nine, and goeth into the mountains, and seeketh that which is gone astray?"

Matthew 18:12

CHAPTER 16
I Hear Him Calling

"Being Groomed to be a Preacher?"
October 31, 2012

The end of Section 2 of this memoir marked the point that I decided to walk out of Summit Church. Ever since then, I've been on a relentless search in the world to find that one thing that would grant me happiness. With ambition, I pursued success in not only acting and spoken-word poetry, but other things in hopes that they granted me the fulfillment that I was desperately seeking. It's been years since the day I walked out of Summit Church, and lately it has become tremendously difficult to avoid the fact that I was missing something essential in my life. So much that while attaining all of my worldly success, I simultaneously replayed the moment that happened years ago when the church elders at Summit offered me the college scholarship to attend school for theology. While toiling in the world, I often wondered, How much happier would I be if I had accepted that offer? Me reminiscing on the day that I had received that offer, reveals how unsatisfied I was with my life. It also conveys that there was nothing that I could do under my own power to attain this fulfillment that I had been desperately searching for. I had failed so miserably in finding fulfillment in the world that all that was left to do was to think back to a time when I stood in front of that elder at Summit Church, and to bask in that momentary euphoric feeling that came with imagining myself accepting his offer instead of denying it.

God simultaneously spoke to me during this vulnerable moment in my life to relay a very important message to me. Starting towards the end of the year 2012, while working as a librarian, I heard His voice. Wait a minute! How did I end up in the humble position of a librarian after working so hard on the performance realm the past several years?

While attending University of the Arts, I got fired from my job as a security guard. This was at a business building in center city Philadelphia called the 1700 Building. As a security guard at this building, some of my duties included sitting at the front desk all night, patrolling the premises, and also checking in anyone (usually workers) that came in during the night to do some work within the building. In the mornings at 7 am when my shift was over, another security guard would come in and relieve me from my post. I then would have to get dressed and make my way to class at the University of the Arts, which was about ten minutes walking distance from the 1700 Building. Sometimes the security guard that was to come in that morning to relieve me from my post would not make it on time. In this case the supervisor on duty would ask another security guard to fill the post until the person that was scheduled to watch that post made it in to work. One particular day after my shift, my supervisor called me on the phone that was at the front desk, and asked me to watch an elevator post (that began at 7am that morning), because the security guard that was supposed to be at the elevator post did not make it on time. I was hesitant with this request of his, because my neutral mask class started at 8 am and making it to class was more important to me. While I spoke to my supervisor over the phone I told him that I would not be able to fill the post because I had a class to get to at 8 am. No matter how much I pleaded, he insisted that I watch the post. Reluctantly agreeing, I told him that I would only be able to remain at the post for so long before I had to make my way to class. He said okay and that he would work on getting someone to come in. I filled in the post, but as every minute went by the more anxious I became because as every minute went by, the closer it got to 8 am, which was the time my class began. When it was about 8 am, I walked away from the elevator post without telling my supervisor, and headed to class. In security work, walking off of a post was a major violation that was enough to get a person fired, and that is exactly what happened to me. My job terminated me, leaving me jobless. Desperate and in need of a job, I searched for a work-study job at the Main Public Library in Philadelphia.

I was unhappy working as a librarian. To me it was an embarrassing situation to be in, simply because it did not add up to me. The past three years since I've been living in Pennsylvania, I worked extremely hard as a performer. Now here in the year 2012, with the desperate need to make money, I was working as a librarian. As I kneeled to the floor to shelve kid's books, I would wonder, How did I end up here? It felt like I was knocked off my high horse. While in this state of confusion, God spoke to me.

On October 31, 2012, while on my shift at this library, I enjoyed creating and posting encouraging messages on my Facebook page. One day while at work, I used my phone to post an uplifting message on Facebook to encourage anyone who read it. Only moments after I posted this message, one of my friends (who has watched me perform spoken-word poetry) responded to my post. His response spoke to me. It read, "After reading your status today, I said to myself, 'He would be a remarkable Preacher!' You ever feel that God is grooming you for such a task? For you have a gift to use your words as a painter uses his brush while he paints on canvas, you paint a picture of hope in the mind of all who hear you...your status gave me hope. Thanks for posting (preacher)."

His message pressed the rewind button on my memories. My thoughts went back to that pivotal event where the elders at Summit Church offered me that scholarship to study theology. I thought about me denying the offer. Right there in that library, years after the fact, I was once again convicted of what God wanted me to do, which is to minister. While I read his words, something was nudging on the inside of me and bringing to my attention a truth that I had tried for years to escape. This voice said, "Thierry, You know the truth, now accept the call!" Years ago, right before I denied the church elder's offer, I heard this same voice telling me accepting the offer is the right thing to do. Now here in the year 2012, I heard the same voice telling me the same thing as I looked at the message that this man sent me on Facebook. It said to me, "Say yes to the call." This was God speaking to me, and I could not deny what he was telling me to do. But I was still afraid to answer the call.

I immediately responded to that man's message. I typed, "I'm glad that it touched you, my brother...yes, I've thought that for a while, but God has been telling me to reach people through my art a lot lately." I found myself fighting to convince myself that this response of mine was true, but I failed to convince myself of this lie, just like years ago when I failed to convince myself that I wanted to become a pharmacist. As I typed my response to him, I said to myself, "Thierry, you are typing a lie and you know it. You are afraid to answer the call! You have been creating a whole other reality in your life over the years and you are afraid to give that up." This was the truth. Over the past few years I have worked extremely hard to build many followers. These followers knew me as a dynamic spoken-word artist and an actor. In other words, for years I've been building this brand. Now what God was asking me to do was to abandon this brand that I had built, surrender to his will, and to go into the direction that he wants me to go. This was a scary thought. I was afraid that if I yielded to God's will, then that would mean that all the performing that I've done over the years would have been done in vain.

When I denied the church elder's offer years ago, I felt like I did the wrong thing in denying the offer. Now it's years later, and I still felt like I was doing the wrong thing in telling that man that I felt like God wanted me to perform instead of being a preacher. Honestly, here in the year 2012, I wanted to accept the call that I had on my life, but my selfishness kept me from it. I thought to myself, What are other people going to think about me if I were to go into the ministry after years of performing? I thought, People already know me as a performer. If I were to go into the ministry now, I would look like a fool. When I initially denied the offer the church elders gave me years ago, it was selfish reasons that kept me from it. I thought to myself, My mother is going to think that I am a fool if I switch my major from pharmacy to theology. Now, here in the year 2012, selfish reasons caused me to deny the still small voice that I heard on the inside of me.

As time went on, no matter how much I tried to portray it on the outside, there was a still small voice on the inside of me saying, "Thierry, you are a minister." The voice inside of me did not win. I continued to run. To where? I was never able to answer this question with an answer that I believed. Every time I tried to answer this question, I would create scenarios for the future that I was never satisfied with. One of these scenarios was possibly becoming some kind of big movie star one day. I guess you can't force yourself to be what you are not. It seemed like I would stop at nothing to get what I wanted (but I never had a clear idea as to what that was). I just simply continued to work hard hoping that the more worldly attainments I gained the happier and more fulfilled that I would be. It's the year 2012, years since I walked out of Summit Church and went out into the world, and it is in this year that I started to clearly hear God's voice telling me that He called me to be a minister. This was only the beginning. God would continue to call.

"Something is Calling Me Out There"
Spring 2013

Right before I dropped out of University of the Arts, I could feel something tugging me out of the school. This thing was like a monkey that I could not get off of my back, and this "pestilence" manifested in the way I performed in class. In acting studio class there was an exercise called "Activities." One of the things that this exercise taught us was how to re-create emotions.

My acting professor would always tell me that my default emotion was "rage." She said this because this was the emotion that was easiest for me to re-create, and she was right. I could remember one of the times that I became my angriest. On this day we were doing activities in class, and my scene partner was a white girl named Rebecca. In the scene that we were assigned, Rebecca played the role of my imaginary wife and mother of my children.

In the scene, Rebecca says to me, "I'm leaving you." After hearing this, I quickly went from 0 to 60 on the angry scale. But still my anger didn't evolve to full blown rage. Feeling threatened by my anger, Rebecca threatens me with the statement, "I'm going to call the cops on you." After hearing this statement in this imaginary world, I thought to myself, The mother of my children is in the wrong for telling me that she is going to leave me. That's strike one! Now she is threatening to call the cops on me. Strike two! Immediately, my anger grew to rage.

Being that my emotions were real, it could have easily caused me to do harm to my scene partner, Rebecca. Our professor, who just sat on a chair against one of the walls of the room, watched on as the scene progressed. When our professor sensed my anger growing to a magnitude that might have been harmful to my scene partner, she quickly commanded me, "Thierry, remain on your side of the room, do not approach her." I yielded to my professor's command, but I was so tempted to approach Rebecca. But I couldn't. As I stood on the other side of the room, furious as ever, my imaginary wife, Rebecca, starts packing her things, for she was preparing to leave me, her husband, and I could not do anything about it. On my side of the room, there was a ladder leaning against the wall. As soon as I realized that I could not stop my imaginary wife from leaving me, I placed both of my hands on the ladder. Then I proceeded to bang it very hard against the wall with all the rage that was in me. Being aware of this default emotion of mine, my acting studio professor requested that I come up with an activity to help me re-create other emotions. Since re-creating rage was so easy for me, I had a difficult time coming up with an activity that would help me re-create another emotion such as happiness. Maybe I had difficulty re-creating this emotion because I was not truly a happy person in real life. I still took on the professor's challenge.

To create this activity, I got in touch with one of my own personal truths. I said to myself, I've been out of the church for years, and over all these years I have not been putting God first. I then thought to myself, Maybe this is the reason why I am so unhappy. With that said, I decided to create an activity that centered on this truth. For my activity, I decided to imagine myself going back to church. Before when I did activities, my goal was to get a good grade in Acting Studio. This was now no longer my goal with this particular activity. My goal now was to figure out why I was such an unhappy person.

I could feel something calling me, and this is what I told my voice and speech professor, right before I decided to drop out of University of the Arts. After noticing that my grades had been slipping lately in my classes, she requested to have a meeting with me in the room where she held her voice and speech classes. Concerned about me, she asked, "What is wrong?" While looking out the window of the classroom, I responded, "Something is calling me out there."

"You Are a Minister!"
May 2013

In Section 4 of my memoir, I mentioned a man named Dr. Henderson who became my mentor not too long after I moved to Lansdowne, Pennsylvania. You've also read that I eventually broke ties with Dr. Henderson. But before Dr. Henderson and I broke ties, he was a person who taught me many things. There is one lesson in particular that is very difficult to get out of my mind. One day I was bragging to him about my ability to make money. Very proudly I exclaimed, "I'm a hustler." Dr. Henderson was not the least bit impressed by this proud statement of mine. He just simply looked at me and said, "Yes, you are hustling, but you are moving without a purpose." This response caught me off guard. This response of his blindsided me so much that I could not give a good comeback. He was speaking the truth-I was hustling without a purpose.

Dr. Henderson did not only teach me lessons, but he would also aid me when I needed financial assistance. In Section 4, in the "Struggling" chapter, you've read that after getting kicked out of Mentor and Leegardy's house in Upper Darby, I moved into an apartment in north Philadelphia. Once again in the year 2013, like the title of the previous chapter "Struggling" suggests, I struggled to keep up with my rent at my north Philadelphia home. While living at this place, and during a time where I desperately needed money, Dr. Henderson emailed me a job offer. In the email he told me that he had just become a director at an after school program in west Philadelphia called ADAC (Anti-Drug and Alcohol Crusaders). In the email he offered me a paying position that was open in the program that he would like for me to fill if I was interested. I quickly accepted this offer. Maurice was right on time. I was lacking in funds so I could not pay my rent, which was due in a couple of days. I did not know where I was going to get the money. In the midst of my troubles, a light shined through in the form of this job offer. Like I said, Maurice was always helping me in any way that he could.

Even though I had this job opportunity, there reached a time where I struggled to keep up with my rent, and I knew that me getting kicked out of the place was on the horizon. Before this could happen, I reached out to Dr. Henderson to help me find another place. He agreed to help me find another place. It was his plan to work things out in such a way that we would be living in the same apartment so that the rent could be split between the both of us. The advantage of the rent being split between both of us would make the load a lighter for each of us. The apartment that he found was directly across the street from the afterschool program, ADAC. The landlord to this apartment owned an eyeglass store that was directly below this apartment, on the first floor.

One day my mentor decided to go speak with this man in regards to the possibility of him renting the apartment that he had available for rent. I tagged along with my mentor as he went to go visit this man. When we walked into the eyeglass store (where this landlord worked), I stood near the door to the store as my mentor, Maurice Henderson, went to speak with him. Me keeping my distance from my mentor was my way of giving him room to speak to this man. I was desperate to find a place to live and the last thing that I wanted to do was get in the way of any negotiation that my mentor was trying to work out in regards to getting this apartment. So while my mentor spoke with this man, I stood close to the front door of the store and leaned on an eyeglass case. I stood there quietly and unnoticeable as possible as my mentor and the landlord became submerged in a conversation.

Almost as soon as they started to converse, the landlord abruptly stopped Dr. Henderson in mid-sentence, and placed his attention on me. He asked me, "Are you a minister?" This question of his shook me to the core. He was asking me this question after I've worked tirelessly for years painting a certain image in the minds of all the people who have come to know me. This was the image of me being simply a performer. I succeeded in not only convincing them, but also convinced myself that I was just a performer and nothing else. With bravado I answered his question with, "No, I'm just a poet and an actor." As soon as this answer of mine rolled off of my lips, something inside me told me that this was not at all true. Once again, I felt like I was lying to myself, just like when I told that man (while I worked at the library) that God wanted me to reach people through my art.

The landlord listened closely to my answer, and simply nodded to show that he was registering what I was saying to him, but in actuality I knew that he was not. I could sense that when he asked me if I was a minister that he was not truly interested in my answer. I could sense that he already knew the answer to his question. I could sense that in his own mind, he had already rejected what I "thought" I was. It was almost as if he saw right through me. After telling him that I was simply a performer, he responded back with a sure tone, "Yes, you are a minister." These words of his hit a nerve within me. Then, as soon as he said this to me, he quickly diverted his attention back to my mentor and resumed their conversation, as if he was not just used by the Almighty God to give me a word of confirmation in regards to the calling on my life.

> "...*Something funny happened. When I went with Maurice Henderson to go talk about a housing situation. The man who he spoke to asked me if I was a minister? I took that as a sign that God is using me or wants me to minister unto other people more often...*"
>
> -May 21, 2013

Chapter 17
Go Back to Church

July 2013

Back in October of 2012, when I was working at the library, I felt a strong conviction that God was calling me. At University of the Arts I could also hear God calling me. And in May 2013, God used the man at the eyeglass store to give me a message of guidance. Though God gave me these great signs of what He wanted me to do, I continued to perform. I continued to move forward like a brakeless, speeding freight train.

It is now July 2013, a little over four years since I've moved to Pennsylvania, and I am going through yet another difficult time in my life. The cycle of not being able to keep up with my rent continued. My rent payment is past due, and I was now on the brink of getting kicked out of my home in north Philadelphia. I could feel it in my whole being. Desperate to make money to pay my rent, I went to my go to method, which was to sell my poetry CDs at an open mic venue. Over the years, I've always sold poetry CDs. I usually sold them at $10 a pop, but if I was really desperate for money I would give them for an open donation (any donation amount that a person was able to afford). The concept of open donations is something that my first mentor Kevon introduced to me years back. This in itself shows you how much of an influence my first mentor had on me. Even after having broken ties with Kevon years ago before I moved out of Jacksonville, Florida, I still used many of the things he taught me in an attempt to further myself.

In the midst of my tumultuous time in the year 2013, I received the opportunity to perform at an artist showcase that was happening at a restaurant in south Philadelphia named Warm Daddy's. This was a well-known bar and restaurant in Philadelphia, where many people held their events. That night I performed my spoken-word poetry for the audience. As always, I blew the crowd away with my performance. After the show, the host, Robert, who was a short, black Christian man who looked to be in his mid-30's-walked up to me while I was standing in the back of the venue, and expressed to me how much he enjoyed my performance. Then he said that his birthday was coming up soon, and that he wanted me to perform at his birthday celebration. Without hesitation, I accepted this Christian man's offer. No, he was not going to compensate me for the performance, but I didn't have any issues with this. Over the years, I became good at selling my poetry CDs. For the past several years of my life, I've performed my poetry at countless venues, and I've pitched my CD to hundreds, maybe thousands of people. As a result, over the years my salesmen skills have been sharpened. So much so that I believed that unless someone did not truly have any money, they would not be able to fight my charm and the fact that my spoken-word was too incredible for them to miss out on the opportunity of having my product in their cars or playing on the stereos within their homes. So when Robert asked me to perform at his birthday party, I quickly agreed, knowing that I would be able to make money off of my CDs.

On the day of Robert's birthday celebration, I prepared my poetry CDs and the DVDs that I had of my one-man shows and placed them into my military transport backpack that I bought at a military shop in center city Philadelphia a few years back. It was my goal to sell as many CDs as I could for the following reasons: To not get kicked out of my room and to buy food.

When Robert invited me to perform for his birthday party, he didn't tell me what kind of venue that it was going to be held in. He just simply gave me the address of the location. I didn't know what kind of venue it was. I didn't know if it was a house, a banquet hall, a restaurant, or a school. So, I didn't know exactly what I was looking for. One bright, sunny day, me along with a spoken-word poet friend of mines named J. Knivez (who was also one of the performers at this birthday celebration), made our way to the venue. On the way to the event, we both got lost. We found ourselves in a north Philadelphia neighborhood near a block full of row homes. Looking at my watch, the time for the show had arrived, and there was no music or people going into the houses to indicate that there was any party happening in the area. After J.Knivez and I walked around for a little longer, I finally decided to call Robert to help guide me to the right place. When I told him what side of town I was on, he told me that J.Knivez and I were on the wrong side of town. This was an easy fix. After being pointed in the right direction, J.Knivez and I caught a public bus that headed in this direction.

Once again, since Robert never told me the venue or setting where his birthday party would be held, I still did not know what I was looking for. But when I arrived on the scene, I discovered that this particular venue was not like any one that I've performed in over the years. It didn't have the same look or atmosphere as the venues that I've grown accustomed to over the years. There wasn't loud, secular music playing. There was no one at the door collecting an admission fee. There wasn't a bar or even a DJ! The atmosphere of this venue was peaceful. I discovered that the venue that I was scheduled to perform in on this day was a church.

After I arrived to the venue, Robert was one of the few people that were there. It was about an hour or so before more people started arriving to the venue. After that time, the festivities began, and I was one of the first people to perform at this event. After I was done performing, with a sense of urgency, I started to walk around the room pitching my CDs to those that were in attendance. I did this while others were still performing. This was something that I was accustomed to doing. Many times when I performed at open mics, I didn't wait until the end of the night to try to sell my CDs. The reason I didn't do this was because once the event was over, audience members started to make their way out of the venue. This emptying of the venue also meant less potential buyers for my product. Since I was already days late on my rent, this was something that I could not afford to happen. Selling my CDs immediately after my performance was a window where my performance would still be lingering in the minds of the audience members. So by the time I walked to them, they would quickly be able to recall my performance. This made is easier to sell my product. This is exactly what I did after my performance at this church.

As I moved around the room with my CDs in hand, something started happening. The performances started to arrest my attention. The more the performances pulled me in, the less concerned I became about my prime objective of selling my CDs. Something about the performances was mesmerizing. So much that I stopped me in my tracks and went back to my seat (which was in the back of the church), put my CDs down, and gave the performers my undivided attention.

What was so captivating about these performances? Well, over the years I watched poets glorify having sex before marriage, and other things that were worldly. But the topics on this night were on the other side of the spectrum. The artists and ministers who were in this church were passionately praising God through their talents and testimonies. This is what got my attention. There was a minister there who even shared his testimony of how God saved him from his drinking habits. This was a subject matter that was the direct opposite of anything that I've experienced at the regular open mic venues that I've grown accustomed to attending. Having been touched by the performers and speakers that night, I totally abandoned the initial mission I had that night, which was to sell as much CDs as I could. This was no longer my concern. My need was much deeper than needing to pay my rent. I had a need for the Word of God.

About two weeks before this night, while organizing one of my one-man shows in Trenton, New Jersey, I received a similar experience. It was on Sunday, July 7, 2013, when I was once again reminded of how far I've strayed from God. The name of the place where I had this experience was called the Conservatory Mansion, and was owned by a black, older gentleman named Sterick. The Conservatory Mansion had a large space on the first floor. Sterick often rented out this space to people that wanted to use it for things such as stage plays or church services. I personally wanted to use it to put on my "Follow Your Dreams" one-man show. One this Sunday, there was a black pastor who was using the space to hold a church service. After speaking to Sterick, in regards to my one-man show, I found myself having a conversation with this pastor who was holding a church service in the Conservatory Mansion that day.

I told him that God did not want me to use my talents as a pastor, but to use them in the arts. When I said this to him, it felt like I was trying to convince myself more than I was trying to convince him. Those words felt far-removed from the truth. I felt like I was lying. In the same way I felt like I was lying to that man that messaged me several months ago when I worked at the library, I felt like I was lying then. As I stood in front of this pastor, I did not believe with all of my heart that God truly was not calling me to be a pastor. I was not only lying to that pastor that day, but I was lying to myself also. This shows that I was trying my best to stay away from a certain truth about myself that was born several years back. After speaking to the pastor, I decided to sit in on the church service that he was having in the Conservatory Mansion. I walked in and sat on a chair in one of the back rows of the church. I don't remember if it was the spiritual music that was being played or what the pastor was preaching about but as I sat on a seat in one of the back rows something powerful about that church service moved me to tears. There was a certain familiarity about this church service, and that something familiar was Jesus Christ. It reminded me of how far that I've strayed away from him. Those tears were rolling down my face because I realized that I had strayed away from God and the church. It hit me hard in that church that I've been shutting my Lord and Savior out of my heart for years, and now I felt him knocking on the door to my heart asking me to let him in.

Now only two weeks after getting this feeling of conviction at this church in Trenton, New Jersey, I now found myself at another church in Philadelphia experiencing the same strong feeling. This feeling was so strong that it caused my original hunger to sell CDs to not seem so important in the light of my need for Jesus. Despite me recognizing this deeper need of mine, I still made a pitiful attempt to sell my CDs after the event was over. The Christians who praised God that night had such an impact on me that it caused me to walk slowly and passively around the room. As I walked with my CDs in hand, I felt defeated to say the least. It's been several years since I walked out of Summit Church. In all those years, I've toiled unceasingly from city to city and from state to state searching for a sense of fulfillment and success, and I never found what I had been searching for. I was defeated. Over all those years, I became so zealous to find success that there have been many days where I was extremely tired mentally and physically and I would just simply ignore this exhaustion to push harder in hopes that I found the fulfillment that I've been searching for. Even after all of my highly respected work ethic, even after all of my hard work, I was still struggling financially. Deep inside I asked myself, Why am I still down on my luck after having worked so hard all these years? With this feeling of defeat wrapped in me, I did not know it then, but I wanted an answer to this question of mine, and God was about to use someone in this venue to give me the answer.

Aimlessly, I walked around the church with my CDs in hand. One of the first people I made an attempt to sell my CDs to was a short, light-skinned, middle-aged woman who was about 5 feet 6 inches tall. She had such a gentle nature about her, that by simply looking at her, you could sense that she was a Christian. Her name was Nicole, but she called herself Pastor Nikki. When I made my attempt to sell her my CD, she politely denied. Usually, when a person denied my CD I would go on to the next person, but I didn't do this at this particular moment. Something told me to just stand there with that woman, and I yielded to this voice. Selling my CDs was no longer my goal. My immediate availability gave Nikki time to strike a conversation with me, and what a powerful conversation it was. She provided me with something that I was not only more in desperate need of, but that would satisfy me better than a couple dollars could. What she gave me were powerful words of guidance.

While she spoke with me, she started to say things that quickly arrested my attention. Looking directly into my eyes (possibly staring deep into my soul) and in a tone that said she knew that she was speaking the truth, she asked me, "You are hungry, right?" and "You need a place to live, right?" I was astonished by her preciseness. I just met this sweet lady moments ago, and she already knew my physical needs. She was right! I didn't have much money so I had not been eating right, and I was on the brink of getting kicked out of my house so I was in a position where I would be needing a place to live soon. Still, I didn't blow my top and scream out "How did you know that!?" I just remained calm and listened to her every word. Little did I know it then, but Pastor Nikki was feeding me the spiritual food that I was in desperate need of. At the beginning of the night I thought I was desperate for money so that I would not get kicked out of my apartment. But in all actuality, I was desperate for an answer from God, and Pastor Nikki was undoubtedly that messenger who was used by God to give me the very important life-changing message that I needed during this time. I recognized that it was indeed God using her to speak to me, so right there in that church I humbly listened closely to what God wanted me to know. She then said to me, "You are a very talented individual." She then asked me, "Do you have a church home?" This question struck another cord within me. This question of hers made me realize how long it's been since I've walked out of Summit Church. I solemnly replied, "No, I do not have a church home." She was thrown aback! She said, "So you are just performing out here without anyone having your back?" I answered, "Yes." She then asked me what was my nationality and I answered, "Haitian." After my response, she recommended I attend a Haitian Church that had an event happening on Sunday night, which was the very next day.

> *"Last night I went to perform at a church where a friend of mine was holding his birthday party: There were a lot of enriching things said at this event that spoke to me…One of the women there encouraged me to attend a Haitian church that was located at 63rd St. & Lancaster…"*
>
> -July 20, 2013

CHAPTER 18
No Glory in the World

Sunday, July 21, 2013

I had reached the end of my rope, and I could feel it. So much that I visited the Haitian church the day after Pastor Nikki recommended I attend it. Over the past several years (after I walked out of Summit Church) with a strong sense of urgency, I rushed to open mic venues, stage plays, film projects, and my one-man shows. I rushed to these places because I felt it was important to be at these places. Now in July 2013, I got my priorities straight again. With the same strong sense of urgency, I was rushing to the house of God, a church.

On this Sunday night in July 2013, I arrived late to the Haitian church service. Though I was late, I arrived right on time. As soon as I stepped foot into the lobby (which came right before the entrance that led into the main sanctuary) the preacher's words quickly found my ears and arrested my attention. His words spoke to me as if he had me in mind while he was composing his sermon. The words filled me up as if they were the exact things that I was being deprived of, and indeed they were. For years I had been toiling tirelessly in the world, in hopes that I would find something in the world that brought me fulfillment, and I didn't. As a result, I felt defeated, as I wondered, Why is it after working so hard over the years, I still haven't found this fulfillment? Using his sermon, the preacher on this night answered this question of mine before I even stepped one foot in the sanctuary. Preaching very loudly and passionately I heard him say, "There is no glory in the World. There are people who leave the church and go out into the world. Then they find out that there is no glory in the world and they come right back to the church."

When he delivered those words, it was as if he was speaking directly to me saying, "Thierry, you have toiled a lot over the past several years and you did not find the fulfillment that you were relentlessly searching for. You did not find it, because true fulfillment does not exist in the world!" These words hit me hard. With these specific words, this preacher brought to light a section of my life who's starting point was about six years ago and who's ending point was marked by me making the conscious decision to attend the church service that night. The person who this preacher was talking about was me! It was me that walked out of the church years ago. It was me who tried to find glory in the world. It was me who failed to find this glory in the world. Now, it was me who this preacher was referring to as I made my way back to church on this night.

When I walked into this church that night, it felt like I just came from a long, tiresome journey. After sitting down on one of the back pews of the church, the preacher continued to speak. My eyes swelled up with tears, for every word of the sermon convinced me of the painful truth that I was the one who finally made my way back to church after having been out of the church for years. After taking a seat on one of the back pews of the church, I noticed something profound. The countless people in attendance looked radiant and refreshed, as if they've never gotten less than eight hours of sleep a day in their life. I knew that this refreshed look was as a result of the rest that only Jesus can offer them. Right before I walked out of Summit, I had this same rested look. Now, I felt tired, defeated, bedraggled, and battered. I did not sit erect like the Christians who were in attendance on this night. On the contrary, my posture was sluggish. Everyone in attendance was dressed nice. I, on the other hand, was dressed like an illegal drug-consuming rock star. I wore skinny jeans and a silver wallet chain dangled from my belt. While I was still attending Summit Church, I did not wear jewelry simply because this was against the Seventh-day Adventist faith. Now, as I sat in the back pew of the church, I was decked out in jewelry. Due to the struggle I've endured after years of being out of the church, I lost a lot of weight. So decked out in these rings and bracelet I resembled a skinny Christmas tree. God desires for each of us to dress modestly. On that night I was not in line with God's will. If I were to go back to Summit Seventh-day Adventist Church dressed like this, the members that have watched me grow in Christ for the better, probably would not have recognized me. They probably would say to themselves, "Is this Thierry, the young, smart leader who has preached for our church?" or

"Is this the young man who is called to be a pastor?" or "What has the world done to you, my son?"

Even the tattoos that I got while I was in the world, told a story of how I strayed away from my hope of salvation, Jesus Christ. One of these read, "I am Hope." How disturbing! There was a time where Jesus was my hope, but now with this tattoo, I was declaring, "I, Thierry Lundy, am Hope!" Many times while I was in the world my mother would tell me in her native tongue of Creole, "You are my hope." As you can see, the idea of me being hope to my mother went to my head so much that I decided to get a tattoo that says it. Since I believed that I was hope I didn't feel a need for a savior.

When I first stepped foot in Summit Church years ago, I was dressed like the world. I would let my pants sag below my butt exactly like the thugs and gangsters that indulged in the things of this God-opposing world. But by God's transforming power to bring me to more of his likeness, the waist of my pants found their way to their rightful place--my waist. Also by God's grace, I replaced my regular street clothes with suits. I didn't know it at the time, but what I was doing was surrendering to God's Holy Spirit to allow these righteous changes to take place in my life. The way that I dressed on Sabbath mornings became reformed as the Holy Spirit convicted me of the worldly ways that I had adopted for quite some time. This was the work that God had done on me right before I walked out of Summit Church. It is now the year 2013, about six long years of marinating in the ways of the world, and I was not dressed simplistically the way I did right before I walked out of Summit Church. Nothing about how I was dressed now, said that I was a God-fearing Christian. The way I dressed went from reformed to deformed.

It was God who guided me to that church that night. He guided me to that church with the purpose of giving me a word of encouragement and guidance. He used that pastor's sermon that night to speak to me. I've heard many sermons in my life, and none of them spoke to me as much as that sermon did that night. And what the preacher told me next suggested the end or completion of something. After the pastor's enlightening sermon was over, everyone in the congregation was instructed to stand side-by-side and to create a circle in the middle of the church. With tears rolling down my face, I also joined the circle. When the circle was created, the pastor grabbed a small bottle full of oil and walked into the middle of the circle. Very composed and collected, he then walked around and anointed everyone in the circle. As he approached me to where I was positioned in this circle, a small voice told me that the pastor was about to tell me something. This voice did not come from the person who was standing to left or right of me. It was a still small voice that only I could hear. And this voice instructed me to be very alert because this pastor was about to tell me something important. Without hesitation, I obeyed.

As the pastor got closer to me, the more alert I became. Before I knew it, we were face to face. He looked at me briefly, dipped his finger into the bottle of oil, and traced a cross on my forehead. He then moved on to the next person. I then said to myself, He did not say a word to me. But I didn't panic; because the Lord comforted me and assured me that this pastor was about to say something to me. I was confident and had faith that God was about to use this pastor to speak to me again. And he did. Almost as soon as the pastor went to the next person in the circle, he came right back to me, leaned into my right ear and whispered, "Now everywhere you go, share your testimony."

As soon as those words entered my ears, I hung my head low as both my eyes flooded with tears. I felt pitiful for having done exactly what I said I would not do. Years ago on the day of my baptism at Summit Church, I recited a poem entitled "I Am a Soldier in God's Army." In this poem, I boldly declared, "I am a volunteer in this army, and I am enlisted for eternity. I will not get out, sell out, be talked out, or pushed out." Now, here I was years later after making this bold declaration, and I did exactly what I said I would not do. I had walked away from the church. With that said, when the pastor instructed me to share my testimony, there was no need for him to be clear on the testimony that I was to share. It was my testimony of leaving the church, failing to find fulfillment in the world, and of how God led me back.

> *Tonight I went to a Haitian church in west Philly and I cried because the sermon spoke to me so much. While the congregation stood in a circle at the end and worshipped, the Pastor stopped at me and whispered in my ear, "Now everywhere you go share your testimony." I cried when he told me this, the Holy Spirit guided him to me. Thank you God for guiding me to that church and giving me the message.*
>
> -July 21, 2013

Chapter 19
"...Take a Leap of Faith."

Sunday, July 28, 2013

Once again, I made it a priority to revisit the Haitian Church the week after I received that spirit-rejuvenating message. After receiving a powerful message like that, wouldn't you? It would almost be insane of me not to have gone back. But I re-visited the church in hopes that I received an experience just like the one I received the week before. A short time after moving to Pennsylvania, I allowed the company that was leasing my Monte Carlo to me to repo it. Not having a car of my own, I was at the mercy of the public transportation system not too long after I moved to Pennsylvania. To catch the bus I've always had weekly bus passes or tokens. On this Sunday, when I revisited the Haitian church, I was not as fortunate. I only had $2, and I used this last bit of change that I had to catch a bus to the church. This church was located on the west side of Philadelphia, and my home at the time was located on the north side of town. It was about a 30-minute drive from the church's location to my place. If I were to walk home, it would have taken me forever. Knowing that I had no ride home, I was still more than willing to exhaust the last couple of bucks in my pocket with the purpose of getting to church. After all, I had a deep need for spiritual guidance, and I knew that the church was the place to find it. I also believed with all my heart that if I attended the church (which I felt like God wanted me to at the time), God would provide me with a way to get back home.

At that Sunday morning service, I was not nearly as moved by this pastor's sermon as I was by the sermon I heard the week before by the much younger pastor who preached. The pastor was a short, old Haitian black man who looked to be in his 60s. I sat there and listened passively as this pastor stood behind the pulpit and hollered passionately about whatever he was speaking on. No matter how much he shouted and yelled, the sermon did not speak to me as much as the sermon did a week before. I guess the message was not meant for me that morning. Maybe all that God wanted me to hear was jam packed into that powerful experience that I had the week before. Maybe the great impact that it made on my life last week was all the impact that it was meant to make on me at this point in my life.

After the church service, I was once again reminded of how far I've strayed from God over the years. A young black woman that was not sitting that far away from me placed her attention on the rings that I proudly wore on my fingers. One ring had a tiger stone in it, and the other had a phantom quartz. Looking at my rings, she asked, "What are the meaning of the stones in your rings?" Like I had grown accustomed to doing for a while now, I confidently explained the meaning of each stone and their power. This God-fearing woman was not impressed with my thorough knowledge on the stones in my rings. With a calm but serious demeanor she responded, "How do you know the stones do that?" What she was really saying with this statement of hers was, "You are placing your faith in the jewelry you wear, when you should be placing your faith in God." She made me feel stupid, because she made me keenly aware of the fact that I had progressively transferred my faith from Jesus to superficial inanimate objects such as the jewelry I proudly wore.

I was at a very pivotal point in my life, and I needed divine guidance more now than ever. Not having received this guidance I thirsted for that day, I walked out of the sanctuary slightly disappointed. After the church service, I could not help but wonder how I was going to get home. The $2 I used to catch a bus to the church was my last, so I had no means of getting back home, which was all the way across town. Despite this grim current circumstance, I was still at total peace as I searched around the church to see if there was anyone who was willing to give me a ride home. For a time I had great difficulty finding a person that was willing to give me a ride home. By this time, many people had already gotten into their cars and gone home. Then I saw the pastor who preached that morning walking through the lobby of the church. I shared my predicament with him and he said that he would look around to see if anyone was willing to give me a ride home. But he was not successful in his search. After waiting around for a little while, I started to become a little discouraged. It was at this point that I saw someone in the church that looked rather familiar. It was Pastor Nikki! This is the woman who God used to invite me to this church in the first place. She was now once again, right before my eyes with a broom in her hand sweeping the lobby of the church. I didn't see her in the sanctuary during service, but now she was right here before my eyes sweeping the lobby of the church. It was almost as if she had appeared out of nowhere. Just like the night I met her at Robert's birthday party, she always seemed to be close by right when I needed her, like a guardian angel or something. She helped me the night of Robert Kelly's birthday party. Now, here she was again at my second visit to the church.

I greeted her, and told her that I did not have a way of getting home. With a big smile on her face she quickly agreed to give me a ride home. She quickly agreed to minister to my need, without me having to work hard to persuade her. She agreed so rapidly that it was almost as if she was placed there at this particular time in my life to be of service to me. After saying that she would give me a ride home, she told me to give her a second to round up her children and then we would be on our way.

On this particular day, it was raining cats and dogs. It was what I would like to call a black and white day and the gloomy weather outside reflected exactly how I felt on the inside. I was several days late on my rent payment at my living arrangement in north Philadelphia, and I still did not have the money to pay it. My thoughts were moving rapidly. I racked my brain trying to figure out where I would live if I were to get kicked out of my place. The thought of having nowhere else to go continued to play in my mind like a broken record. I became totally submerged in my own thoughts. After Pastor Nikki rounded up all of her children, we all piled into her family minivan. I sat on the passenger seat right next to her. As she drove along, she spoke almost endlessly. As a direct result of the noise that was in my head, I drowned out everything around me, including Pastor Nikki's words.

When we were only a few blocks from my home, something shifted in the words that Pastor Nikki spoke to me. She started to say things that quickly arrested my attention. Once again, her words got my attention in the same way they did on the night of Robert's birthday party. Her words demanded my attention like the preacher's sermon the first night I visited the Haitian Church. The inflection in her voice changed, and the words spoke to me so much that they felt personal. Now, when we were only a few blocks from reaching my home, her words changed from being a blur to becoming so authoritative that they demanded that I listened. I knew then that it was no longer her words, but God's.

She asked me, "When was the last time you paid your tithes?" This question spoke to me because the truth was that I had not paid my tithes in years. Most of all, as soon as I heard her question, I could not help but think how long it has been since I walked out of Summit Church. I could not help but think about that day that I denied the offer to attend Oakwood University. I thought to myself, I have not paid my tithes in years! Like the first night I met Pastor Nikki, she succeeded in reminding me of how long it has been since I left Summit Seventh-day Adventist Church. Having been out of the church for years was the elephant in the room. In this case, it was the elephant in the minivan. My crisis at this time was way deeper than me being on the brink of getting kicked out of my home. It was something that laid dormant inside me for years, and that thing is the truth that for the past several years of my life I had placed Jesus Christ, my Lord and savior, on the back burner, and now lately God had been showing me sign after sign that He wanted me to accept the calling that He had on my life a long time ago. Now Pastor Nikki's question in regards to tithes woke up this truth that was within me. I knew God was calling me, and as I sat in that car with Pastor Nikki, with my whole being I could hear Him speaking to me.

I answered, "It's been years since I paid my tithes." She then gave me instruction to always pay my tithes. She said, "Even if you don't attend church service one week always make sure you drop off your tithes." I listened and absorbed this instruction of hers. As she spoke to me about the importance of paying my tithes, her demeanor suggested that the reason that I had a lack of money is because I've neglected to pay my tithes for years. Once again God was using Pastor Nikki. He did not only use her to give me a ride home, but also to speak life-changing words into my life. He was using her to speak to me at a time when I was humbled enough to listen. I was in one of the darkest moments in my life and I knew that I had to look in higher places for an answer. God was shining through the darkness like the light that He is. But He was not done yet. He continued to speak through her. Hungry for an answer for "Why I was broke and getting kicked out of my house, even with all of my hard work over the years?" I listened very closely in hopes that I was about to hear the answer that I was so thirsty for.

After she encouraged me to pay my tithes, she asked me another question that was of another magnitude. Her next question was like the punch that KO'd me. As soon as this particular question left her lips, it went into my ears and filled my soul with a certain familiarity. This question caused my eyes to quickly swell up with tears. Very calmly Pastor Nikki asked me, "Thierry, who is the pastor in your family?" I've felt the calling in my life to be a pastor for years. Not only this but not too long after I met Pastor Nikki, God had been speaking through other people to tell me that it is my calling to be a minister. With that said, as soon as she asked me the question, I knew immediately that she was about to suggest that I am the one in my family who is the pastor.

Right there in her minivan, her question floated around in my head. My thoughts quickly traveled years back to when the church elders at Summit Church saw my calling in me way before I did. I thought back to when they would put me in position to write and preach my own sermons. I thought back to when they told me that I was a leader and that I had to set a better example. I thought back to when they gave me an offer to help me pay my tuition at Oakwood University, if I studied theology. I thought back to when I said no to the offer. I've been running from my calling for years and it was finally catching up to me. I ran into the world and started a journey towards fulfillment and did not find it, now as I sat in that car on this rainy day with this woman, I found my life doing a 180 degree turn back to what God originally intended for me to do, and that is to be a minister.

Even though I knew the answer to Nikki's question, I still attempted to run from it, like I've been doing the past several years of my life. As I sat there in the van, I thought about the occupations of my family members, desperately hoping that one of them was a pastor. My logic was, if I could find at least one person in my family that was a pastor, then that would mean that I was not the pastor. In my mind I scrolled through all of my family members and thought about what they did for a living. As I scrolled through the names, Pastor Nikki waited patiently for me to reveal the answer. I thought long and hard hoping that my search brought up someone in my family who was a pastor. To no avail, my search came up empty. There was no one in my family that was a pastor. Not one.

Then, with a pitiful look on my face and tears swelling up in my eyes, I looked at Pastor Nikki and mumbled my answer, "No one." The reason I mumbled the answer is because I was so afraid of the truth that she was about to tell me. I don't know if Nikki did not truly hear my answer or if she was joking, but with a knowing look on her face she asked me to speak a little louder with her question, "What was that?" Once again I mumbled, "No one in my family is a pastor." When those words crept out of my mouth, I felt something swell up within me. Something inside me told me the answer before she gave me the answer. Before I even got my answer out she interrupted it and said, "You are the pastor...you can't run forever! Take a leap of faith." These words were so thunderous, that I could not bring myself to look at her. I just continued to look forward towards the front of the van. When those words came out of her mouth, they were very loud as if someone else were speaking through her. That sweet tone she owned so well, escaped her. Now, her voice was more like a roar that shook me to the core. I could feel that those words were not her own, because I never shared my story of walking out of the church with her. There is no way that she could have known that information. Only an omniscient God would know information like that. Therefore I knew that it was God speaking through her. Right there in the passenger seat of that van, the guilt of running from my calling for so long was so strong that I could not bring myself to look at her. As soon as God used Pastor Nikki to give me this important message of guidance, the swelling that I felt within me came out in the form of a single tear that rolled down from my left eye. I thought to myself, Thierry, you knew it. You always knew you were called to be a pastor.

> "...The most recent indication of my life purpose was a couple days ago while coming from a Haitian church in west Philly, a woman who is also a prophetess gave me a ride home and said during the ride, "Who in your family is a pastor?" I thought about it and nothing came to mind. Then I said, "No one is a pastor in my family." She quickly answered, "You Are the Pastor! You can't keep running forever." When she said this, tears rolled down my face, because what she said was true. I've been running from this reality for what seemed like forever, and she hit the nail right on the head. It's time to stop playing around and start taking action toward my calling into the ministry..."
>
> -July 31, 2013

Chapter 20
He Brought Me Full Circle

After Pastor Nikki gave me a ride home from the church, I walked into my apartment to find a sight that was not normal. Piled high in the dining room area, were several big black garbage bags filled with something. My first thought was, My roommates were probably cleaning the apartment and have used these garbage bags to fill them with trash. When I walked into my room, my eyes fell upon a disheartening sight that told me that my guess was wrong. All of my belongings (except for a mini refrigerator that I kept in my room) were gone! As my eyes took in the emptiness of my room, it immediately hit me that those trash bags were filled with all of my things, not trash. My heart sunk. This depressing sight told me that the couple who rented the room out to me wanted me to move out immediately. So much that, while I was out, they took it upon their own selves to go into my room and pack all of my belongings for me.

As I stood in this empty room, I could feel a darkness closing in around me. I leaned against one of the walls of the room and tears proceeded to swell up in my eyes. I thought to myself, Where am I going to live? While in this realm of bewilderment, I was comforted by Pastor Nikki's words to me right before she dropped me off moments ago. "You are the pastor, you can't run forever. Take a leap of faith." Yes, I was indeed getting kicked out of my room with not the slightest idea of where I was going next, but Pastor Nikki's revelation to me functioned as the silver lining around the dark cloud of me being evicted. As I leaned against the wall of my room with tears continuing to roll down my face, I optimistically viewed this seemingly dark situation as God's way of moving me out of a dark world and into the light of purpose and fulfillment.

Though I did a great job on focusing on the greener grass on the other side, I still had a question that needed answering. "Where was I going to live?" Then it hit me that I should try calling a poet friend of mine who had his own place in Philadelphia. His name was Christopher "K.P" Brown. Though I knew K.P had roommates, and might not have room for me, I still picked up my cell phone and dialed his number. When he answered his phone, very humbly I told him, "I'm getting kicked out of my house and I need a place to live until I find my own place." He told me, "Both my roommates are out of town so I will allow you to stay in my apartment for two weeks or until you are able to get back on your feet." This was a great relief, because the people who rented the house to me wanted me out that day. Once again, those garbage bags filled with my belongings sent across the same message.

It was good news that I had a place to lay my head for the night, but there was one more problem: Since I didn't own a car I didn't have a way of transporting my belongings to K.P's home. And I had too many things to bring on the bus or train with me. So after getting off the phone with K.P, I told the people who rented the room out to me that I had a place to stay for the night, and that I would have to stop by and pick up my things another day once I found someone with a car. They agreed with this as long as it didn't take too long for me to come back and get my things.

The place I was getting kicked out of was located on the north side of Philadelphia, and my friend K.P lived on the opposite side of town near west Philadelphia. Since I didn't have a car, I had to catch a bus and a train to K.P's house, which I didn't have the money for-I was totally broke! If I had money, I would catch a bus to Broad and Olney Street, which is where the Broad Street line was located. But on this day I was totally broke, so I had to walk about 30 to 45 minutes to the Broad and Olney train station. To catch the train, usually I would either use a one-week pass that cost $22 or some tokens. On this particular day, I had neither of these things. My only options were to sneak onto the train or to beg one of the Septa sales representatives to let me on the train. It was very difficult to sneak onto the train at the time because the sales representative--who sat in a glass-encased booth at the time was on watch. They were stationed too close to the entrance for them not to notice me sneaking onto the train. Therefore my only option now was to beg the sales representative to let me onto the train. I explained my situation to the sales representative in hopes that they would sympathize with me and let me on the train, but they didn't.

After I was refused access at the Olney stop, I decided that I would walk to the next train station and attempt to woo the Septa sales representative that was there. It was about a 20-minute walk from the Olney station to the next bus stop. When I got to the next bus stop I managed to convince the Septa sales representative to let me on the train. I was on my way to K.P's house.

K.P provided me with a place to sleep and take a shower for about a month. But he also told me that I would have to pay $100 for that month that he allowed me to stay in his house. I quickly agreed to this deal. To me it was a good deal. After all, it was better than sleeping on the streets. I was expecting some money to come to me from a gig where I did my "Follow Your Dreams" One-Man Show for some youth at a Summer Camp in New Jersey. This gig paid me about $500, and I planned to pay K.P that $100 using those funds.

Original Plan
While at K.P's house I thought about what Pastor Nikki said to me when she gave me that ride home from the Haitian church: "You are the Pastor, you can't run forever." These words continued to replay in my ears like a broken record. Her words along with the words of all the other people that God used to tell me that I was a minister, continued to ring in my ears. Such as the time that I worked at the library when that man told me that I would make an awesome preacher. And also that time when my mentor went to speak to that landlord that owned the eyeglass store, and that landlord telling me that I was a minister. All of these messages were ringing in my ears. Dwelling on the idea that God had been lately calling me to be a minister was taking me along for a ride. Over the years I had created a groove with performing that I became comfortable with. Every day I woke up and pretty much knew what I was going to do with my life, and that is to perform! Now God was extracting me from what I had grown used to, so that He could guide me into a whole new direction. With that said, my mind was spinning out of control like a plane that had been shot out of the sky. I felt like a fish being pulled out of water, and like that fish, I was flailing and gasping for oxygen.

I guided myself the past few years of my life when I was doing my will. Now that I could feel the Lord telling me his ways are far above my will, I knew that I could not guide myself. I could feel that the Lord was guiding me to a place that I could not see, so out of uncertainty about where he was taking me, I reached out to an old friend for guidance. When it came to being in the world performing, I didn't need anyone to guide me into that. But now when it came to getting spiritual advice, I had to reach out to someone who I knew was spiritual--an uncompromising soldier in God's army. This particular person was not someone who I met recently. This was not someone who I met while I was in the world. This person was someone who knew me ever since I first walked through the doors at Summit SDA Church. This was a person who watched me grow spiritually from the time I walked into Summit, to the time that I walked out. This was a person who watched me walk into the Seventh-day Adventist Church with my pants sagging, and watched as the waist of my pants found its rightful place, at my waist! She watched me go from a regular kid from the streets to being baptized into the church and being ordained as a Deacon of the church. Her name was Sister Audrey. This was the same church elder who asked me to stand in the middle of the Sabbath lunch years ago while I attended Summit Church. This was the same woman who told me right there at that lunch in the midst of all of my peers that I needed to set a better example because I had a major influence on them. This was the same elder who introduced me as a pharmacy major years ago right before I preached for "Youth Day" at Summit Church. She was one of the elders who saw the leader in me way before I did. Now, it was the year 2013, years after I've walked out of Summit Church, and I found myself desperately reaching out to her for some guidance. I knew that if anyone could give me the spiritual guidance that I needed at this pivotal point in my life, it was her.

Just like that fish out of water, I was shaking and trembling as I spoke on the phone with Sister Audrey. With a trembling voice I told her, "I think that God wants me to be a pastor." When I said this to her, her demeanor was calm as if she was not the least bit surprised by this "revelation" of mine. Almost as if she were totally aware of what I had been going through lately, she responded very casually, "The Holy Spirit has been tugging at you, huh?" I answered, "Yes." She then said, "I was wondering what was taking you so long. Thierry, you always knew that you were supposed to be a pastor ever since you saw Pierre go to school for it." Pierre was the young man who faithfully lived out the calling on his life while I was still attending Summit Church. This eventually led him to enroll in school to become a pastor. While Pierre was moving faithfully in the direction that God wanted him to go, I was stubborn and did not yield to the direction that God wanted me to go. I was much more interested in doing my will and my family's will. When I sat in that Bible study that Pierre was facilitating at Summit years ago, I felt the conviction of God telling me that he wanted me to do exactly what Pierre was doing, which is to share the word of God. But I fought hard to brush off God's voice, and to tug into the opposite direction. I continued to tug in the opposite direction, until I finally decided to walk out of the church to try to find fulfillment in the world. Now here I was, it's the year 2013 (years after I walked out of the church), and Sister Audrey was reminding me of a calling I felt years ago to become a pastor.

As I spoke to Sister Audrey here in the year 2013, I explained to her that I refused to surrender to my calling while I was in the world, because I was afraid that if I went to school for pastoral ministry, that all the work that I did in the performance realm would have been done in vain. In a comforting tone, she said to me, "No, it would not mean that you did it for nothing, because performing has given you the confidence that you need to do God's work in the ministry. God needs strong, confident young men like you to spread the gospel." When she said these words to me, I felt like the weight of the whole world came off my shoulders as I stood in the living room of K.P.'s apartment. For the first time in years, I was finally letting go of my need to be in control of my own life, and taking conscious steps towards surrendering to God's will for my life. The beginning of the process of letting go felt good, and right there while I was on the phone with her, I felt a feeling of peace come over me.

Sister Audrey did not remain on the phone long. Her final words were: "I'm going to text you a list of schools that offer a theology degree. Research these schools, see which one you like, and contact me if you need further help." When Sister Audrey gave me the names of the schools, it was almost as if she had been waiting forever to do it, so that I could finally begin to pursue the obvious calling on my life! After all, I had been running from my calling for about six years! Sister Audrey told me about two schools. One of these schools was Oakwood University. This was the exact same school that the elders at Summit Church wanted me to attend years ago! In the world I had become ambitious to find something in the world. I became ambitious to do everything but do what God wanted me to do. Now here I was, after years of toiling in the world, right back to square one. I was right back where God wanted me to be. I didn't spend too much time looking at Southern University. Since Oakwood was the school that I first heard about, that was the school I gravitated towards. This was the school that the elders tried to get me to attend years ago! Right in my friend K.P's apartment, I quickly applied to Oakwood University on my laptop. God brought me full circle!

Lansdowne

After years of running from the calling in my life, God was bringing me full circle in more ways than one. After getting kicked out of my home in north Philadelphia, my friend K.P allowed me to move in with him. Being that his roommates were out of town for a limited time, I knew that I had to find another place to live when the time came for me to move on.

In August 2013, while still living with K.P, I received the opportunity to perform at Poetry Slam Nationals, which was being held in Boston, Massachusetts. Before I left for finals with my team, I made moves towards finding another place to live. I found out that a man was renting out some rooms in a house that was located in west Philadelphia. When I met with this landlord, I told him that I was interested in the room. The cost was $200 to rent this room. This was money that I did not have. So I reached out to a man named Paul, to see if he can lend me the money. Paul was a nice, white middle-aged man with a bubbly personality who was the new owner of my cousin's dance studio in west Philadelphia. When I asked him to borrow $200, without hesitation, he said that he would lend it to me.

While in Boston, I feared that the landlord would give the room to someone else while I was away. So while I was in Boston, I contacted my good friend Kina and told her to go get the $200 from Paul at the dance studio and to then meet with the landlord to hand him the funds. This would guarantee that the room was reserved for me so that I could have a place to lay my head once I got back to Philadelphia from Boston. But there were some complications with getting the money over to the landlord. For some reason Kina was not able to meet with the landlord to hand him the money. So Kina had no choice but to hold onto the money, so that once I got back to Philadelphia I could get the money from her and to then pay the landlord myself.

Once I got back to Philadelphia from Poetry Nationals my teammate drove me by Kina's house so that I could get the money. After receiving the money, I then contacted the landlord and told him that I was ready to meet up with him to hand him the money. But to my dismay, he told me that he had already given the room to someone else. My heart was broken. That room was my only hope, and I was now officially homeless.

While homeless, I was in a very embarrassing situation. I had to ask my friend Amun if I could sleep over his house for a night. The very act of having to ask him if I could sleep over his house was embarrassing to me because of the prestige and respect that I had gained from him and many others who have seen me perform time and time again. Amun was also a poet, and sold jewelry more often than he performed his spoken-word poetry on stage. He would often sell his jewelry within the venues where I performed. He would set up his table and place all of his jewelry on top of the table to be sold to the people that were in attendance. From this table, many times while he was busy making new jewelry pieces, he watched me as I performed.

I remember sitting outside of a Cosi's restaurant when I called Amun. After years of working hard to be the best performer that I could be, I found it difficult to put my pride aside. So much that when Amun answered his phone, I lied to him to protect my ego. I told him that I had found a new home and that this place was not ready for me to move in. I then told him that I needed a place to stay for the night. Here I was, the "great performer" Thierry Lundy asking one of his fans if he could crash on their couch for the night. And that is exactly what I did, I just slept at his house for the night, and I was out on the streets as a homeless man again.

It is the night of August 23, 2013, and being homeless, I walked through some unfamiliar dark streets near Lansdowne, Pennsylvania. Soon, I saw two black men conversing on the front steps of a church. In desperate need for a place to sleep that night, I stopped and asked them if I would be able to sleep within the church that night. They said that they didn't know anything about the services that the church offered. So I continued to walk through a dark unfamiliar neighborhood with no place to lay my head.

Eventually, I reached a gas station, where I stood for a while. Not too long after I got there a man who worked in the gas station walked out, and we struck up a conversation. I shared with him my predicament of not having a place to sleep that night. He told me that he would have allowed me to sleep in his home if he lived alone, which he didn't. Then he pointed me to a fire station that was in the area and recommended that I look to see if they would allow me to lay my head there for the night. I walked up to the fire station and knocked on the door, but there was no answer. After knocking a few more times, I gave up, and decided to move on. After a while I came to a familiar bus stop in the city of Lansdowne, Pennsylvania. I took a seat on one of the benches that was there. I decided that I would wait there until a bus came along, which was a few hours later. When it was about 6 or 7 o'clock in the morning a bus finally came along and got me to the 69th Septa Train Station. From here, as a homeless man, I started my day.

> *I'm homeless right now with no money to get a new apartment, at the moment I'm sitting at the Darby Bus Station waiting for the bus...I know that God is going to lead me out of this, I have faith. I'm homeless, but I'm still comforted and have faith that things are going to work out for the better. Amen.*
>
> -August 23, 2013

Desperate for a place to live, I eventually made my way back to my aunt and uncle's house in Lansdowne, Pennsylvania. Wait a minute! This was the first house that I moved into when I just moved from Jacksonville to Lansdowne in the year 2009! This was the first house I lived in four years ago when I had just started to hit the ground running in Pennsylvania. Now it's the year 2013, and I was right back at this house. I had come full circle, just like a dog chasing his own tail.

Initially, I lived in my aunt and uncle's house in Lansdowne, Pennsylvania. Then when I moved from there I lived in a house that was located in west Philadelphia. When I got kicked out of that house due to failure to keep up with the rent, I got kicked out. I then moved in with some family friends in Upper Darby, Pennsylvania, for a time. Then I moved to a house in north Philadelphia. When I got kicked out of this house (also due to my failure to keep up with the rent), I moved in with my friend KP. When I could not stay at KP's house anymore, I slept at my friend Amun's house for a night. After all of this moving around, I found myself back at the first house I lived in when I moved to Pennsylvania. Once again, when I believed that I was progressing in the world, I was only going around in circles!

Actively Ministering to Others

In the world, I was not interested in praying for others. I was not interested in ministering to them. I was not trying to find out the condition of their present relationship with Jesus Christ. I was only concerned about being successful according to the world's standards. It's only because of God's grace, did this focus of mine gradually start to change. It was only by divine providence was I able to get back to doing the work that God originally intended for me to do. Once again, God was bringing me full circle.

I found myself ministering more actively. One of the people I ministered to was my friend Kina. She was a woman who I met on the poetry scene. She was one of those people that did not have that strong relationship with Jesus Christ. Having sex with this woman more than once, it was never my intentions to minister to her. I just viewed her as an object to satisfy my fleshly lust. This shows how far from my calling I was. Now four years after I moved to Pennsylvania, I found myself actively ministering to her, like a Godly man would do. Here at my aunt and uncle's house in Lansdowne, Pennsylvania, in one of the upstairs rooms of the house I conversed with her on the phone. After our conversation, I prayed with her, and as soon as the first words of my prayer rolled off of my lips, I listened to Kina as she started to cry. To me, the tears said that she had realized that she was far from God. Those tears were the beginning of a healing process for her. God used me to minister to her that night. Like I said, I had walked out of the church years ago and strayed far from my calling and God was now bringing me full circle to what He originally intended for me to do.

"Pastoring"

> *"I've been ministering a lot frequently and I'm referring to one-on-one ministering, and it has been the same woman Kina. She's been finding it hard to surrender to God, and I told her that she had to let go of whatever she has been holding on to, and allow God to take control of her life..."*
>
> -August 24, 2013

My Poetry

Not only was I actively ministering to others through prayer, but God was also bringing the very nature of my secular poetry full circle. The Holy Spirit started to do such a number on my heart that I started glorifying God in my poems! When I initially created a particular poem of mine entitled "I Know How It Feels," I did not glorify God in it. I added it later when I was starting to feel God calling me back. This was my attempt to make up ground for all the years that I've wasted in being of the world and outside of God's perfect will for my life. The following excerpt from this poem has a special anatomy. In a nutshell, it conveys my testimony of leaving the church, turning my back on God, searching for glory in the world, and after discovering that there was no glory in the world, this excerpt conveys that I was now starting to take steps back to God.

> *"...It feels like letting go of God's hand, the I Am*
> *Thinking you are the man, like 'Do you know who I am?'*
> *Then run back to God when things start to hit the fan..."*

SECTION 6
God's Goodness

"When Jesus therefore had received the vinegar, he said,
It is finished:
and he bowed his head, and gave up the ghost."

John 19:30

Chapter 21
"It Is Finished"

As a child growing up in Miami, I had a limited understanding of God. Catholic school was a place where I could have learned more about Him, but this learning was cut short. As a result, the Catholic ways and religion quickly faded away in my life. Though my mother was still Catholic, she didn't push religion down my throat as a little boy. So things that encompassed a Christian lifestyle, such as reading the Bible, was not enforced in my household. There were instances where I visited a few churches growing up, but I never remained in any one church long enough for me to build a relationship with Jesus. Nevertheless, unbeknownst to me the little knowledge that I did have about God was a seed that was planted in my heart. A spiritual seed that would one day receive a sufficient amount of water and sunlight to grow into a magnificent plant of righteousness, changing the whole course of my life!

With this seed planted in me, by the age of 15, I had grown-by far-more familiar with the streets of Miami than I was with the word of God. Before I continue, I feel that it is very important to say that naturally, we are inclined to do our will. Naturally, we are inclined to go against the word of God and His plan for our lives. And the public school system in the United States assists us in doing our will. As a matter of fact, it is pushed on us as children! Through our families and our teachers, we are taught to follow our dreams. This teaching goes directly against biblical teaching. According to the Bible, we are to deny ourselves. We are to deny our dreams and personal ambitions, and to place God's will for our lives first. When we are in Christ, we are to have new desires, purposes, and motives leading to a new life. We are to become new creatures aligned with His perfect will. As a young man growing up in Miami,

I had zero understanding of this biblical truth. With my own mind, I created and pursued my own plans for my life. With that said, when I moved from Miami to Boynton Beach, Florida, at the age of 15, I held on to my dream to one-day play basketball in the National Basketball Association. What I did not know was that God had a perfect plan for my life that transcended my hoop dreams. Not being knowledgeable about His plans, I continued my quest to be a great basketball player. But when I failed to make the Boynton Beach JV team, I no longer had any plans for my life. Til this day, I believe that it was my almighty creator, God who kept my mind from retaining those basketball options. I believe He did it to prevent me from going down a road that would keep me from His plan for my life. Though my passion for the sport remained, I quickly lost interest in making it to the NBA. This dream of mine dissipated as if I were not truly dedicated to it in the first place. I strongly believe it faded so quickly because making it to the NBA was not part of God's perfect plan for my life. Though I still enjoyed playing basketball, there was a void within me that needed to be filled with purpose and fulfillment.

When I did not make it on the Boynton Beach junior varsity basketball team, my mother felt no need for me to remain at Boynton Beach High and had me transferred to a high school closer to home (which was in the city of West Palm Beach). Not too long after I moved to West Palm Beach in the year 2001, I became friends with a Seventh-day Adventist Christian named Junior Bennett. When Junior felt the time was right, he invited me to attend "Summit" church. It would be here at Summit that I would first hear God sharing with me the calling that He had placed on my life. Now in my mid-teens, while at Summit Church, God was calling me to my purpose.

Not knowing that God had a plan for me, made it difficult for me to surrender to His plan. As time went on, as a member of Summit Church, the more I felt the calling on my life to be a minister of the Gospel. God's still small voice would say to me, "You are a leader and a minister." But every time I heard the call, I immediately ignored it, and tried my best to push it to the back of my mind. Almost as soon as I started attending Summit Seventh-day Adventist Church, God used the elders of the church as tools to help put me on the path of being His co-shepherd. The elders would beckon me to write and preach sermons to the youth as well as the adults of the church. They were also constantly encouraging me to stand out as a leader amongst my peers. But

I tried my best to fight the direction that God was trying to get me to go in by trying to blend in with my peers. At Summit, it became a battle of what I have grown to know and what God was sharing with me. I knew the truth of my purpose, but I did not want to step into my purpose because I was afraid that I would look like a sell out to my friends. While I was trying to blend in with my friends, God was calling me to stand out.

Though I tried my best to reject the notion of me being a pastor, I continued to hear God's call on my life. My effort to ignore Him and to do my own will was not successful. His voice would always resurface. I continued to ignore the calling that God had placed on my life for the rest of my time in high school. After I graduated, I didn't have a clear idea on what I wanted to do after high school. I would rack my brain and depend on my own understanding to find where I fit in this world. After high school, I decided to pursue a degree in pharmacy.

While attending school towards a pharmacy career, the elders of Summit continued to push me into the direction of being a minister. One day they encouraged me to be the main youth speaker for a major Seventh-day Adventist event called "Youth Day." The elders saw so much promise in me as a minister that they entrusted me with the task of preaching the word of God to the 300 people that were in attendance on this big day. Still, after preaching at this event, I did not warm up to the idea of me being chosen by God to be a minister.

All of the earnest encouragements that the elders gave me to stand out and be much more of a leader, all of the sermons that they chose me to preach culminated into one powerful event that had the power to change the whole course of my life right on the spot. One Sabbath morning, when I was just arriving to Summit church, one of the elders walked right up to me outside of the church and gave me an offer that was difficult to refuse. The elder said to me, "Some of the church elders had a meeting where you were the topic." He continued to speak to me and said, "We have decided to help you pay your tuition at Oakwood University if you decide to study theology there." Oakwood University is a highly accredited school that was founded by Seventh-day Adventists in the year 1896. This school was known for generating great ministers of the gospel. The fact that the church elders wanted to invest in my education if I wanted to study theology their, testifies of the fact that they saw a lot of promise in me to become a great minister. A part of me wanted to accept the offer, and another part of me was tugging away from it. A combination of things kept me from accepting this great offer, but the main thing was my mother. I was afraid of what she would think if I switched my major again. I had already switched my college major once. When I did, my mother was a little disappointed in me and said in an angry tone, "You don't know what you want to do!" Now here I was standing in front of this elder and he was asking me to change my major for the second time and to pursue theology. As I replayed my mother's words in my head I thought to myself, If I tell my mother that I'm going from pharmacy to theology to do the Lord's work, she's really going to think that I am out of my mind. This greatly influenced my decision. I denied the offer.

When I denied that scholarship, many of the church elders started to act differently towards me. At one time I was the golden boy of the church and all their attention was on me. Now after I denied their offer, they no longer gave me the same attention as they used to. Something about the way that they now acted towards me made me feel uncomfortable. The atmosphere of the church now felt highly claustrophobic to me, so I made up my mind that I would leave the church as a whole. I walked out of the church and I did not look back.

When I no longer attended church, I quickly strayed away from building a relationship with my Lord and Savior, Jesus Christ. I stopped doing things like reading my Bible and praying. As the years went on, church became lower and lower on my priority list. Instead of yielding to God's perfect will for my life, I tried to find fulfillment on my own. I tried to find it in studying pharmacy, journalism, and acting. I tried to find it in creating an organization that was against violence and gangs. I tried to find it by creating my own one-man shows. I even tried to find this fulfillment in people like Kevon and Maurice.

Several years after walking out of Summit Church, I felt emptier than ever. During this time, God started to get my attention in powerful ways. He would send people who I knew and did not know to tell me that I am a minister. The more people that He sent to me the more convicted I was of the truth that I am indeed a minister and that He has a special work for me to do.

The Vision and Commission
September of 2013

While looking at the depressing state of this dark world and their current circumstances, many question, "Is God truly good?" They are easily deceived into believing the lie that He is not. This belief causes those who were once in the faith to stray away from it, and keeps those who were never in the faith from coming into it. I am a witness that God is not only good, but He is also the initiator of goodness towards us. He is the Great Initiator! In the gospel, God's goodness was shown on Calvary. When we didn't ask Him to, He took the initiative and reconciled a sinful people unto Himself through His son Jesus Christ. Better yet, God himself came in the form of man to save us from our sins. He is the one who initiated this goodness towards us, not us towards Him!

In the gospels, Jesus Christ declared, "It is finished…" right before taking his final breath on the cross. With these words, he was signifying that his perfect substitutionary sacrifice had come to a completion. It is because of this work on the cross that our sins can be forgiven and we can appear blameless before a holy God. To emphasize God's goodness, this work of salvation was solely initiated by Him, and not us. God is the great initiator, not us.

Out of His goodness, God's invisible hands are still heavily involved in our lives today. In the same way He did on the cross, God is still finishing things in our lives for our good. In the year 2013, God brought a beautiful story to completion in my life. In a sense, in completing this story, He was saying, "It is finished." With that said, I can testify of the depths of His goodness, by painting a clear picture of how good He has been to me. In the last few months of living in Philadelphia, God spoke to me in profound and life-changing ways, but He was far from being done with me yet. In the tail end of the year 2013 (I was 27 years old), after receiving all these powerful messages from God, I still went back to doing what I have grown acclimated to, which is performing. It is then that God would speak to me in a way that was more profound than all the ways that He has spoken to me in those last few months of living in Philly. Not only would He choose to speak to me in the most profound way then what I have already experienced, but He would place an exclamation mark on all these events with a powerful revelation!

After moving back into my aunt and uncle's home in Lansdowne, Pennsylvania, I decided to move back to Jacksonville, Florida, with my mother. While here, I took a trip to Atlanta, Georgia, to perform spoken-word at an open mic venue there.

"I'm on my way to perform at a few venues in Atlanta…"
-Friday, September 6, 2013

After the performance, I spent the night at my friend's apartment, which was located in Atlanta. After everyone in the apartment went to sleep, I remained awake on the living room couch (which was my bed for the night) as I continued a phone conversation with one of my lady friends back in Philadelphia. Her name was Tyesha, and lately I have been talking to her to see if she was the woman for me. Not long after we started conversing, the Holy Spirit came over me, and instructed me to immediately tell Tyesha to let go of something that she was holding onto. Right there in the midst of our conversation, I commanded, "Let it go, just let it go." As I continued repeating these words to her, I could feel a deep empathy and sense of concern for her. My eyes started to swell up with tears. I continued, "Let it go, just let it go." As I repeated these words to her, I noticed how eerily silent she became on the line. Judging by her silence, I knew that the words that I was repeating resonated with her. I knew immediately that there was indeed something that she has been having a difficult time of letting go for quite some time now. I don't know what this thing was, but God knew, and He was using me in a powerful way on this night to help free Tyesha from this bondage.

Immediately after God used me to give my friend Tyesha this message, the phone conversation I was having with her was interrupted yet again! This time, God shared something with me that was meant for me. There, that night as I sat on my friend's couch, God shared something with me through a vision. Yes, you read it right. While I was still on the phone with Tyesha, God started to feed some images to me through a vision. This vision, like a movie, was playing right before my eyes! While being fed this divine revelation, I remained on the phone with Tyesha. Afraid to miss a thing, when God started to reveal these personal truths to me, I immediately redirected my attention from Tyesha to what God was saying and revealing to me at that moment.

God was sharing a particular story with me. Not just any story, but my story. It was not just my story, but also His story. It was a story that I could not have possibly conceived with my own finite mind. The very nature of this story was so beautiful and imaginative that only an all-knowing and infinite God could have come up with it, and I was in awe by its beauty. As I sat on the living room couch in my friend's apartment, I was so amazed by the story and how God was revealing it to me. I was so stunned that I couldn't find words adequate enough to describe what I was seeing and the way that I felt.

This vision began with God showing me in clear detail an event that happened several years ago. Years before I moved to Pennsylvania, and even before I decided to move from West Palm Beach to Jacksonville, Florida. This was an event that happened before I decided to walk out of Summit Church, which is the church where I did not only get baptized at, but also the church where I learned how to build a close relationship with my Lord and Savior Jesus Christ. This event was when I refused to study theology by not accepting a scholarship that the elders of Summit offered me. As the vision played right before my eyes, God replayed the exact event (as it actually happened years ago) of me denying the scholarship offer of the Summit Church elders. It was as if God had pressed the rewind button on my life and was now replaying this pivotal moment right before my eyes many years after the actual event took place. While He replayed the event of me denying that scholarship to attend school for theology, He also narrated this revelation. He said to me, "When you denied that offer the church elders gave you years ago, you also denied the calling that I had placed on your life. Also, the exact moment that you denied the scholarship to study theology was the exact moment that you started to run from your calling."

After showing me these images, He then replayed images of myself immediately going out into the world and submerging myself in the spoken-word poetry community after denying the offer. While this image played before my eyes, He narrated it by saying, "After denying the calling on your life, you tried to run and hide from it by submerging yourself in the spoken-word community." As I sat there with these images flashing before my eyes, I was nearly speechless, for I was astonished by the truths that were being revealed to me. Once again there are no words sufficient enough in meaning to describe how amazed I was by the truths that the Creator of the universe was revealing to me.

The vision did not stop there. Next, God revealed something profound to me. Before I tell you what he revealed to me, there is something very important to mention. Years after I walked out of Summit Church, when God revealed my calling to me again, I had pity on myself because I accepted the idea that I had wasted a lot of time by not ministering to others while I was outside of God's will for my life. I felt as though I had already wasted many years branding myself as an actor and a poet, so much that I neglected what God originally intended me to do, which is to serve Him by ministering to others. Now due to the major events that have been happening in my life (before I received this vision) I started to actively minister to others. You reader have gotten a sense of this in Section 5, in the "He Brought Me Full Circle" chapter. I started to actively minister to my friend Kina by telling her about God. I also felt so convicted of the calling on my life that I even started to incorporate God into my poetry! I was in the world for years after I denied that church elder's offer to pursue a degree in theology. I was in the world foolishly following my will, and being impressively driven by money, fame, and worldly success. I was not totally driven by ministering to others. Now, towards the end of the year 2013, I was making a desperate attempt to make up all the time that I had wasted by spending years running from the calling on my life. As I sat there on my buddy's couch in Atlanta, Georgia, I was under the impression that I had just recently started to serve God by ministering to others. Which suggests that while I was running I was not ministering to anyone. What God revealed to me next in the vision was that this was not at all a true statement. As a matter of fact, it was far removed from the truth!

The vision continued. God showed me myself submerging myself in the spoken-word performance scene. He narrated this scene by saying to me, "I had been simultaneously and strategically positioning you to minister to others from the point that you denied the calling on your life until now, and I have been using your spoken-word poetry in order to do so." When this truth was revealed to me, I was shocked and relieved at the same time. I thought to myself, Then that means when I became selfish over the years, God still used me to do something selfless, and that is to encourage and inspire countless souls who probably were dying in discouragement. I received this vision around the time that I started to accept the fact that I was called to be a servant of the Lord and to minister to others. With that said, I thought that I failed in not ministering to others because I spent too much time running from my calling and doing my own will. What God was now revealing to me in the tail end of the year 2013 showed me that this was not at all true. He revealed the truth to me that He was using me the whole time to minister to others.

In the gospel, right before Jesus Christ died on the cross for our sins, he exclaimed the words: "It is finished..." These words indicated that Christ's perfect substitutionary sacrifice had come to a completion. So now through him we too can have victory over sin thereby enabling us to live a new life. With that said, during the vision, God said to me, "Because of my goodness, while you were denying the calling I placed on your life to minister to others, I used you to minister to others regardless. Because of my goodness, I have already used you to minister to countless souls over the years. Even while things of the world took your focus off ministering to others, I still guided you in such a way that you still ministered to people that really needed it." Just like Jesus Christ said on the cross, it was like God was telling me, "It is finished!" It was like he was telling me, "I have already used you to finish the work of ministering to the many people that you came in contact with in the world, while you were running from your calling."

As a performing artist, God knew that I would come in contact with many people, and used this to His advantage. When He revealed to me that He had used me to complete such a work, the interjection "Whoa," slowly crept out of my mouth, as if I could not think of any other word that was sufficient enough to describe the beauty, the love, and the goodness that was wrapped up in what God was revealing to me. In a state of amazement, almost paralyzed by the magnificence of what God was revealing to me, I slowly repeated the words, "God is good," three times in a row. With the words "God is good" I was communicating to God, "Thank you for using me to do something great when I foolishly turned my back on you."

Once again paralyzed by the beauty of what God was revealing to me in the vision, I didn't say much. I was very careful not to speak because I didn't want to miss anything from what could have been a once in a lifetime experience. This revelation was like a good movie that was hard to pull away from. Nonetheless, I was too excited by what God was revealing to me, for me to keep it to myself. I shared these things with my friend Tyesha (who I was on the phone with during the vision). Greatly amazed, I said to Tyesha, "He (God) was using me to touch people the whole time!" With this statement, I was saying to her, "He used me the whole time that I was out of the church." The reason why I was so in awe was for the simple fact that during all those years that God was using me, I was focused on another selfish agenda that was not of God. For years, I was more concerned about finding fulfillment for myself and I became more obsessed and determined to find success and glory in the world. Now, when God showed me that he had been using me the whole time to do something selfless that transcended my own selfish agenda, I was in awe and I praised him right where I sat repeating the words, "God is good." While I was running from my calling, I became more frustrated having not found what I was looking for. As a matter of fact, there was a void within me that I did not succeed in filling up with the things of the world. I became frustrated and tired. Then God showed me that because of him, the running that I was doing, was not in vain. He used me wherever I ran to so that I could minister to people there. I was being used as a minister in the world, and I did not know it!!

In the vision, I was also shown a particular scene where God used me on the spoken-word scene to minister to people that were in the audience. I saw an image of me performing on stage at a spoken-word venue called Studio 41 in west Philadelphia not too long before I received this vision. God narrated this scene by saying, "You didn't know it, but there was someone in particular sitting in the audience who was in desperate need of encouragement, and I used your poetry on this night to minister to them." Once again, I was in awe at this revelation.

Another thing that is profound is that God used me to minister up until the time that I received the vision. This shows me that He has definitely called me to be a minister. Not only did He use me to minister to people in the past several years of my life, He used me to minister to my friend Tyesha right before He spoke to me through the vision. To show you how far removed I was from the calling that God had placed on my life, it was never my intention to minister to Tyesha. I was pursuing her with the goal of making her my girlfriend. I do not reject the possibility that God only allowed Tyesha and me to cross paths, so that I could minister to her.

The vision did not end there. At the conclusion of it, God commissioned me just like He commissioned Noah to build the Ark. He said, "Now I want you to write a book. In this book, I want you to show my goodness to others, by revealing to them everything I have just shown you in this vision." Then He said to me, "This book will be successful." After He commissioned me to write this book, He very briefly revealed the concept of my future memoir. The concept was so impressive that it was a concept that I could not have conceived with my own finite mind. It was so impressively mind blowing that it was clear to me why the book would be successful as He promised it would. This concept quickly flashed in my mind and was impressed on my brain ever since then. Here is the concept: While I was running from my calling, God's hands were guiding me to specific places so that I could minister to specific people.

> "...a few days ago I was talking to Tyesha from one night early into the next morning, and something came over me (The Holy Spirit) and told me to tell her to "Let go" of whatever she was holding onto in the past. I remember repeating to her over and over again to let go of whatever she was holding onto. I asked her if she was holding onto something, and she said "yes" she is. And I remember repeatedly telling her to let go of whatever she was holding on to, and judging by her silence, she knew that she was holding on to something. Afterwards, I had this vision that showed me what God wanted me to create. He wants me to create a book that shows how he has used me, despite the fact that I did not initially listen to my calling to be a pastor. In this vision, he showed me that it was going to be a successful book."

-September 8, 2013

Chapter 22
God Has Been Placing Me into Position

"For as the heavens are higher than the earth,
so are my ways higher than your ways,
and my thoughts than your thoughts."

Isaiah 55:9

Having gotten this far in my memoir, you reader should now have a great sense of how far it was from my agenda to minister to others. Over the years, I rapidly grew more concerned about being successful based on the world's idea of success, instead of aiming to please God. I became deeply concerned about attaining money, prestige, and also pleasing my family. Regardless of my selfish mission and stubbornness to yield to the calling on my life, God used me to minister to others. This testifies of His goodness.

Earlier in the "Spoken-Word Poetry" chapter of my memoir, you've read about when I first became a spoken-word poet. While reading this memoir, you might have been wondering, Why didn't Thierry go into depth with the poetry performances he did over the years? Well, I didn't give you more insight into these performances so that you as the reader could get a clear sense of my failure to find fulfillment in the things of this world. Also, in the "It Is Finished" chapter of this memoir, you've read how God has been specifically and strategically using my poetry to minister to others while I was running from my calling. So naturally, I felt the need to separate these special instances from my sad story of failing to find fulfillment in the things of this world.

In the midst of searching for fulfillment in the world, I performed spoken-word in as many places as I could and as often as I could. I've performed in various states and cities. Places such as Oklahoma, Iowa, Lansdowne, Pennsylvania, Philadelphia, New Jersey, New York, Delaware, Georgia, Washington D.C., Boston, Connecticut, among many others. I've performed at many open mic venues, elementary schools, universities, celebrations, and on radio stations. I've performed for numerous people in various places and walks of life. I've performed on countless stages for the rich, the poor, and everyone in between. I've performed for people in urban and affluent communities. I've performed for Caucasians, African Americans, Hispanics, and Asians etc. I've performed for the young and old. I've had kids younger than 10 years old express to me how much they have enjoyed my work. I've also had elderly people who have done the same. All these people have gained something positive from my performances. They were given hope. They were encouraged. They were given light in the midst of darkness, and they were inspired. I've inspired people to improve their craft of writing and acting. I've inspired people to start writing poetry. I've inspired people to keep pushing through their trials and tribulations and to not give up. I've inspired people to work hard to get what they want. I've inspired people to not be afraid to reach for the stars. I've inspired people to be great! Most importantly, I've inspired them to put God first.

I could remember after attending a performance one night in Philadelphia, I ran into a man who watched me perform in times past. This black man was much older than me. Therefore, I considered him to be my elder. Well on this particular night, the tables turned dramatically. As soon as he laid his eyes on me, he said, "Let me know when you are performing again, I will follow you anywhere." This statement of his shows how much I have influenced him with my art. As a result of my toiling on the poetry scene, he was willing to follow me anywhere that I performed. Based on that interaction alone, I have no doubt in my mind there are a plethora of other people that I have performed for that would probably make the same bold statement as this man. I have no doubt in my mind that they would follow me from performance to performance in town or out of town. That night, this man gave me a strong sense of the impression that I have made on people as a result of my attainments in the performance realm.

Being that I've visited so many places over all the years that I've been out of the church, it would be virtually impossible to document every single person that God has used me to reach with my art. Luckily, in the year 2012 (while I was living in Philadelphia), I started to keep journals. This became my pastime, because I believed that I was going to finally blow up and make it to the big times. This statement in itself conveys once again that ministering to others was far from my focus. Now that I've written this memoir (relying heavily on these journal entries), I see now that it was nothing but divine providence that compelled me to start keeping journals. I say this because it is in these journals that I was able to clearly document the many instances of people I've ministered to with my spoken-word performances, not knowing that I would be writing this memoir one day. Now, relying purely on my memory, I've also documented specific instances of me reaching people with my art that I did not record in my journals. If I did not start keeping journals, I would not have been able to do any justice in conveying a clear picture of the depths of God's goodness.

Since I started keeping journals in the year 2012, while living in Philadelphia, I was able to document the people I've touched from the winter of 2012 to the summer of 2013. In the "It Is Finished" chapter, God revealed to me that He specifically used my spoken-word poetry to minister to others. However, I have grounds to believe that He has also been using other projects such as my one-man shows and stage plays to do the same. Therefore, I made sure that I also documented those instances. Now, I've documented the people that I know for sure that I've been a blessing to. This includes instances that occurred when I lived in West Palm Beach and Jacksonville, Florida, and the many cities that I have traveled to over the years. With that said, I've included instances when I attended Palm Beach Community College, Florida Community College, and when I lived in Pennsylvania. In the year 2013, when I moved out of Pennsylvania to Jacksonville, Florida, I've run into people that have told me that they clearly remembered a performance of mine that I did way back when I lived in Jacksonville, Florida. I've included these instances also. I was also performing spoken-word while I was attending Summit Church, so I've documented instances of me reaching people before I walked out of the church.

I've performed for way more people than the ones I remember. I've also been performing much longer than what I have documented from a part of the years 2012 and 2013. "So how much more people has God used me to minister to that did not tell me so?" If God revealed the answer to this question to me, this memoir would not be one book but a series of books jam packed with meaningful experiences of God using me to bless others. You, the reader, have read my memoir. You've gotten a sense of the various places I've performed. With that said, use your imagination to get a better sense of God's goodness by figuring out how much more people He used me to minister to. Chances are you will only get a very rough estimate of this number. One thing is for sure...by God's grace I've ministered to countless individuals!

While I was confused to what my purpose was in life, God was using me to give others a sense of purpose. While I was in darkness and suffering pain from running from my calling, He was using me to heal others. While I was concerned about fame and money, He was using me to touch to others. When I had a difficult time taking care of myself, He used me to enrich malnourished souls. When I thought that I was in a room full of people who wanted to see a dynamic performance, there were people in there that were searching for healing. When I believed that I was on a journey to find fulfillment, God used me to give a person encouragement. When I believed that it was about me, He said, "No, it's about them." When I believed that I was guiding myself, He was guiding me to be a guide to others. When I was in darkness, He said, "I've used you to give others light." When I was lost, He said, "I'm using you to help others find their way back to the fold." And the many times I thought I was standing on a stage in front of an audience, He said, "No, every stage you stepped on was a pulpit and the audience was your congregation." When I finally decided to stop running from my calling, He said, "It is finished, for I have been using you to minister to others."

You, reader, have read my visible and depressing story of running from my calling and trying to find fulfillment in the dark things of this world. Below I do not continue this depressing story. Instead, I tell another. It is the uplifting story of how God's invisible hand has worked in my life to spread light in a dark world. Enjoy.

He's Encouraged
West Palm Beach, Florida

One of my earliest experiences of having touched someone with my poetry was very early on in my spoken-word career while living in West Palm Beach. Inspired by a rap song by a famous black rap artist named Jay-Z, I decided to create this poem. The name of this song is "Feeling It." Titling my poem after this song, I named my poem "When I'm Feeling It." It was simply my goal with this original poem of mine to tell my listeners the action I take when I am inspired to create a new poem. In this original poem of mine, it was simply my goal to explain to my readers that I do not waste any time when I feel the inspiration to create a new poem. I did not know that this poem of mine would touch any of my listeners in a deep place. Quite honestly, my goal was for people to simply notice my ability to write well.

"The Stage" open mic event was located in the city of West Palm Beach. This event was put on within a Haitian-owned restaurant called C & N Café. Early on in my spoken-word career, this was the spoken-word event that I performed at the most. One night, I passionately performed my "When I'm Feeling It" poem for the audience there. I received great feedback from the crowd.

At the end of the night, an older black gentleman walked up to me and shook my hand. In a sincere tone, he told me that he had been going through some hard times lately and that my poem inspired him to not give up and to keep pushing. This discouraged man was quite possibly on the brink of giving up, and my poem inspired him to keep on pushing through whatever he was going through at the time. The following is my "When I'm Feeling It" poem:

"When I'm Feeling It"

She sang with so much soul, and I loved it.
She sang, "If you're feeling it, raise your hands in the sky."

Her voice was beautiful, but I didn't agree with her words though,
because when I am feeling it, my first reaction is not to raise my hands in the sky,
As to indicate when Ms. Inspiration is moving me.
My first response is to keep my hands right where they are,

because that is where my pen and my pad agreed to meet me.
Why would I choose to waste my time when there is a lot of writing to be done?
Why would I waste my time swaying my arms back and forth when I am feeling it?
That's like someone throwing up a strong peace sign when they don't support the message that's behind it.
That's like someone buying a roll of toilet paper when they are not doing shit.
A WASTE OF TIME!

And in this profession, there is no time for hesitation.
So as soon as I feel it, like when I'm feeling Ms. Hip Hop as soon as the beat drops,
I GET DOWN TO ACTION!
I get my writing on while my head is still rocking and Ms. Inspiration has me in a bind like a reticulated python, and there is no telling when she will let go.
So as soon as she hits me, I start writing immediately!
Creating massive waves of words with a pen that has less than an ounce of ink in it,
and a sheet of paper that does not have the depth of a small puddle.
I start writing immediately!
Keeping both of my hands down and focused on the task at hand.
Ms. Inspiration is here for a limited time only,
and I've got to grasp this opportunity before she no longer grants me the ability to make a few thoughts expand into Spoken-Word Poetry.

When I am feeling it, I do not reach for dioxide.
Instead, I reach for the feeling that I have on the inside to create a unity and peace between words that they may together produce a work that is hard-hitting, mind splitting, and in your face like HD television.
USE…YOUR…IMAGINATION!

When I am feeling it, I frantically search for my notebook and when it's finally in my possession, I spread the cover of it open and sex the pages with my Bic;

Letting loose on every page until I am no longer feeling it.
You see, I don't waste anytime flailing my arms back and forth when I am feeling it,
I love poetry too much to spend another minute from it,
I get down to business when Ms. Inspiration whispers to me "LET'S GET IT!"

When you're feeling it, put your pen on a pad and start writing it,
Lay your fingers on the strings and start plucking it,
Don't waste anytime and just do it.

Don't worry, you will still feel the hype,
and when you're done, you could put your hands in the sky.

"He Likes "Generation X"
West Palm Beach, Florida

Also one night at "The Stage" open mic I performed an original poem of mine entitled "Generation X." This was a poem that I wrote out of a place of anger and frustration. I was angry at the fact that my generation (or my peers and I) was deemed "Generation X." The letter "X" in this label signifies the unknown. This "X" conveyed the statement "We don't know what this generation is going to amount to." The older generations believed that my generation would not amount to anything. This view made me furious enough to create this poem. With this poem I wanted to tell the older generations that my generation had the potential to become something great. One of the people that did not hesitate to tell me that he enjoyed my poem was a very spiritual man named Isaiah. He attended "The Stage" often to watch the performances and to promote his Christian-based t-shirt company. One night, while Isaiah and I were at The Stage, he told me how much he enjoyed my "Generation X" poem. Below is my "Generation X" poem.

"Generation X"

My motivation is to be distinct.
I dread the thought of blending in.
I don't fear the beauty of standing out.

So I bring the dogs out,
Which symbolizes my skills and talents and I let them go off.
I let them loose on your neighborhood streets late at night while you sleep.
Growling and barking the message "Wake up and get up. Open your mind and start pacing.
Stop procrastinating and run on the steam of your motivation."

The time is now to stand out, to strive to become out of the ordinary.
Make your primary aim standing out.
Become an outcast, be seen.
But remember, when you are doing all of these things to keep it clean.

Wake up and get up.

Grab your DJ systems and pick up your guitars.
Slap unique paint onto your tricked out race cars.

Speak up and speak out.
What's your perspective?
How do you see things?
What's your idea of a solution?
Don't let laziness cripple you!
Run on the endurance generated by your motivation!

They say that you are "Generation X" and that you will not amount to anything.
Hold on, they made a mistake.
They meant to say that we can and we will amount to everything.

So let's prove them wrong and wake up and get up.

Let's prove them wrong and speak up and speak out.
They are also asking their selves, "Are they going to make it?"
Let us scream out "No doubt!"

Time waits on no one and you better believe it is moving.
On a quest to be different is what gets me out of the bed every morning.
What's your motivation?

My motivation is the woman that gave birth to me.
I've been so defiant for so long blaming the premature man in me.
All the while it was the ignorance that I didn't see.
But she, the woman that gave birth to me understood that I was going through a slow process, though I didn't, and continued to hold me.

She, my favorite lady, the woman that gave birth to me is
the epitome of what a strong woman is supposed to be.
The strength that she possesses has earned much respect from me and has awakened a monster of limitless determination within me.

The strength that she possesses has made me determined to make a brighter future for her not only me.
It has made me determined to, "Get up, get out, and get something",
And not blame my adversities.
Whatever does not kill me is only going to help feed that monster of motivation that has been awakened so abruptly within me.

Whatever does not kill me is going to become my motivation,
My mode of transportation to get me to my goals and destinations,
To prove to the previous generations that I am not part of what they have deemed the X Generation.
We, the teens of the new generation have our minds set to
"Get up, get out, and get something".

Let us wake up and get up.
Speak up and speak out,
And get out and get something.

"I Gave It to Her" Poem
Stillwater, Oklahoma

One memorable out of state performance was when I performed at Oklahoma State University with my first mentor Kevon. He was scheduled to do one of his seminars there. Before we both visited the school, Kevon requested that I perform one of my spoken-word pieces entitled "I Gave It to Her" at his seminar. Kevon is the person who requested that I create this poem in the first place. This particular poem of mine depicted the devastating effects of the AIDS virus. Initially, I had great difficulty finding the inspiration to create this poem, but eventually I received the inspiration to create this powerful 45-second poem that would strike at the hearts of countless people over the years.

The way that Kevon and I went about doing the performance at the seminar was strategic and organized. He instructed me to sit in the back of the room in the midst of some of the students. He said that once he cued me to begin performing my "I Gave It Her" poem, I would stand up from my seat and begin performing from the back of the room, as I made my way to the middle of the room in front of all the students that attended his seminar. Kevon's cue for me to begin performing was him turning his back to the audience. Remember, Kevon was a seasoned performer who was studying theater in school, so as a performer, he knew ways of staging a performance to make it more dynamic.

Sitting in the back of the room and blending in with the students, they had no idea that I was a performer. As soon as Kevon gave me the cue, I stood up and powerfully recited my "I Gave It to Her" Poem while I epically walked down from the back of the room to the front of the audience. Also at this workshop, I brought some product with me. This product of mine was a DVD of me reciting my "I Gave It to Her" poem in the form of a short film. This was the first product I had for sale early on in my spoken-word career. At the culmination of the seminar, eager to receive this product of mine, some of the female students who were in attendance that day walked up to me with big smiles on their faces. Their smiles told me that they enjoyed my performance that day.

Lake Worth, Florida

Oklahoma State University was not the only place that I have performed this poem. I also performed it at a fundraiser on the campus of Palm Beach Community College, before I decided to drop out of the school. This fundraiser was organized by an organization on the campus of PBCC called the Black Student Union. For this fundraiser, female students were being auctioned off to the highest bidder. The highest bidder won a date with the woman being auctioned off.

At this fundraiser, performers also had a segment where they would be able to showcase their talents. I was one of those performers, and I performed my "I Gave It to Her" poem. The stage was a wooden platform that was placed in front of all the tables that were in the cafeteria, so that everyone sitting at the tables would be able to see what was happening on the stage. When it was my time to perform, I stood on this makeshift stage and I recited my piece. This particular poem of mine was new, so many (if not all) of the students that were in attendance that day had never heard this new poem of mine.

Like I said before, my "I Gave It to Her" poem-with the approximate length of 45 seconds-is one of the shortest poems that I have ever written. I crafted it in a way so that it had a crescendo rhythm to it that built up to a surprising climax. This poem's purpose was to educate others about HIV, but when I stepped on stage I didn't usually tell the audience what the poem was about, and I did this for a purpose. Doing this added more of an element of surprise to the poem. Not using a mic, I would simply step on stage and once I prepared my mind, I would start to perform this poem very loudly and passionately.

In this poem, it was my goal to make my audience think that I was talking about one thing and then to ultimately surprise them by suddenly revealing that I was not talking about this thing at all. The expression "I gave it to her" is often used to mean that I gave my male genitalia to woman during sex. So during the poem, I repeatedly say to my audience that I'm penetrating a woman. This action is often seen as being respectable in the eyes of many. With that said, the crowd was enjoying the poem. Some women during the performance were screaming out "Give it to me! Give it to me!" as I performed my piece. They were engrossed and captivated by the poem, so by the time I got to the end of the poem I had them in somewhat of a snare. After making them think that I was talking about something that I was not talking about at all, I dropped them off at a location they didn't expect to find themselves. After making them think that I was simply talking about sex, I revealed at the end of my poem that the thing that I was giving the woman the whole time was not simply the pleasure of sex, but the fatal HIV virus.

When I ended my poem with "…I had HIV and I gave it to her," the crowd was stunned. Many people let out a gasp. After begging for me to "give it to her," one woman quickly changed her mind and said, "I don't want that!" Some of my poet friends, who were there at the time, were also shocked and amazed by the unexpected conclusion of the poem. Having enjoyed this poem, they laughed and shook my hands with admiration. When I started to perform, the audience thought it was an erotic piece. Then when I got deeper into the piece, their attitude changed. They wondered, Where is he going with this? By the time I got to the end of the poem I quite possibly compelled the audience members to take an HIV test. With this short and powerful poem, I brought the audience back down to earth. The following is my HIV/AIDS awareness poem "I Gave It to Her":

"I Gave It to Her"

She told me that she wanted it…
So I gave it to her.

She told me that she just couldn't wait,
So I gave it to her.

She told me that all I had to do was
pull out whenever I felt
myself cumming…
So I gave it to her.

She said she would call me a "punk" if I didn't…
So I gave it to her.

She told me that her mother would be
home in an hour…
SO I GAVE IT TO HER…

I GAVE IT TO HER

YES! I GAVE IT TO HER!

I HAD HIV...and I GAVE IT TO...HER.

Great Reactions
Lakeworth, Florida

I've had many other opportunities to perform on the campus of Palm Beach Community College before I dropped out of the school. One of these opportunities was a talent show that was taking place on campus in a theater called the Duncan Theater. This was a time where my stage name was Hiku. Also a part of this talent show was a poet friend of mine who I met on the West Palm Beach spoken-word poetry scene. His name was Pureblood. Since Pureblood and I performed at a lot of the same events, we knew each other well. Not only this, but Pureblood and I grew to respect each other as spoken-word performers.

Before this talent show, Pureblood and I both thought that it would be a great idea if we did a friendly battle against each other at the talent show. When I say battle, I do not mean us using weapons to inflict physical harm to each other. We mutually decided that we would use the words in our poetry with the intention of hurting each other. In essence, we decided to wield our poetry pieces like swords to see which one of us was the best writer.

I was excited and fired up about this great opportunity. I worked hard to write this poem, as I pushed my mental capacities to the limit to come up with the most effective words or poetry lines that would best hurt Pureblood. When the day of the show arrived, I was excited. I performed this piece with everything that I had in me. With power and clarity, I delivered this poem to the audience. I won the battle that night. The audience hung on my every word and carefully followed my every line as I delivered my poem. Oohs and ahs radiated from the audience, to show that they enjoyed my work. I had the audiences hooked from the very start of the poem with the following lines:

> "I don't know what you've been told.
> But everything I touch turns to gold.
> And whatever you touch...rusts.

The only way you can have what I have is if you become a mechanic
Like I've got the Midas touch…"

Below is the battle piece that the audience enjoyed so much on this night.

"Pureblood Dis"

I don't know what you've been told.
But everything I touch turns to gold.
And whatever you touch…rusts.

The only way you can have what I have is if you become a mechanic
Like I've got the Midas touch.
And the only reason why you can't hear them screaming my name
Is because I'm a mouthful and you are not saying much.
So stop while you are ahead.
The only time that I've been touched was when I first saw the movie "Remember the Titans,"
Or heard the song Untouchables.

I'm heavy like 17 syllables.
And you are five:
"He's not serious."
I'm not five syllables!
But if I were I would be more like
"Armed and dangerous."

When it comes to poetry I get straight A's
And you get C's when you are at your best
The only time you get good grades is when you get paid and use that money to
Get two A's on your chest.
So grab your perm and relax.

Because, little lady, you can't hold me.
Let alone catch up to me.
Your speedometer reads zero, and mine reads: dot dot dot infinity.
You're a Ford Focus and I'm like the car from the Back to the Future movie.
Yellow and red traffic lights do not apply to me.
Because I don't believe in doing anything less than my best.
I grace stages with finesse.
And you remind me of the story of the lochness.
Every now and then an individual claims they've seen something
Great in you but we still haven't seen any proof yet.

I don't have pureblood.
I'm half human and half robot
Like the terminator.
Arnold Schwarzenegger.
I lead like the Governor
And you're just satisfied with just being the mayor.

You are such a poet.
I'm a great performer.

You're a spark, I'm a taser.
You're a lizard, I'm a gator.
You come up short like flashlights.
I go long like lasers.

With thoughts speeding like a motorcycle
And a pen full of fire.
I become my own Ghostwriter.
When evolutionists talk about the big bang theory that was me
When I sneezed.
 And you're just a brushfire.
Show me who nicknamed you spitfire.
Whoever it is, is obviously a liar.

You hug blocks I break down rock to build empires.

Hiku is synonymous with:
Wow,
Great,
Did you see that?
And um um good.

Today marks the day
Of the contamination of Pureblood.

Church Members Enjoy My Poetry
Boynton Beach, Florida

While I was attending Summit Church, I performed at a Seventh-day Adventist Christian Church in Boynton Beach, Florida, called Bethel. I was invited by a young black man named Ron to perform at this church, which he was a member of. The poem I performed that night was entitled "Not Arrogant, Overly Confident." After I performed my piece that day, I received a standing ovation. The church members, who were my audience that day, truly enjoyed my poem. They all could relate to the subject matter of it. Below is my poem "Not Arrogant, I'm Overly Confident."

"Not Arrogant, I'm Overly Confident"

I don't see myself as arrogant. I see myself as being confident.
How Confident?
So confident that you can see it dripping off my gestures when I speak,
And when I recite my poems it's a must that I apply anti-per spirant to my speech.

Arrogant? I am a speaker.
I came here to reach an audience.
It just wouldn't work if I were a timid and shy talker.

My words shoot from my mouth with urgency just like rapid fire from an

AK-47,
because the Lord is the foundation of my inspiration.
I'm not dealing with anything weak.
So every time I speak,
my emotions leak and it's as if I'm mad and I start to rage with a body loaded with arrogance. But please try to understand, that I am the General aka the Pastor that
my innermost feelings have chosen to guide them off the page.
So, it is almost like a requirement that I'm assertive and confident.

I wouldn't exactly call myself arrogant.
I would label myself as being confident.
 Yeah, I'm confident.

I drape this word over my body like armor.
I wear the letter C on my chest everywhere I go like the superman logo.
When I walk, I don't stumble and my head is held up high.
When I talk, I don't stutter or mumble and I definitely don't sing out this familiar tune
"I'm so fly. I've got money so that's a good enough reason to buy the things that I buy."

To be real with you, I'm in debt.
I've got no money in the bank.
But even if I were rich, I wouldn't be singing like Lloyd Banks.
I would be too concerned about sharing the dough, not bragging about swimming in cash flow.
That's real.

I'm overly confident!
Because I believe with all my heart that in this life when
I slip off my broken ladder of trials and tribulations the Lord will catch me when I fall.
And that's real.
I wouldn't call it arrogance; I would call it umm…confidence.

What do you do with something that is no use to you?
You either give it away, or just simply throw it away.
Well, arrogance is no use to me.
And I'm not going to give it away.
Man, I'm throwing it away!
And not in the recycling bin,
Because I don't want this tainted way of life coming back again.
And not on the side of the street visible for all to see,
Because I don't want it to be brought back into someone's home again.

Arrogance!
If you really want it, you can have it.
I don't want to shrivel up.
I'd rather live a prosperous way of life, by accepting confidence.
It's only right that I am confident and not arrogant,
Because I am aware that it is the Lord that works through me to do the things that I do.
It is the Lord that constructed my mind and body and inspired me to write these words that I have brought to you.

So you see, I can't be arrogant because I don't do things under my own power.
The Lord is my strength!
The God of the lifetime, the God of the year, the God of the month, the God of the day, and the God of the hour.

I'm overly confident.

Famous Actor Enjoys My Poetry
Miami, Florida

The next person who was touched by my work is not a regular old Joe. This next person is a famous person and is known by many people. This was an actor who I've watched on television ever since I was a little kid time and time again on various shows. The name of this actor is Malcolm Jamal Warner. One of the shows he became famous for was a long-running television show called

"The Cosby Show." In this widely known show, he acted alongside the famous actor and comedian Bill Cosby.

While living in West Palm Beach, I had opportunities to not only perform in West Palm Beach, but also in Miami. Many times I drove down to Miami to perform at a venue called "The Literary Café." A well-known poet named Will da Real One hosted this particular event. Will da Real One was what you call a Def Poet. A Def Poet was someone who has performed at least one time on the nationally televised show named Russell Simmons Def Poetry Jam. Many poets dreamed and strived to be on this show. The reason why they had this common aim was because being on this show was considered to be the pinnacle that a spoken-word artist could reach. It was one of those platforms that if you made it there, it said that you have "made it" as a spoken-word artist. It says that you have worked so hard on your craft that you are now polished enough to share your wonderful works with the world via television. If you are a Def Poet you had more doors opened for you than poets that were not Def Poets. Anyways, it was at this Def Poet's event that I met the famous actor Malcolm Jamal Warner.

On this night, I performed my well-known and loved poem about roaches entitled "Why Must They Die?" This poem went through a whole war theme about killing roaches. The roaches in the poem were not symbolic for anything else. In the poem I simply referred to the little critters that many people found crawling around their homes.

To give you a little background, this poem was inspired by a young lady who attended Palm Beach Community College (the first college that I attended). While I listened to her very heartfelt poem on the genocide that was happening in Darfur at the time, I was immediately inspired to create my "Why Must They Die?" poem. In her poem she referred to actual people who were being murdered, and she asks in her poem the question, "Why must they die?" (referring to the people who were being killed). Me, on the other hand, I took the seriousness away from the poem and created a more comedic poem about roaches. As I look back in retrospect, I should have been taking the topic of genocide more seriously, than taking the seriousness out of this monstrosity by creating a comedic poem about roaches.

Now I was seeing Malcolm Jamal Warner in real life, with him performing in the same venue as me. Malcolm was also a musician who played his guitar that night. Sometime after I was done performing in this venue, I walked out to get some air. While I was standing outside, Malcolm Jamal Warner also walked out of the venue. When he saw me, he told me very sincerely how much he enjoyed my roach poem. Needless to say, it made me feel good on the inside that a famous person like him would complement my poetry. After all, I was still a young black man (I think in my early twenties) striving to make a name for myself on the spoken-word poetry scene. Below is my "Why Must They Die?" poem.

"Why Must They Die?"

They make my home their home,
and they know it.
Because every time I shine a light on them,
they quickly scatter into the little cracks and
crevices in my kitchen.

Why must they die?

Well…they have the nerve to have sex within my
home while I am sleeping.
When I wake up in the morning and grab a
box of cereal from the cabinet,
I find some of the females in labor,
and because I just woke up,
I don't have the energy to squash her with my slipper.

Why must they die?

They are always waking me up in the middle of the night,
crawling onto my face and asking me stupid questions like:
Hey, where did you put the gummy bears?

Why must they die?

They are always pooping on my food.
When I get home after a hard day of work,
it makes me angry when I get a mouth full of bread,
only to find out that those droppings were not pepper.

Why must they die?

I always find them in my cereal.
And NO ONE, I mean, NO ONE messes with my cereal.

So, I will make sure that the cause of
their death is ruthless,
to set an example to all the roaches worldwide;
a modern-day holocaust.
But no survivors,
not even enough to do a monologue.

This mass genocide is going to be
premeditated to perfection.
Every day for two weeks before the killing,
I'm going to be conditioning my mind with
videos, CDs, and books on how to kill roaches.

The videos are going to star the
best exterminators in history,
who show you the correct way to
make yourself inconspicuous...
and how to KILL, KILL, and KILL roaches without MERCY.

I'm going to visit the library and check out the
audio CD called: "The Life and Times of Exterminators"
Where they play the sweet sounds of roaches,
crumbling under the wrath of bug killers.

When the day comes, I will be mentally and physically ready.

With compliments to the grocery store,
I will be armed with more artillery than the Marines,
the Army, and an Iraqi.
I WILL BE READY to get rid of enough roaches to fill a football stadium,
making open stadiums out of their craniums.

I will have four extra large Raid cans,
one strapped to each of my legs,
and the other two on my back, nice and snug in my
self-manufactured-20 ounce-extra large-Raid can-capable BACKPACK!

And also on my back,
next to the raid are two five gallon sacks,
full of little hotels where roaches check in… but never check out.

The time is 10 o'clock and we see Thierry standing outside of his house.
And he looks like a fireman ready to rock.
And because the roaches kept
him up the night before, we also see that
his eyes are blood shot.
But he is focused!

HE KICKS THE DOOR IN!!
He starts throwing some hotels out,
HE'S GOING CRAZY!
He could have sworn that he heard the LOX in
the back of his mind telling him to…
WILD OUT!!!
And he does…

He reaches for his foggers and throws three into the bedroom,
three into the bathroom,
and the rest into the kitchen…
then all the roaches come out screaming!

If you ever cross that line
I guarantee you there will be nothing to save ya.
I've got a couple more cans and a lot more hotels and
I'm coming to get ya.
Coming from a life of grime, trying to be on my best behavior
Yeah, my poems are getting bigger, but still this same dude will spray at you buggers.

DON'T TAKE WHAT'S MINES...
DON'T SHIT ON WHAT'S MINES....
DON'T EMBARRASS ME IN FRONT OF MY DIME...
I WILL LOSE MY MIND...
If you ever cross that line.

Audience at Poetry Slam Enjoys Me
Ft. Lauderdale, Florida

While I was still living in West Palm Beach, I received an opportunity to be a part of a poetry slam that was being held in Ft. Lauderdale. A poetry slam was a competition where poets wielded their poems like swords. This is a competition where the spoken-word artist's literary skills and ability to perform were judged. I drove from West Palm Beach to Ft. Lauderdale, Florida, to be a part of this competition and for very good reason. The prize for the night was $300. The venue that was hosting this event was smack dab in the middle of an urban neighborhood. When I pulled up into the parking lot of this venue, I saw that there was a light-skinned gentleman standing on the outside of it with his cell phone in hand. Later on that evening I would find out that this poet was the very talented Bert from Miami, Florida. As I pulled up in my Monte Carlo with my driver window down, I looked at him and he looked at me very intently. Poetry slams are a very serious matter for spoken-word artists take their crafts seriously. Especially when a large amount of money it involved. The money involved makes each poet question if their poems are good enough to win that night, and as a result they look at every other poet in the competition with a very close eye as they wonder, Who is that guy? I wonder how great of a poet he is. Before the actual competition begins, poets would look at other poets with an analytical eye, wondering what that other poet can do with words. As I arrived to that venue that night with full intention to win the money that night, Bert looked at me with that analytical eye that said, "I wonder if he is one of the poets competing tonight?"

The venue where this competition was being held was spacious. It was dimly lit and had tables everywhere. The place also had food available for purchase for the people who were attending this poetry slam on this night. This poetry competition had spoken-word artists coming from all over. Bert was the name of the poet who I saw standing in front of the venue when I first arrived. He drove all the way up from Miami to be at this competition. When the competition was underway, all of the spoken-word artists were called up front to the stage (which was in front of all the tables where many people were sitting). As all of us spoken word artists lined up along one side of the room, we all had on our game faces. We all knew what we were there for and that was to win $300 using our literary works in this battle. So there was no place for a smile.

I was hungry for that big prize, so I worked hard that night to earn it. Putting all into my performances, I was able to advance to the next round. The other poets whose performances were not up to par were eliminated. The audience members that night grew to love me. Judging by the audience's reactions to my performances, I felt that I had a good chance of winning this money. Bert, the poet from Miami, was also a very good performer, and had a good chance of winning on this night.

This momentum that I was building throughout the competition would soon come to an end. Midway through one of my poems, I struggled on one of the lines. It was at this point that I knew that I no longer had a chance of winning this competition. In poetry competitions, the goal was to be as perfect as possible with the delivery of your poem, and to not stumble. The judges were looking at you closely and once you messed up on one line, they would dock you for that mistake. In other words they would penalize you greatly for your unfortunate mistake and it would show in your score. So, I messed up on my piece and as soon as I messed up on my line, I could hear the audience exhaling in a moan that stabbed my ego like a sharp knife. With this reaction of theirs, they were telling me that they noticed my mistake and they felt that I had a less likely chance of winning the $300 that night. I did not win the poetry slam that night. The poet Bert took the money home that night. I went home empty handed. Though I was greatly disappointed, it was obvious that many of the people that were in attendance that night were touched by my work.

He Remembers My Performance
Jacksonville, Florida

While it was hard for me to remain consistent and submerge myself in my studies at Florida Community College of Jacksonville, I totally submerged myself in the performance realm. I created (possibly in search for fulfillment) a form of poetry called "Drive by Poetry." As the name suggests, as abrupt as a drive by shooting, I would, without warning start to perform poetry in a public place. One day I decided to stand on a chair and perform one of my poems right in the middle of the campus cafeteria. On this particular day, the campus was busy with students that were eating and socializing with their friends. When I finally mustered up the strength, I grabbed one of the cafeteria chairs, stood on it, and started to recite one of my poems. Many of the students that were deeply engrossed in their business now froze to watch this random act of mine. After my performance I felt so proud of myself for having the guts to stand on a chair in a room full of strangers to perform my poetry.

I did another act of drive by poetry on the campus of FCCJ. This time it was within the student activity center. This activity center was located right above the cafeteria and had many games there for students to play, such as pool. When I arrived to the student activities center, there were a few people (male and female students) that were engaged in the game of pool along with another group of men that were deeply engaged the game of ping-pong. It was a very lively atmosphere of college students trying to enjoy themselves between classes.

Before I started reciting my poem, I asked a lady who was a student at FCCJ to hold onto a small hand camera that I had with me. I wanted her to video tape me while I recited my poem. She agreed. When I was ready, I stood in the middle of the activity center, and began to recite an original poem of mind entitled "Poison." In this poem I was exposing hip-hop artists and talking about the negative messages that they send to our youth. I express to the youth in this poem that Hip Hop artists do not truly care about them. Once I started to recite my poem, the couple that was playing pool stopped immediately, got real close to each other and watched my performance as if they were at the theaters snuggled up together watching a very interesting movie. There were also some other white males there who stopped with their pools sticks in their hands to watch me perform. Some of the males who were engaged in the game of ping-pong also stopped and watched my performance. When I recited my "Poison" poem in the SAC Lounge, there was a white woman who was sitting in a chair directly behind me. She had on a set of headphones probably listening to music. Once I started to recite my poem very loudly behind her, she turned around in her seat to watch my performance.

When I was done with my performance, a few of my audience members applauded. Sometime after these two random acts of what I call "Drive By Poetry" a young white male who was one of my colleagues approached me one day and asked, "Are you the one who was performing poetry the other day?" I responded, "Yes." With a bright smile on his face he expressed to me how much he enjoyed my performance. The following is the poem that I recited in FCCJ Student Activities Center:

"Poison"

I'm not talking about quarters and dimes when I say "It's time for a change."
Many of us want to see change…it's our aim,
but because we don't want to give up the sounds of Lil' Wayne or
The Game, our aim is pointless,
because pointless-blank-lyrics have us shooting blanks at point blank range.

I'm speeding!!

Rick Ross and his Platinum chain has you fiending for the fast lane,
He has your head in the clouds like "Cocaine should be easy to maintain,"
forgetting that the main thing is to remain sane in order to dodge those bullets
When they come crashing through your windowpane.
In other words, you've got to be speeding if you're going to be in the fast lane.

One wrong move…well, there is no coming back.
Even if you had 100 stacks of greenbacks accompanied with a couple of packs of Rogaine.
Your money might be able to get you to the laundromat, but the detergent won't
Be able to reverse the bloodstain.

And Ross could care less,
Afterall, your blood didn't come from his veins.
Blood is thicker than water.
And his dollar is thicker than your slaughter.
So let's proceed to kill the future.
For that is the formula to make cheddar.

Hey Mr. Carter!
I mean…Hey Mr. Killer.
I must admit, Lil' Wayne has a twisted brain but he can't make it rain without a twist of
Mary Jane.
Yet you support his fame.
You pop in his album and listen to everything.
You live by everything he says in his bars.
In that case, I challenge you to challenge him to do those things when he's not high enough to eat a star.

The only things today's rappers talk about are money, hoes, and cars
It's all they talk about so it's all they are
They Hip-Hop on television and create an illusion
because they know that you would not buy a CD if they were portrayed to
be as poor as you are.

So make-up artist, cover up my scars.
And the pictures of my homies that are dead or doing time behind bars.

Hurry up! We've got a show to put on.

I've got to make another cool million.

Even if it means destroying the potential of today's children.

Performing "True Graffiti"
Jacksonville, Florida

When I was no longer in the church I decided on my own that I would be an anti-gang activist. So as a performer I started to create anti-gang monologues. I could remember performing one of these monologues entitled "True Graffiti" one night in the city of Jacksonville, Florida. The whole goal of the piece was to deter young people from this dangerous lifestyle. I performed this piece for a group of grown adult professionals. This particular piece was centered on the lives of two gang members that did not enjoy the gangster lifestyle that they were living. I received the idea to create this monologue from documentaries that I've watched on gangs. In these documentaries I've watched as gang members expressed with deep lament on how they did not enjoy the lifestyle that they were living. I created "True Graffiti" around these documentaries, and on this particular night while I was living in the city of Jacksonville, Florida, I performed it for a large group of adults.

"True Graffiti" was a one-man piece, meaning that I was the only person who performed it. Nonetheless, the piece depicted the lives of two people. So that the audience can see the other character in the play, I spoke to this imaginary character throughout the whole piece. The character of the other person in the play would then be left to the imaginations of the audience members.

When "True Graffiti" begins, the first thing the audience sees is me running into the scene. When I come into the scene I'm frantic and somewhat paranoid. The other person that is in the scene is my fellow homie, or gang member. During the scene I would periodically ask my gang member friend to hand me spray paint out of an imaginary bag that is in his possession. With these spray cans I would spray paint one by one on the wall in front of us various words that described how being a gang member made us feel. "Angry" and "Frustrated" were the first couple of words that my character proudly spray-painted on the imaginary wall. After each word that was successfully spray painted on the wall in front of me, my character would then take a step back from the wall and we would look at each word with satisfaction. This satisfaction confirmed that the words that were being tagged on the wall were the exact way that the gang members felt as a result of living the dangerous lifestyle that they were living.

As a writer and performer, I found it very fun to add unforeseen twists to my pieces. To shock and surprise the audience members that watched my pieces was my goal. With that said, in the piece "True Graffiti" you have two gang members that have grown bitter as a result of being gang members. They have become sick and tired of living this type of lifestyle. Now keeping that in mind, during the scene I would periodically tell my gang member friend that the sooner that we completed the task of tagging the wall with all of these sad words, the sooner we will be able to go home. Now the audience has been hearing the phrase "going home" the whole time that they have been watching, but do not know what my character means by it. My whole goal was to pull my audience into thinking that I was simply talking about going home to my family, which was not what my character meant at all. I was only doing this to set the audience up for the surprise.

Remember, the scene is made up of my character spray painting words on the wall that described perfectly how it made him feel to be living a gangster lifestyle. With that said, the last word that my character spray paints on the wall is the one that he is the most satisfied with for a reason that the audience would later find out. After tagging this particular word on the wall, my character takes a step back like he always did, but this time he drops the spray can as if to say "My mission has been accomplished." From this position, he looks at the final word long and hard with a sad countenance. He then expresses how the final word encapsulates all of the turmoil that was going on within him as a gang member. Then finally my character says the word loud enough for the audience to hear and the word is "Suicidal." He then repeats again the words "It's time to go home now" and asks his fellow homie to hand him something else out the bag that was in his possession. But this time what his homie hands him is not a spray can but a handgun. My character grabs the handgun and holds it up to his head. When my character did this, I heard several of the audience members gasp. They were shocked that my character was about to take his life. After closing his eyes and holding his breath (to brace himself), he shoots himself and falls to the ground dead. My piece "True Graffiti" touched the adults in a deep place that night.

Performing "Ben & Jerry's, not Haagen Daz!"
Jacksonville, Florida

I was greatly influenced by my mentor Kevon. Imitating him, I created and performed pieces called Confessional Narratives just like he always did. On stage these pieces resemble the monologues that actors often pulled out of stage plays for auditions. Though they looked similar there were five distinct components that made confessional narratives different from regular monologues.

While I was living in Jacksonville, Florida, I received an opportunity to perform at a school that was called Florida Community College of Jacksonville. This was not the campus that I attended. There were several of these campuses throughout Jacksonville. The one that I attended was the South Campus, and I performed at the Downtown Campus. Like its name suggests, it was located in downtown Jacksonville.

The event that I was scheduled to perform in was located in the campus cafeteria. On this particular day the cafeteria was full of students who were there for the event. When it was my turn to perform, I performed a confessional narrative just like my mentor Kevon. The name of this piece was entitled "Haagen Daz." Yes, that is right! The confessional narrative was about the famous brand of ice cream. When I am about to perform this piece, I do not give away the title of it, so that the audience would not be able to figure out the twist that I placed at the end of the piece.

In the beginning of the confessional narrative, I'm in an office within my home and I'm pacing back and forth, and I'm obviously worried. With this confessional narrative, I intentionally give the audience the idea that I'm some kind of mob leader or leader of some gang. While pacing back and forth in my home, I proclaim very loudly, "He was supposed to be here by now!" Then I say, "I gave him only one job to do and he could not even do that." Then I say, "If he comes back with the wrong thing, the boss is going to kill me." Once again, the reason why I say this line is to give the audience the impression that I'm part of a mob, and I sent one of my men out not to long ago to do a job for me. After building enough suspense, someone then comes into the room and tells me that the person that I sent out to a do a job for me just got back from doing the job. I hesitate and then command the person that came to give me the news to ask him to come in. Then I start to pace back and forth again repeating the words, "If he comes back with the wrong one, the boss is going to kill me." When the person finally walks in I re-direct my attention to an imaginary item that is in his hands. I then look at the person that is holding the item and ask him, "Is that it?" He tells me, "Yes." I then say "if that is the wrong one, the boss is going to kill me!" I then ask the person to come over to me, but he hesitates as if he were scared of what I might do to him. I reassure him that he does not have to be afraid and I ask him to come over to me. As soon as he comes over to me, I smack him on the back of his head. As this imaginary person is crouched over, I ask him to get back up.

Not after long, I ask him to hand me the item that I've been waiting for a while now. I take the item to my desk and say to him that the item is too wet (to make my audience think that the item that I am dealing with is a bloody body part of some sort). After all, by this time I've already done a good job in giving them the impression that I was part of a dangerous mob.

After taking a deep breath, I finally open the item that was before me and in my gestures I show the audience that I am obviously disappointed with what I am looking at. I immediately start to yell at the person that I sent to do the job for me. Now here comes the twist that blows the audience away. After all of this I say to the imaginary person, "I gave you one job to do and you couldn't do it! One job! How many times do I have to tell you that my wife likes Haggen Daz and not Ben & Jerry's?"

The audience discovers the fact that I was in my house the whole entire time, and not in an office of some high-rise building. They discover that my boss was actually my wife, and I was not some kind of mob lieutenant, but a fearful husband. And the person who I sent out was not sent out to kill anyone, but was sent to the store to get my wife (aka my boss) some ice cream. The audience members fell out of their seats with laughter after I revealed these truths. They enjoyed the piece.

She Remembers My Performance
Jacksonville, Florida

"In the year 2007 or 2008 I performed one of my original monologues at a school named Florida Community College of Jacksonville. All the students enjoyed my performance.

In the year 2014, about six years after this particular performance, I met a young black woman who was actually at the performance. She was sitting in the audience while I was performing at a Theatre called the Ritz in Jacksonville, Florida. While I was walking around the room selling my poetry CDs eventually I walked up to her and she said that she remembered me from the performance that I did years ago at Florida Community College of Jacksonville. When she told me this I was thrown aback because it amazed me that she still remembered me after all those years since the performance.

This told me that my performance left a long lasting impression on her."
-October 11, 2014

Performing at Patterson's Palace
Philadelphia, Pennsylvania

I could remember performing at a place called Patterson's Palace. This was a venue that was located near the Temple University campus in Philadelphia, Pennsylvania. This was one of the first places that I performed when I moved to Lansdowne, Pennsylvania. Patterson's Palace was a dimly lit room with a stage and a lot of chairs and tables. On this stage I performed many of my original works. One man in particular who did not make it a secret that he enjoyed my poetry was a young black artist that called himself Back Fia.

Performing at the Harvest Open Mic
Philadelphia, Pennsylvania

"Two" is an original poem of mine that was inspired by a hurtful experience that I have had in my life. I was inspired to write this poem after I cheated on an ex-girlfriend of mine with two women. Hence, why I chose to entitle this poem "Two." Once again, I have always been a fan of twists in my poetry works. I've always had a hunger to create a concept in my poetry pieces that my audience would not see coming. I call this the art of surprise, and "Two" is definitely one of those poems that I added an element of surprise to.

I begin my poem "Two" by first painting a vivid picture of how close my ex and me used to be. After expressing how inseparable my ex and me were and how much I adored her, midway through the piece, I suddenly reveal to my audience that I cheated on her. After taking the audience for a ride, I dropped them off at an unexpected location. Once I drop them off at this location, the audience members would gasp with shock after being caught off guard. This was a reaction I received when I performed one night at an open-mic event in Philadelphia called "The Harvest." On this particular night, it was probably one of the best reactions that I've ever received for this poem. There were easily over 100 people in attendance that night I performed the poem. The following is my original poem "Two":

"TWO"

TWO, was the age I was when I was first shown pictures of you,
and taught to picture you and I in a picture or TWO.

At the age of TWO,
I was tied down to a chair, and told to watch you on TWO TV screens,
and then handed TWO magazines that only talked about you.

YOU ARE ALL I KNOW.
SO PLEASE DON'T WALK OUT THAT DOOR.

Just try to picture us married, bride and groom.
Or us standing next to a child or TWO.
Or us, getting so old that the only way to
Remain standing would be for you to lean on me,
And for me to lean on you.
Come sit with me,
and let me rub your feet for you.
I want us to converse about the TWO years that we spent into each other...

How we were so intertwined that when we
walked down the street together,
people confused us for one person and not TWO...
How we were so into each other that every time my heart beat,
it beat for you.

YOU ARE ALL I KNOW…

I don't have the slightest clue when it comes to the answer for
TWO plus TWO.
The only equation that I've ever known was me plus you equals
TOO hot to be bottled in a bottle of hot sauce or TWO.
TOO explosive to be compared to World War TWO.

TUE- SDAY and Wednesday were the days I cheated on you.
TWO women within TWO days,
TWO condom wrappers thrown to the bedside,
right where you found them,
with your TWO eyes.

We've been separated for four years,
and I just realized that
These TWO women put together would not be able to get in tune
with your vibe,
Even if they had you tutor them for TWO years on how to be a Queen,

TUE-SDAY and Wednesday were the days I messed up,
so to show you that you come before them,
On a Monday, I would wake up TWO o'clock in the morning,
head out into TWO degree weather,
wearing a tutu that is TWO sizes too small,
on my TWO feet,
walk twenty-TWO blocks to
IHOP to get you a TOOtie Frootie,
because I know how much you love it, so I'm trying hard to get
it to you before I have to go to work at 3.

BABY DON'T LEAVE!
YOU ARE ALL I KNOW!

So if you walk out that door,
all I will be left with is TWO tears rolling
down my face clutching onto TWO photos of you,

thinking how you were just too sexy.
And how I was too stupid for cheating on you with TWO women, in TWO days, STAY!

Because if you leave, there will be too many miseries,
PLEASE DON'T LEAVE ME!

The End

Performing Roach Poem at Billie's Black
Harlem, New York

Over the years, my roach poem "Why Must They Die?" is a piece that my fans would not allow me to retire. They have grown to love the piece this much! After seeing me perform this poem one day, Renair Amin, the host of the "Speak Your Myne" open mic event in Harlem, New York invited me to be the feature performer for her event. Billy Black's was a cozy and quaint African-American restaurant that served soul food. It was very dimly lit and had various works of art on the walls. These works of art that were placed on display were usually by African-American artists. There were also tables that were set up for the customers who were dining in. The stage was positioned in front of all of the tables. On this stage was a DJ who was responsible for the music that was often playing. Billy Black's was like a Juke Joint. The "Speak Your Myne" open mic had a very diverse crowd. There were black, white, gay, straight, young, and old people. At the time I performed there, I labeled myself a "comedic actor" and "playwright." I performed more than one poem that night which included my "Why Must They Die?" poem. I performed this piece off the stage. I walked throughout the crowd while I performed this comedic poem for them. It was very funny and everyone enjoyed my performance that night.

My Fame Is Spreading in New York
New York

One night, when I was in New York, Renair, the host of "Speak Your Myne" told me something powerful that showed that I was touching many people with my art. She said my fame was spreading throughout New York. More specifically, she said many people that saw me perform in New York, were talking about me. These people knew who I was and what I did! This reveals that my art had touched many people there.

Educating at Duckery Elementary
Philadelphia, Pennsylvania

While living in Pennsylvania, I've had an ample amount of opportunities arise for me to perform for younger generations. One day I received the opportunity to perform at an elementary school in north Philadelphia named Duckery. I received this opportunity through a black woman named Clarity. Like most people I knew in Pennsylvania, I met her on the Philadelphia spoken-word scene. There was a fundraising event organized at Duckery with the goal of raising money for the victims of the Haiti Earthquake that shook the island in January 2010. She asked me to perform at this event. The cafeteria (where I was scheduled to perform) was packed with many children. For them, I performed acting skits that I had written myself. The children loved my performance.

Performed This Piece at First Fridays on Vine
Philadelphia, Pennsylvania

One open mic event in Philadelphia I could remember performing in often was called First Fridays on Vine. This event was located in a building near center city Philadelphia. A middle-aged black woman named Aziza Kenteh hosted this particular event. It was a venue that had a very distinct feel about it. Once you walked in you found that there was African art everywhere and bongo drums. It was a very eclectic place. Various musicians would come and play instruments that ranged from the acoustic guitar to interesting one-of-a-kind instruments that looked as if they originated in Africa. Here at this event, I performed my "What Goes Up, Must Come Down" One-Man Show. When I performed this piece of mine, people were in awe. They appreciated my energy.

Young Black Men Are Touched
Philadelphia, Pennsylvania

I could remember standing outside of my cousin's dance studio one bright and sunny day in west Philadelphia. Also standing outside of the dance studio were a group of young black teenage boys. The aura that they let off told me immediately that these young men were from the inner city. They didn't seem like the type to be interested in Latin or ballroom dancing, which are some of the dance forms that my cousin taught within his studio. By simply looking at them, they seemed more like the types to be interested in rap music and hip-hop dancing.

Anyways, while standing on the outside of the dance studio, one of the young men said something to me. As soon as this kid laid his eyes on me, he exclaimed, "You are the dude that did the poem about roaches!" This young man knew who I was! As a spoken-word artist, I did in fact have a poem about roaches. He was referring to my "Why Must They Die?" poem that I wrote years ago while I was living in West Palm Beach, Florida. The fact that this young man recognized me so quickly told me that my performance had made a major impact on him. Flattered that he recognized me, I looked at him and simply responded, "Yes, I am!" He then continued to express how much he enjoyed my original poem "Why Must They Die?"

Ministered to an Inner City Man
Philadelphia, Pennsylvania

One day while I was walking out of my home in west Philadelphia, I saw a black man who was dressed in urban attire. With that said, he did not seem like the type of person to be interested in spoken word. As soon as he saw me, he said, "You are the one that did the roach poem." My performance left such a lasting impression on this man that he remembered me.

Gang Member Recognizes Me
Philadelphia, Pennsylvania

One night while I was riding the Septa Train in Philadelphia, a group of Blood Gang members rushed onto the train. I knew that they were Bloods because of the red bandanna that hung outside of their back right pockets. They were joking and laughing with each other. As they laughed and joked around with each other, I just sat there and observed them.

While they were joking and carrying on, one of them made eye contact with me and came running over to where I was sitting. He told me that he recognized me from one of my spoken word performances. More specifically, he told me that he recognized me from when I performed my roach poem. While he sat there next to me on the train, he had a big smile on his face and could not stop smiling. He was so happy that he ran into the poet Thierry Lundy on the train. Extremely excited, he looked back at his friends and told them who I was, but they didn't care too much. I don't remember ever meeting this gentleman, but he sure did remember me. My poem left such a lasting impression on him that he recognized me as soon as he laid eyes on me.

Performing at Catherine Zickgraff's Open Mic Venue
Augusta, Georgia

After performing my poetry at an open mic venue in Philadelphia called "Word Flow" I met a white woman named Catherine Zickgraf. After watching me perform at this event, Catherine and her husband expressed to me how impressed they were by my performance and they invited me to be a feature performer at the open mic venue they hosted in Augusta, Georgia. I performed my roach poem while I was there and the audience enjoyed my performance. After my performance, several people purchased my poetry CD and wanted me to autograph their copy of it.

Standing Ovation
Philadelphia, Pennsylvania

One day I wrote a poem entitled "I Know How It Feels." One night I performed this poem at one of my lady friends' poetry event. Her name was Mary, and the event was located in a space that was located in south Philadelphia. When it was my time to perform I walked up front through the middle aisle, which split all of the audience members into two groups, one group on either side of the aisle. So this means that as I walked up front to perform, there were people at either side of me. When I stood in front of this crowd of about sixty people I performed my heart out. While I recited the poem, I felt so deeply connected with it. I have performed many of my original works over the years, but this probably was the most connected that I've ever felt with any of them. It was almost as if I received an extra boost of energy that did not derive from me, but came from another force. As a result of my connection with the poem, the audience members hung on my every word. As I stood in front of the crowd delivering my poem, I could hear certain audience members reacting to my words. When my performance came to an end, everyone in the crowd gave me a standing ovation. Like I said before there was an aisle that split the audience into two sections. So as I walked down the aisle trying to simmer down from the power that I felt on stage, I could feel all the members of the audience members standing to either side of me applauding my performance.

I Keep Her at The Edge of Her Seat

On Facebook, a woman who saw my performance the night before said that I always keep her at the edge of her seat and she can't wait to hear what comes next. This says that there is something captivating about my performance.
-December 20, 2012

They Love the Roach Poem

Ever since I stepped on the stage and performed my roach poem for the first time, I never stopped performing it. The reason is because my fans enjoyed it so much. People would often request this poem when I performed at various venues. They would either request that I perform the poem, or when I am pitching my spoken-word CD to them, they would ask if the poem is on it. People enjoyed the poem so much because they never heard a poem about roaches. When I would begin my poem the audience's initial reaction would be, "Is this really a poem about roaches?" Immediately after they figure out that it is indeed a poem about roaches, they would smile really hard as if they were thinking, I've got to hear this! Over the years, many people have come up to me after my performance and told me how much they really enjoyed the poem. They would even mimic the acting components that I've added to it. When I wrote this poem initially, I never thought that it would leave such a long-lasting impression on people. It has left such an impression on people that they would go home and tell their friends and family about it.

> *"People love my Roach Poem. They hear it, and tell their friends and family about it. That is refreshing to know. People always remember me for my Roach Poem..."*
>
> -December 21, 2012
> 6:41 pm

Lyrical Thought Wants to Learn from Me

I enjoyed performing a lot, but I never thought that I would get to the point where people would want to learn from me. After years of performing, there were now artists that were interested in learning from me. One of these artists was Lyrical Thought. She was a short, heavyset light brown-skinned woman who really enjoyed spoken-word. One day she told me how much she respects me as an artist and said that she would like to learn from me. I told her yes I would be happy to help her with her writing. This was really flattering to me that she would ask me to help her improve her writing.

> *"I had an enriching conversation with Lyrical Thought...She told me how much she respects me as a poet, and how much she would like to learn from me. I am so honored and humbled at the thought that a good poet would come to me for some pointers..."*
>
> -December 23, 2012
> 4:39 pm

I Left an Impression on the DJ
Philadelphia, Pennsylvania

One night I featured at a venue in south Philadelphia called "The Reef." The poetry event was hosted by a man everyone called Mally Mal. The venue had two floors. On the bottom floor was a restaurant and bar area. The top floor also had a restaurant and bar area, but there was also a DJ booth and a stage. This is where the open mic was held. Since I've performed countless of times at this particular venue, the DJ has seen several of my performances. When the event host, Mally Mal, finally introduced me on this night, the DJ played a particular song as I made my way up to the stage. He played a rap song called "Power" by a famous rap artist named Kanye West. With the song, the DJ let me--and everyone in the room--know what he thought about me as a performer. As the song continued to the hook, it said, "...No one man should have all that power!" With this hook, the DJ was saying that he viewed me as a powerful performer!

> *I was thinking to myself, the time that I featured at Reef open mic venue in south Philly. Mally Mal was the person who was hosting, and when it was time for me to perform, the DJ played*

the song "Power" by Kanye West. This shows me that they think that I am a powerful artist. That was a profound experience!

-December 24, 2012
12:23 pm

I Inspired Whisper

I think the first time I met Whisper was at an open mic event called Coffee After Dark. She was a spoken-word artist just like me and she was the author of her very own poetry book. As her name suggests, she was very soft spoken when anyone would converse with her, and when she performed her work. She would often come to an open mic event dressed in nursing scrubs. This did not only show me that she was just getting off work, but it also revealed to me how dedicated and passionate she was about the craft of spoken-word poetry. She has seen me perform countless times. One day I was on the online social network named Facebook. While on there I found a message from Whisper. In her message, she expressed to me how much of an inspiration I was to her.

Okay, people telling me that I am an inspiration seems to be a recurring thing. Another poet by the name of Whisper Facebook messaged me and told me that I am an inspiration to her. This shows me that in the midst of your troubles you are still able to inspire others. :)

-December 23, 2012
8:39 pm

Recognized in UPENN Bookstore
Philadelphia, Pennsylvania

I performed in a lounge area one night in Philly. There was an open mic event that was happening there that night. This place had a bar and there were a lot of grown people in the venue. I performed my famous roach poem that night. Sometime after I performed at this event, I was at a bookstore near the campus of UPENN. I often came here to create and promote my one-man shows. While I was in the bookstore on this day looking at some merchandise, a black male who was about my age startled me. As soon as he recognized me he shouted very loudly in the store to get my attention. He recognized me from that lounge where I performed a little while back. This shows me that my performance left a long lasting impression on him. Since he enjoyed my work I immediately gave him an autographed copy of my poetry CD (the Roach Piece was also featured on my CD). He was excited, almost beyond words, for the gift that I gave him.

> "While I was hanging out at the PENN bookstore, a young black man came up to me and said he recognized me. He was so excited to see me…This shows that I leave a lasting impression on people who see my work. :) I gave him an autographed copy of my CD, and he was so excited…"
>
> -December 28, 2012
> 5:20 pm

Troy Enjoys My Work
Philadelphia

Troy is an event host who I met at a poetry venue that he was hosting. He was a young black man who looked to be in his early 20s. He was also very down to earth and friendly. I don't remember if he bought one of my poetry CDs or if I just gave him one for free. Nonetheless, the fact remains that he owned one of my CDs. He enjoyed my work so much that he let me know on Facebook how much he enjoyed it. In the journal entry below, you can read what he had to say about me and my poetry.

> "While I was on Facebook, a man named Troy Goodwin put up his status saying: 'Chillin listening to Thierry Lundy's poetry CD. This guy is an amazing poet.' Many people have included me in their statuses to this capacity…"
>
> -Sunday, December 23, 2012
> 3:14 pm

Performing at Poetz Realm
Bridgeport, Connecticut

One night, I received the opportunity to perform at an open mic event in Connecticut that was named "Poetz Realm." As the name suggests, it was an open mic event where spoken-word artists could share their works in front of an audience composed of poetry lovers.

The event was held in a small room that had chairs and couches for people to sit on. It was here in front of these makeshift pews that I would get the opportunity to speak in front of these poetry lovers. That night I performed my much-loved Roach Poem, and it blew the audience members away. The audience members were reacting throughout my performance. They enjoyed my theatrics and how I brought the poem to life on stage.

> *"Last night, I went to go perform at a venue in Connecticut. I was well received. A beautiful woman sitting in the front during my performance said that she respected me. Made me feel good...people enjoy my work..."*
>
> -December 28, 2012

> *"A Haitian gentleman who was at the show in Connecticut sat down with me afterwards and expressed how he thought that my poetry was really diverse, and he told me that he would come out and support the show… People are not or do not only enjoy my work, they are inspired by my work."*
>
> -December 28, 2012
2:40 pm

He's Inspired by Roscoe the Roach
Philadelphia, Pennsylvania

There was a woman who was in attendance at my "Roscoe the Roach's Story" One-Man Show. Her name is Diaspora. Her job had to do with counseling prisoners. Sometime after my show, she told me that my "Roscoe the Roach's Story" One-Man Show had inspired one of the prisoners who she was counseling. She told me that this man had been in and out of jail for years, because he had continued to make the same mistakes over and over again. This man was fed up with making the same mistakes that would land him in prison over and over again. Well, after watching my one-man show Diaspora went back to this man and explained the message of the show to him and he was touched.

She told him about Roscoe's recurring line "Roscoe is Standing Now!" This incarcerated man took this line and said that it was time for him to stop making the same mistakes and to stand now. This is amazing! This man was not even at my show, but the message of the show found its way to him via my friend Diaspora who was counseling him. Diaspora also told me that this man wanted to meet me.

> *"Diaspora is a woman who attended my "Roscoe the Roach's Story" One-Man Show. She called me this morning and told me that one of her patients was inspired by my show. This gentleman has been incarcerated for 30 years, because he continued to do the same things that got him incarcerated. My show made him want to "Stand Now." He's even quoting lines from the show…"*
>
> -January 17, 2013

Anna in the Tropics Stage Play
Philadelphia, Pennsylvania

Before I dropped out of University of the Arts, I had opportunities to act in a few stage plays on the campus of the school. Anna in the Tropics was one of these stage plays.

> *"Today, we had our first run of Anna in the Tropics, and it was fun! I made an effort not to over-think things, and it paid off. When I was on that stage I felt alive. My colleagues who were in the audience really enjoyed my performance and did not fail in telling me that they did…"*
>
> -January 24, 2013
> 1:46 pm

Neal Is Inspired
Philadelphia, Pennsylvania

Neal is a homeless black man who I met in Philadelphia. Though he was homeless he was always in good spirits, and I admired that about him. Another thing that was special about Neal is that he enjoyed the crafts of poetry and acting. Often times he would quote Shakespeare lines.

One night on my way home from watching some of my older poetic brothers perform in a show called "Am I My Brother's Keeper" I ran into Neal on the train. He was selling his newspapers on the Broad Street Train. While conversing with him he shared something with me that I did not know. He told me that he has taken things from my performances and has applied these techniques to his own work. This was truly inspiring and motivating.

> *"When I came from 'Am I My Brother's Keeper' I ran into Neal, who is a good friend of mine who wants to be an actor and he told me that he has taken things from my performances and has applied some of my techniques to his work…"*
>
> -March 3, 2013
8:17 pm

Performance in Baltimore
Baltimore, Maryland

Last night I featured at a venue called "5 Seasons" in Baltimore, Maryland. It was a really fun performance and everyone enjoyed it. I performed:

- *"Checkers"*
- *"Two"*
- *"I Know How You Feel"*
- *"Roaches"*

> *"People were buzzing off the roach poem with the slow-time component. The host of the show expressed to me that she thought my performance was awesome. She really enjoyed it. It was also a gentleman's birthday, and he Facebook messaged me and expressed how glad he was that I brought in his birthday…People genuinely love my works…"*
>
> -March 28, 2013
11:43 pm
Thursday

> *"Not Enough Money to make it back to Philly, and one more event in Baltimore"*
>
> *"I performed at a venue in Baltimore and I got good feedback from some of the people. There was a gentleman there who said that more people need to hear me..."*
>
> -March 29, 2013
2:10 am
Friday

Inspired Him to Write Poetry
Philadelphia, Pennsylvania

One night in Philly I was heading to my home in north Philadelphia. While I waited for the bus on the corner of Broad and Olney Street, I had a very powerful encounter with a black man who looked to be a few years older than I was. While I waited there, he took one look at me and said he remembered me from a performance that I did a year ago at a major Black History Event that was in Philadelphia. As we stood there at the bus stop that night on Broad and Olney, he expressed to me how much he enjoyed that performance and how much it had impacted his life. After expressing to me how much he enjoyed this performance of mine, he told me he had been writing poetry a lot lately. He said "Over the past year, I wrote over 400 poems." I then felt impressed to ask him, "What inspired you to write all those poems?" He looked at me and gave me a response that sent chills running down my spine. In response to my curiosity he simply said, "You." Unknowingly, I inspired that black man to start writing poetry. Talk about having an impact.

> *"While I was waiting for my bus to go home at Broad and Olney, a black gentleman greeted me and said that he remembered one of my performances from last February at a Black History event. He said that he started writing recently and said that he wrote over 400 poems. When I asked him what inspired him he told me that I was the one that inspired him to start writing poetry..."*
>
> -July 4, 2013

Owner of Barber Shop Remembers My Performance
Galloway Township, New Jersey

One time while I was living in Philadelphia, I was invited to an event called "Rhythm and Rhymes" in Galloway Township in New Jersey. This event was created by a poet friend of mind named Loreal. She invited me to feature at this event one day. This event was located within a barbershop called "Kingdom Kutts." The pieces that I performed that day were my poem "Two" and my poem "I Know How It Feels." Years later I was told by Loreal that the owner of the shop asked about me. He asked how I was doing. In his words, he asked "How is the skinny fella (referring to me) doing?" This man remembered me after all of that time. This shows that my performance left a long lasting impression on him. People have told me that I perform my poems with a lot of passion, and that my words stand out in people's minds. I would like to suggest that that man remembered me because my passionate performance was highly memorable.

You Never Cease to Amaze Me
Trenton, New Jersey

Though the first one-man show I put on in Trenton, New Jersey, had a rough turn out, the second one I did only a week after that had a much better turn out. One of the people who came to see me was an African American millionaire named Tracey D. Syphax. After my show via an online social network, the following is what Tracey expressed to me in regards to my show:

> *"Great show, Beloved!" You always seem to amaze me with your gifts and talents! Thanks. #FollowYourDreams #AntonioAntonio"*
> -July 9, 2013

They Love the Roach Poem
Eastern Shore, Maryland

One of my biggest gigs was in Eastern Shore, Maryland. I performed my Roach Poem at this event. The people were amazed by my performance. They reacted as if it was the best thing they have ever seen. They would laugh hysterically at my words, movements, and facial expressions. After the show, I sold many of my poetry CDs. A married couple expressed to me how much they enjoyed my performance. They also purchased one of my poetry CDs. Lisa, the host of the show, told me that many people were coming up to her after the show and expressing to her how much they enjoyed my performance.

Honored to Be Sitting Next to Me
Philadelphia, Pennsylvania

One night while coming from a poetry venue, I got into a car along with some other poets. One of these poets was the famous Def Poet from Philadelphia named Black Ice. Before I met this black man in person, I watched his Def Poetry performances over and over again on YouTube. I've also watched him deliver a rap freestyle on the famous BET Network show called the Rap Basement.

On this particular night, this well-known profound spoken-word artist was sitting next to me (who was widely known on a smaller scale then he was). I had a moment where I felt the need to express how honored I was to be sitting next to him. I exclaimed, "I'm sitting next to Black Ice!" He looked at me and said, "I'm sitting next to Thierry Lundy!" I was caught off guard by his response. I felt honored that the famous Black Ice was honored to be sitting next to me.

> *Last night after I left the Coffee After Dark Open Mic, I was sitting in the back seat of a friend of KP's, and in the back seat with me was the Def Poet "Black Ice." When I expressed my excitement about sitting next to Black Ice, Black Ice responds, "I'm sitting next to Thierry Lundy!" Man this was a mutual respect! I'm stoked..."*
>
> -August 9, 2013

You Are Talented!
New Jersey

Out of all the poems that I've written, there is one topic that showed up quite often in my poetry. And this topic is me breaking up with my ex-girlfriend. All of these pieces have one thing in common and that is the deep feeling of remorse that I felt for doing such an insensitive act. One day while I was living in Philadelphia, Pennsylvania, I decided to write yet another poem on this topic. I titled the poem "Turn Back the Hands of Time."

I received a strong feeling of inspiration to create this poem, as a result of a song that was written by a very famous singer named R.Kelly. The song is a very solemn song where R. Kelly is pouring out his heart and expressing how he wishes that he could turn back the hands of time. Because he says that if he could do such a thing, the woman who he is singing about would still be with him. This song inspired me to write this new spoken-word piece where I express in about three minutes or so of how I wish I could turn back the hands of time to make it so I never lost my girlfriend.

In my poem "Turn Back the Hands of Time" I first speak about the heartbreak of my ex girlfriend and I breaking up and then I say, "If I could turn back the hands of time." And then I do exactly this for the rest of the poem. The poem is rewinding back to the point that I made the decision to have sex with another woman, and in the poem I make it so that I would have made another decision that would have saved my relationship with my ex. I had to work very hard to make this concept manifest on paper. As I sat there in the early morning hours in my room, I racked my brain on trying to figure how one would write backwards. In other words, my goal was to put words together into sentences, to make it so that when someone hears or reads the poem, it would tell them a story that was rewinding in the same way that a video would rewind. This was not an easy task. As I wrote, I repeatedly replayed the painful event of me cheating on my ex-girlfriend in my head and I figured out how this event would sound if it were to rewind. I was successful in accomplishing this difficult task. I started the poem around 10 or 11 o'clock at night and completed it around 3 o'clock in the morning the next day.

I could remember performing this piece with background music at my friend Gandhi's events in New Jersey. Ghandi was a friend of mine who hosted one of the first events that I performed in New Jersey. He called this open mic event "GPS." The first "GPS" event I performed in was in a very dimly lit restaurant in Trenton, New Jersey. Now it's a few years later and it is now located in a restaurant in Willingboro, New Jersey, called Fat Boyz Kitchen. In this venue one night I performed "Turn Back the Hands of Time."

Before this night, I had already performed this piece on several occasions so I had gotten a good handle on it. Having fully memorized this poem, I now knew the piece like the back of my hand, so now it was time to play! On this night there was a band in the building. When it was time for me to perform,

I asked the band to play something a little mellow. It was my plan to recite my piece while the band played in the background. With full force I recited my poem against the music in the same way that a rapper would flow on an instrumental. This was the first time that I had done this with this poem of mine. Reciting a spoken-word piece over music was somewhat tricky. If you were already used to reciting a piece at a certain pace or rhythm, you would have to slow down or speed up with the music, depending on the speed of the rhythm. On this particular night, the mellow music I asked for was slow and mellow. So it took hold of me and caused me to recite my poem slower than I was used to. I did not sweat. I owned the music and recited my piece as if this music and poetry thing was premeditated, but it was not. It felt good as I recited my poem to the audience. It felt as though the music and I became one. I recited my piece so effortlessly that it made Ghandi think that I've done it like that before, but I did not. It was the first time that I've done the poem over any kind of music at all. Some days after that night, I could remember sitting in a back room in Gandhi's house. He was in the room with me when he asked me, "That night you performed your poem Turn Back the Hands of Time at Fat Boyz, did you plan to do it like that?" And I looked at him and answered, "No." He responded back with, "You are talented." The following is my "If I Could Turn Back the Hands of Time" Poem:

"If I Could Turn Back the Hands of Time"

I've been losing my mind for four years.
Every morning since you left I woke up
and reached hungrily for my cell phone,
thinking by some miracle I'd still get that "Good morning" text from you.

I don't go out as much as I used to,
and my bedroom became an insane asylum,
where I used my fingernails to etch the date of when I first met you
into the walls over and over again,
hoping that you could see my ability to focus on one thing
and you would come running into my life again.

I've been thrown into the back of a cop car time and time again,
because over the period of four years,
I've trashed hundreds of stores, knocking things over,
because none of the clocks they sold could take me back in time so that
I could reverse your tears.

If I found out that I could turn back the hands of time,
I would go back to the year 2008.
We are in my bedroom; It's 11 am, Wednesday morning,
On the floor next to the bed, there is a condom wrapper,
a pen, and a few sheets of paper.
Back on the bed there are two people wide awake,
me and a woman that is not you.

After a minute or two, the whole scene starts to progress.
Her and I close our eyes back up, as if we were trying to get more rest.
After a few minutes, we are fast asleep.
During the night, there is a lot of rolling back and forth,
pulling and tugging on the bed sheets,
and me waking up occasionally like, "Damn she got some cold feet!"

It's now 5 am, and neither one of us are moving,
until the hours of 3 and 4 when the blanket on our backs starts shifting.
I get up, pull the blanket off of my body,
And backwards, I stagger, as if my legs were sore,
out of the room on the other side of the bedroom door.

A few seconds later, there is the sound of rusty hinges, and a toilet flush.
I can now hear my footsteps getting closer to the room
I walk in, and my energy level is not much.
My soldier, just came from war so it's barely standing up.
The condom is filled with semen,
the woman turns over from her finished position, onto her back, and
spreads her legs open.

I climb back onto the bed and place myself between her thighs,
but before I dive in, my soldier stands up,
my ejaculation reverses,
the condom empties of my juices
then comes penetration,
I'm talking a whole lot of smack, and periodically I would ask her if she feels the sensation.
Her screams subside into moans and groans,
"What in the hell was I thinking?"

My thrusting goes from fast to slow,
It goes from wanting her back to blow,
and trying to see her curl her toes,
to "I better take this slow, because it's way too early to let my load go."

It's 1 am now, we are both naked, and before we started to go,
I detach myself from her,
As if I were saying, "This is wrong, I've got to go."
I pull the condom off, she closes her legs shut,
The condom wrapper elevates off the ground into my hands,
I put the condom into the wrapper,
and the wrapper reseals itself back up.
She says, "Okay, let's do this, now that you got it up."

I put the unopened condom onto the dresser,
I move closer to kiss and caress her,
I go from touching her thighs and breasts,
and licking on her flesh,
to now moving fast and working hard to put her bra back on
to cover her chest.

By this time, my room is a mess.
Our clothes are everywhere, and pens and paper are on the floor
from being knocked off of my work desk.

We continue to viciously kiss each other,
While falling to the floor,
Then my room starts to look like a scene from the Twilight Zone.
Her clothes start floating up from the ground and flying off of my bookshelves,
my clothes start to fly towards me,
as we both quickly re-clothed ourselves.

We get up from the ground, put the rest of our clothes on.
From the floor, we move towards the wall of my room, by this time,
I've already got a hard on.
We land on my work desk, take our hands off of each other,
The pens and papers that were knocked to the floor earlier, quickly reclaimed
their place, on my desk, next to a black folder.

We walk slowly out of my bedroom,
and make our way out of my apartment,
I take my keys out of my pocket, and try to open my front door,
and it's a pitiful attempt,
because at the same time, I've got my arms around her
whispering things into her ears that are not meant.

I throw my keys back into my pocket,
and walked her back to her car without saying a word,
I opened her car door, watched her get in, but this time
I don't say a word.

12 am is the time.
Both cars start, first hers, and then mine,
Then backwards, we both are driving fast, weaving in and out of traffic,
I'm going back now, at this point I'm longer thinking with my penis,
I'm now using logic.

So, when me and this woman get back to that empty parking lot,

I'm going to tell her, "No! We can't exchange numbers,
and you can't come to my spot!"
I would watch as she looks at me crazy,
Watch as she walks away from me,
And watch me not looking at her
Because I'd be too busy thinking about you.

If someone told me that I could turn back the hands of time,
Without hesitation, I would do it, just so I could watch myself get into my car
And this time drive straight to you.

My Poem Resonated with Bill
Vineland, New Jersey

One day I performed at a place called Sweet Life Bakery in Vineland, New Jersey. I was the only black person in attendance. Everyone else was white including the employees of the bakery. I was the feature performer for this event. Being that there were not much performers in attendance I was allowed to perform as many pieces as I wanted. One of the pieces I performed was called "On This Road."

    One of the people in attendance was a very quiet white man who looked to be in his 30's. His name was Bill. He was very slim, wore prescription glasses, and a straw hat. After the show, the event host, Bill, and I all went to a buffet to eat lunch. While here, Bill expressed to me how much my poem "On This Road" resonated with him.

> *"Today, I performed at sweet life bakery in Vineland, New Jersey. There was a gentleman there by the name of Bill who came kind of late and Bill afterwards told me that he was touched by my "On This Road" piece. He said that it really spoke to him..."*
>
>   -May 11, 2013

The Women Enjoyed my "On This Road" Poem
Philadelphia, Pennsylvania

> *"Tonight, I did my "On This Road" poem, and the audience was touched. Two of the women in particular enjoyed it. One of them cried, and gave me a hug when I sat down after the performance…"*
>
> -May 22, 2013

"On This Road"

There is a road.
An arduous road filled with danger.
A road that has struck fear in billions and billions of hearts
and has the power to send a shudder running through your body
and chills running down your spine, just by simply thinking about going down that road.

On this Road, there is a possibility that you will be abandoned by
Your family, friends, and everyone else that you thought would be there for you 'til the end.
Because no matter how much they try,
they just can't see what you see in the road.
They just can't seem to bring themselves to understand why you are so attracted to the road.
Their lack of comprehension causes them to disappear like ghosts in thin air,
Leaving you there all alone on the road.

And all alone, you will experience the darkest nights you will ever experience,
for they camp out and make their home on the road.
They remain very vigilant, and can't wait to see you coming down this road,
to bully you,
to test you,
is what these dark days have been trained to do.

Your patience and persistence will have to be made into a wool coat,
a pair of gloves, a scarf, and some boots,
for the cold that you will run into on this road.
The blizzard is a thief and is eyeing your courage and pride,
and it has been making plans to steal all the energy that you have mustered up inside.

This road will make you weary,
It will provoke you to curse it.
It will make you shed tears of pain and disappointment.
Your blood will easily find its way out of your body and onto the road.
The pressure put on you will have blood dripping out of your ears and your nose.
Your body collapses!
But you are still breathing, get back on your toes!

You will run into military tanks and infantry soldiers on this road,

When you see them,
Do not fall back!
Do not retreat!
Hold your ground!
Remain on your two feet!
Take a deep breath,
And let out the war cry, "THIS IS MY ROAD!"

This is your road!
This is your visions and your goals!
Devote yourself to your road!
Don't let your road die, nourish your road,
Show affection, and embrace your road.
Don't betray your road.

There will be countless billboards on the side of the road that will try to

seduce you,
they will tell you to separate yourself from the road,
they will offer you alternatives to your journey,
They will tell you that you can still turn back.
They will tell you that you don't really have to be on this road.
Don't fall in the trap,
Tell them "It's either follow my dreams or die!"

This road is made to test you,
Many times it will seem like it wants to kill you.
But the road is not testing because it hates you.
The road is testing you to show you that your body was designed to make it through.

So hold your head up high, and don't be discouraged.
Believe with all your heart that you are built for this road.
Believe that everything that you have been through in the past has conditioned you specifically for this road.
Believe that long before your parents existed, the road was already there.
Just waiting there like a beautiful Clydesdale with long hair
Waiting patiently for you to come along to take the reins.

Even with all the rain,
The road does not hate you.
This road has been given a job, and that job is to make you!
It's trying to show you that you have what it takes to push through!
So keep your head up high, push through, and allow it to make you.
Allow it to prepare you, for the good things that were made just for you.

So when you are on the road, and you find yourself alone.
Do not panic,
remain calm,
Take a deep breath, and say to yourself,
"This road, is my road. This is my mission, my vision, and my goals.
I will rest if I have to, but I will not walk off my road.

Suicide Prevention
Philadelphia, Pennsylvania

"Jus Words" is another open mic event located in north Philadelphia where I often performed my works. This event was located within a venue called "Dowling's Palace." One particular night in the year 2013, I unknowingly ministered to a young lady who had attended the venue that night. Her name was Gemar. What I did not know was that she had been going through a tough time lately. Her boyfriend abandoned her after finding out she was pregnant with his child. She was so depressed that she lost hope in God. To escape this darkness, she made a couple unsuccessful attempts to commit suicide. She even wrote farewell letters to the people who were close to her. While in this dark place, Gemar remained in her dorm room for three weeks reflecting on her troubles. She posed herself the question, "Where did I go wrong?" Wanting Gemar to get out of her dorm room, one day her friend invited her out to the "Jus Words" open mic on a night where I was performing there.

At the end of the night, I walked up to Gemar as she was preparing to walk out of the venue and in a friendly manner I introduced myself. I then handed her one of my poetry CDs, and told her that it was for her. I did not know it at the time, but my performance that night helped in preventing Gemar from committing suicide that night. Below is a message that Gemar sent me via the social network of Facebook in the year 2014 (several months after I moved out of Philadelphia). In this message she expressed how I helped her get through this particular tough time in her life.

> "I had to find you. You changed my life one night…when I was visiting Dowling's Palace. You spoke a poem and then at the end of it you said it was for me. :) I loved that. You also gave me your CD that I just have been able to find. I know this random message may never probably be read by you but your poem helped stop me from trying to commit suicide that night. Thank You. :) BTW I think you are amazing."
>
> -April 14, 2014

"It is finished"
John 19:30

Epilogue: God Is Good

God is real, and He loves us all dearly. He loves us so much that while we were yet sinners, He initiated His goodness towards us by sending His only begotten son to die for our sins. His goodness and mercy can clearly be seen in my testimony. Though I strayed away from Him, He still used me to bless others. All the years that I was running from His plan, He used me to do something that was still a part of His plan: He used me to minister to people through my art while I was out in the world. What makes this demonstration of God's goodness so powerful is the fact that He started to use me from the very point I denied the calling that He had placed on my life. After denying the call on my life, I was in the world for almost seven years. In all those years, I've performed in countless places for countless people. Unbeknownst to me, God used me to minister to many, if not all of these people. Though I turned my back on Him, out of His goodness He still used me to do exactly what He called me to do years ago before I walked out of Summit Church. The way He worked in my life when I strayed away from Him transcended my reality. It transcended everything that I could hear, smell, taste, touch, and see. The whole time that I was submerged in the ways of a dark world I became totally selfish. Often times thinking about myself, I was always trying to find fulfillment in the world. In the year 2013, years after turning my back on Him, He showed me that it was never about me or my perverted desires, but about the people who I came in contact with. It was all about feeding His sheep. I would like to encourage you reader, to not allow "the world" to persuade you that God is not good. He is good all the time, and all the time He is good. After reading my memoir, you can see that His goodness permeates my testimony. With that said, if you feel the Lord knocking on the door to your heart, accept him as your personal Lord and Savior. If you have strayed away from the fold where Jesus Christ is the shepherd, I would like to encourage you to make your way back. When you do find your way back, yield to him with all of your heart and soul, and allow him to lead your life. This dark and decaying world is quickly coming to an end, and our Lord Jesus Christ is coming very soon to gather those that kept their faith in him. If you can feel him knocking on the door to your heart, let him in!

God Bless You.